MASADA
THOU SHALT NOT KILL

SHIMON AVISH

Developmental Editing by Julie Gray
Copy Editing by Daniel Cross, The Open Book Editor
Cover Design by Tim Barber, Dissect Designs
Internal Formatting by Formatted Books

Library of Congress Control Number: 2021924966

Paperback ISBN: 979-8-9854304-1-7
eBook ISBN: 979-8-9854304-0-0

MarbleStone Press, Salem, Massachusetts 01970
www.MarbleStonePress.com

Foreword

This novel is a dramatization of the story of Masada. I have taken some license for dramatic effect, and I have speculated on some events since we know so little beyond the fact that the Romans mounted a siege at Masada. This is my attempt to explain some of the unknowable. The Historical Afterword provides a more detailed examination of why I made some of the choices I did.

My love of Masada derives from being stationed in the area for more than a year while serving with an Israel Defense Forces patrol unit. After completing nighttime patrols, my lieutenant would often have us climb the Snake Path to the top, which I despised at the time, functioning, as I was, on only three hours of sleep. But today, I cherish those memories of getting to know Masada intimately. I've been fascinated with it ever since, and I hope you will enjoy my speculations about what could have happened there as much as I have enjoyed writing them.

CHAPTER

1

I stood by the arched entryway to my parents' home. My cheek still tingled from the blow Father had dealt me moments before. I let the cool stone of the archway and nighttime summer air relieve the sting, but not the memory of the slap. How could he hit me? Isn't it a parent's role to nurture and protect their children, and doesn't thou shalt not kill also mean thou shalt not resort to violence to force your son to agree with you?

Unable to remain so close to him, I ran away from the house and down the main alleyway until I had to stop and catch my breath. Then, pausing partway across the Zion Bridge, which spans from the Upper City to the Temple entrance, I tried to calm myself by leaning against the rough stone of the balustrade. But looking up at the massive triple-arched portico of the Temple Mount and then down on my favorite view of Jerusalem toward the Siloam Pool, I still could not soothe my heart or mind.

Standing in silence on the bridge and slowing my breath, I noticed voices approaching and the jingling of little bells to my left, close to the Temple Mount gate. I watched as the High Priest, Mattathias, and his retinue drew near the stairs leading from the Temple onto the bridge. Mattathias led the procession from the front, dressed in his finest indigo robes with dangling tiny gold bells and tassels, his head held high and shoulders back, strutting quickly, as he was prone to do.

Suddenly, a man in a filthy tunic with wild hair shoved past me on the bridge and ran toward Mattathias. I caught sight of another, younger man as he drew near the High Priest from between the arches of the Temple Mount gate. The unruly-haired fellow headed straight at Mattathias as the other man closed fast from behind, lurching forward and striking the High Priest in the back as if tripping on a crack in the paving stones. He shoved the High Priest and sent him flying into the waiting arms of the first assailant.

With infinitesimal, almost undetectable movements, the wild-haired attacker drew a blade from between the folds of his robe and forced it up under Mattathias's rib cage. Then he twisted the dagger and pulled it out, wiping the bloodied blade on the priest's robes as he eased him onto the ground. Stepping back, he looked around to see if there were any other witnesses to his actions, and missing me in the darkness, he gathered his men to him with a high-pitched whistle.

What was happening? Who were these people? My heart pounding, I moved into the shadows of the bridge to hide. Was that the notorious Sicarii—the dagger-men of Jerusalem? Did I just witness an assassination?

Gathering my courage, I yelled, "Guards!" to the sentries near the Temple gate. "Look, the High Priest!" I pointed across the bridge to where Mattathias laid in a heap, his entourage surrounding him, making useless sounds like a brood of hens.

I looked for signs of the attackers, but the dagger-men had already vanished into the night.

I could not believe what I was seeing. I knew that attacks on the Temple priests were becoming more common, but the Sicarii had never struck this close to home, nor had they ever assassinated a High Priest before. I had to tell Father.

Before I had managed two steps, someone caught me by my belt.

"Be quiet," this someone hissed while grabbing and then twisting my right arm high behind my back. The pain was unbearable, but sensing the danger I was in, I clenched hard with my already aching jaw to keep myself from screaming in pain.

Earlier that day, I had awoken to a sense of foreboding because the morning sky foretold of a coming sandstorm. The leading edge of the storm would arrive soon, and the air was already thick with dust, making it difficult to see. On such days, most people stayed indoors, or if they had to be out, they covered their mouths and noses. I knew I would not be able to gaze upon Jerusalem's honey-colored stones this day. I also knew my twin brother, Jonathan, and I would struggle to study; the weather's fug and oppressiveness would be a source of distraction. But Father did not rest for sandstorms, and I was sure he had already left our study assignments for the day.

Dread of the approaching storm was much like the frequent apprehension I felt from living in turbulent times; not knowing if today would be the day the Jewish rebels or our Roman overlords would change our lives forever. Thank God the Roman occupation rarely touched my life unless the Sicarii assassinated a priest. Then Mother would become hysterical, and Father would disappear into himself for days.

Jonathan and I were eighteen and spent our days studying from dawn to dusk, learning the holy scrolls and our responsibilities as future Temple priests. After completing his daily priestly duties, Father returned from the Temple to grill Jonathan and me about our lessons before allowing us our evening meal. I'm reasonably sure boys in other priestly homes were not subjected to such daily abuse. The only good thing about these torturous examination sessions is that Father would also not eat until we completed the oral examination to his satisfaction. Many an evening, I suspect the depth of his questioning depended on how hungry he was, and sometimes I heard his stomach rumble while waiting for me to finish explaining a more nuanced point of law. Nevertheless, I do have to admit, it gave me a great deal of satisfaction to inflict on him an equal measure of discomfort to the discomfort he imposed on Jonathan and me.

Ours was not a truly happy household, and sometimes, it felt more like a battlefield as our parents tried to shape us into what they thought we should be to bestow honor upon them and be a credit to our family. To illustrate, Mother had recently announced that Jonathan and I were to be married.

"Jonathan will marry Rivka, and Daniel will marry Rachel, her younger sister. They are the daughters of Mattathias and will maintain the purity of our bloodline and ensure our descendants will be priests forevermore."

Jonathan and I already knew of the young ladies and objected vociferously but to no avail. As Mother explained in her clipped speech, "There will be no discussion. Only these two young ladies meet all the criteria Father and I require of your future wives."

Lying quietly on my pallet as I struggled to wake up, I heard the sounds of morning in our household. Crows cawed incessantly outside my window, and the kitchen staff chatted and banged away as they prepared the morning meal.

"Daniel, Daniel?"

My brother's voice, as always, interrupted my thoughts. Knowing I would be spending the next eight hours closeted in a room with him, studying whatever esoteric texts Father had chosen for us, I decided to ignore him and rolled over.

"Daniel," Jonathan said again, this time louder. I sighed and rolled over to face him.

Jonathan, whose hair was a lighter shade of brown than my own but whose eyes resembled mine in their intense blueness, appeared anxious as he tried to get my attention.

"What was that sound?"

"I didn't hear anything," I said, just as I, too, heard a racket from downstairs.

"Stop, thief!" a voice rang out.

"Come on. We'd better go find out what's happening," I said as I dragged myself off my pallet, with Jonathan following close behind. We descended the marble stairs in our bare feet and crossed the honeysuckle-scented atrium to the kitchens, where the shouting continued. Mother's chef was holding onto the wrist of a beggar she had captured.

"Look what I caught," said Cook, as she was losing the battle to restrain the thief while he dragged her along the slick white marble floor, struggling to escape with the loaf of bread he clutched in his bony hands. "Stop trying to escape! And quit dragging me!"

"What's this all about?" I asked as I entered the kitchen while Jonathan took up position in the passageway from the dining room. Meanwhile, with a frantic look on his face, the unfortunate man desperately tried to flee before Jonathan and I got involved and brought the authorities.

"I caught this thief stealing bread from the cooling rack," Cook explained more animatedly than I could have managed so early in the morning.

I stepped back to look at the scoundrel and positioned myself between him and the alley doorway.

"Why, Cook," I said, "look at him. He's wasting away. His cheeks are sunken, his beard scraggly, and his arms are stick-thin. The dirt on his tunic weighs more than he does."

I disentangled the vagrant from Cook's grip, and he stood before me; his eyes locked on my face; his expression a mix of pride and fear.

"What are you doing here? I asked.

"I'm taking food to feed my family," he said.

I blocked his exit. "What makes you think you can just take our food?"

"You have a lot of bread, and out there, we have none."

"Out where?"

"Outside your door, there is no flour for bread. Don't you know that? People are starving to death. Haven't you heard?" the thief said while looking me up and down. "No. You don't look like you've ever missed a meal a day in your life."

"Why is there no flour?" I asked, looking at Cook, who nodded in agreement with the thief. "So, where do we get our flour?"

Obviously not wanting to say in front of the thief, Cook whispered, "We draw our flour from the Temple stores."

"And I can't," said the thief, "and my family is starving. We've only had a rotten onion to share between the three of us. How is it you don't know people are starving?"

"What is happening here?" Mother had arrived and stood in the hall outside the kitchen behind Jonathan. I had not yet offered my morning devotions, yet Mother appeared perfectly coiffed, dressed in a blue silk tunic, with a string of pearls at her neck. Her graying hair was done up in some intricate arrangement, and she smelled like a costly perfume. "Who is this creature, and why is he in our kitchen?"

"I caught—" Cook said, but I interrupted her.

"He is a brother Jew down on his luck, Mother, so I offered him a loaf of bread from the generosity of our home."

Mother took a step toward me but couldn't get past Jonathan. She gave him her notorious glare, but he held fast.

"Yes, Mother?" Jonathan was ever the wit, but Mother pushed past him.

"You are giving away our food?" she managed, planting herself in front of me and gracing me with a penetrating stare.

"Mother, it's just this one occasion. Right, Cook?" I said while I winked at Cook and the other kitchen staff over the thief's shoulder.

"Yes, Mother," chimed in Jonathan, not happy Mother had slipped by him to confront me.

"Just wait until I tell your father about this at supper."

Suddenly, the kitchen door burst open, and three Roman soldiers rushed in.

"Is this the rebel?" asked the commander as they grabbed the thief and threw him to the ground.

"What's happening here? Who called you?" I demanded.

"A servant brought us an urgent message saying a rebel was here," the centurion said gruffly. Mother had apparently heard the ruckus while still in her rooms and sent a servant to fetch the Roman soldiers.

"I sent the messenger, Daniel," Mother interjected imperiously. "Now, let these men do their duty and take him away. These rebels are a blight on us all."

"But he's not a rebel. He's just a starving Jew, Mother. What have you done?"

"You don't know that, Daniel. And he's a thief. So, take him away," she said in a tone that allowed for no more discussion.

Turning to the commander, I asked, "What will happen to him?"

"It doesn't matter if he's a rebel or a thief. Either way, he's a criminal, and he'll be found guilty and crucified, just like all the other criminals." Then, signaling to his men, he said, "Lift him up and bind him and let's get going. We've spent enough time with these Jews."

They had to drag the thief to a standing position to tie his arms behind his back. Not so hostile now, the fellow appeared just a poor Jew, unable to feed his family because of circumstances beyond his control. And my mother, from her rigid place of privilege that didn't let her see past her own powdered nose, had just sentenced him to death. Jonathan and I were mortified and cast our eyes to the floor as the squad of Roman soldiers dragged the poor fellow off to meet his fate. Just one of so many other Jews to be crucified that day.

"I cannot believe she called the Romans and not King Agrippa's troops." Agrippa's palace is closer than the Antonia Fortress, where the Roman troops are stationed. "And why did she lie about him being a rebel? The Romans will crucify him."

Jonathan and I were supposed to be studying, but I found it impossible. Not after what had just happened. Instead, we returned to our room, and Jonathan sat quietly on his pallet as I ranted and paced back and forth furiously. "I won't ever pretend to understand Mother. How could she call another human being a blight? He is a starving father with a family."

"With every new assassination of a priest, Mother becomes more afraid," he said. "What would she do if something happened to Father? What is she without him?"

"Brother dear, you always try to find the best in people, don't you?" I said, as pleasantly surprised by Jonathan's generosity of spirit as ever.

"Yes, Daniel, I have to find the best because if I don't, all I'm left with is the worst. And I don't want that. Come, let's go see what Father has left for us today."

CHAPTER

2

On a typical day, it was a pleasure to study in Father's library. Its clerestory windows allowed sunlight to illuminate the room all day long, and its two exterior doorways, one facing north and the other west, enabled gentle breezes to cool the room. But today was not a regular day. With the sky tinged dull red and the shocking events in the kitchen, I already wanted it to end.

"What has Father left for us?" asked Jonathan, sitting across from me on the other side of Father's enormous teak desk, which he had had built to make scroll-viewing easier. It had been carved in Rome and transported to Jerusalem at great expense. Father's instructions sat in the middle of the desk, and I picked them up and read aloud:

"Jonathan will study the eighth commandment, thou shalt not steal, and Daniel will study the sixth commandment, thou shalt not murder, and you will both be ready to present your thoughts on the implications of these commandments for the Jewish people at supper."

Was Father prescient? It's almost as if he knew a thief would pay us a visit today and that Mother would send him to his death. "I'm not sure I can manage this today," I said to Jonathan. "Both these topics are too real for me, given this morning's happenings, brother."

"You know Father as well as I do. He won't let us get away with not providing our analysis."

And, of course, Jonathan was right.

Father's library contained hundreds of scrolls, and we spent the next few hours looking up and comparing sources before formulating our positions. By late morning, Jonathan was getting impatient with me since he'd finished first. This was often the case; he was competitive by nature.

"I'm going to the kitchen to get us something to eat. Keep working," Jonathan said as he headed off.

With Jonathan away, my thoughts began to wander. I could not help thinking about the fellow who stole bread from us that morning and how he would always be connected in my mind to the commandment, thou shalt not kill, since Mother brought the Romans down on him, which will inevitably lead to his death.

"Are you finished?" Jonathan asked as he entered the room with a tray of food for me.

"Yes, but I have so many questions. I feel so isolated in this close-knit little world we live in. I had no idea things were so bad out there. Jonathan, can you tell me more about the poverty and starvation our thief spoke of?"

Handing me the tray, Jonathan looked at me quizzically from the other side of Father's desk. "You really must spend more time with other people, Daniel. How could you not know these things?"

"You are right, but you know me. I have always preferred the quiet life of reading and writing. You are the adventurous one. So, what have you learned in your wanderings?"

"Well, do you remember the ceremony, two years ago, when the Temple was completed and sanctified?"

"Certainly. Mother entertained for a week."

"So, you remember the celebrations. But did you realize the dedication of the Temple also brought the employment of eighteen thousand artisans to an end? Or how once the artisans had no income, the merchants who supplied their worldly goods also suffered?"

"But hadn't the workers saved for just that eventuality over the years when they were working?"

Jonathan gave an audible sigh and said, "Perhaps, but the people are heavily taxed by the Romans, who collect head and water taxes and excise taxes on foods, such as produce, meat, bread, and salt. And there are road taxes, collected at the juncture of every road. And on and on. And our fellow Jews still have to provide yearly half-shekel tithes to the Temple to maintain the priesthood and the costs of animal sacrifices they incur at each of the three required visits to the Temple during the pilgrimage festivals. Oh, and in addition, there is the tithe for the redemption of the firstborn, and they have to send their first fruits. If you combine all of the taxes and levies, do you know how much the people pay annually?"

"I have no idea, but I think you are about to tell me," I said as I arranged the scrolls I had perused during our morning studies.

"More than one-third of their annual income, that's how much. All these taxes and levies lead to impoverishment here in Jerusalem and starvation in the rural areas, where farmers can work the whole year and still not have enough to feed their families. In Galilee, they hate the Romans and the priests. They see us as parasites sucking them dry, and they are joining the ultranationalist Zealots in droves to help push the Romans out of Judea and reestablish Jewish independence."

"Are they succeeding?" I asked as I pushed back from Father's desk and opened one of the exterior doors to see how the sandstorm was progressing.

"They will never push the Romans out. Rome is an empire with a voracious appetite for conquest and the military might to overcome any opposition. But unfortunately, Rome also has an appetite for the wealth it steals from those it conquers. Much of Rome recently burned in a massive fire, and Emperor Nero needs funds to rebuild the city and build a new palace." So is that why the Roman governor, Gessius Florus, stole seventeen talents from the Temple?" asked Jonathan. "Exactly, where better to find riches than from the Temple in Jerusalem?"

"Surely the priests cannot be happy about the theft of seventeen talents?" I asked.

"Of course not, but they don't want to challenge the Romans for fear they will stop our daily sacrifices at the Temple. They are trying to protect our way of worship. But the Zealots and their splinter group, the Sicarii assassins, see this as collaborating with Rome."

Perplexed, I said, "But the priests don't collaborate with Rome. Look at Father. Do you hear him supporting the Romans?"

"Daniel, you're so naïve. Father's function at the Temple is to obtain the necessary ingredients for the incense used to anoint the holy utensils. He has contracted with a Roman purveyor to import the items he cannot get locally and has a side deal with his Roman contact to export balsam oil from Ein

Gedi, which is sold throughout the Roman Empire to make a costly perfume."

"Like the scent Mother wears?"

"Yes, and where do you think Father's wealth came from to build this extravagant house?"

"I have no idea. I always assumed this is what is due to priests for their hard work. So, Father is a collaborator?"

"I wouldn't call him that. The connections between the priesthood and Romans came about because our priests wanted to maintain the status quo in the way we worship at the Temple. And it worked. The Romans allowed special dispensation for us to continue worshiping as we have been, and that only came about because the priesthood convinced the Romans that denying traditional worship would cause more instability than not."

Having finished eating my midday meal now, I put the tray to the side, hoping I would remember to return it to the kitchen later. Father did not tolerate food in his library, and it was always best to remove the evidence.

Feeling like it was time to get back to our studies, I said, "Interesting times in which we live, Jonathan. Thank you for your explanations, but these problems seem intractable, and this conversation is getting us nowhere. Let's continue preparing our responses for Father."

Jonathan found a scroll he referenced earlier in the day and, opening it, said, "My lesson seems simple enough. Thou shalt not steal is simply stated and means exactly that. It is never acceptable to steal."

"You might think so," I said. "And if it is that simple, then thou shalt not kill is just as straightforward. But what about that poor fellow who stole from us this morning? He and his family are starving. So, shouldn't his theft be acceptable to prevent starvation, or should he just be allowed to die? Especially since he was stealing from a family that has never known hunger."

"You are overcomplicating the issue," said Jonathan. "If God meant for there to be exceptions, wouldn't the commandment be thou shalt not steal, unless you are starving?"

"I can say the same for murder," I said as I stood and paced the room. "Aren't there exceptions for defending oneself? For example, if a thug enters your home and threatens to kill your family, would God want you to let them, or would it be permissible to defend your family to the point of killing the invader? And what about accidents? What does the commandment say when a stonemason slips, dropping a building block on a passerby, resulting in their death?" I could see by Jonathan's face he was becoming bored, having likely thought through and disposed of all these concerns already.

Bouncing up from his seat, Jonathan said, "Again, I would argue you are overthinking this. I say the commandments are straightforward; don't steal, so don't steal, and don't kill, so don't kill. There's no need to examine every angle or every imaginable situation. Just don't. That's how God fit the commandments on two tablets that were small enough for Moses to carry down from Mount Sinai by himself."

"You're entitled to your interpretation, Jonathan. You present your understanding to Father at supper, and I'll present mine, and we'll see who's right."

Leaving Jonathan to mull over his straightforward explanation to Father, I slipped out of the library door into the atrium, where rainwater was gathered in a reflecting pool to irrigate the flora Mother had planted there. Then I took a walk through the neighborhood. It was good to move after so many hours of sitting and thinking, and it gave me a chance to wander aimlessly through my beloved Jerusalem. I stopped near Agrippa's Palace, where one can see over the outer wall to the hills beyond. The Romans had decorated the peaks of Jerusalem with crosses of those they considered criminals, crucified, and left to dangle like jewels on some grotesque necklace. I wondered if our bread thief was among them.

The family convened in the dining room as the sun began its final descent. Mother and Father spared no expense to decorate the space next to the atrium, and with its floral mosaics on the floor and multi-colored bird frescoes on the walls, it was my favorite room in the house. The Roman artisans who painted the frescoes had mixed pearl dust into the paint, causing the room to sparkle as it reflected light from the atrium in the courtyard during the day and from wall sconces at night. But not today; the sand-filled skies dampened the usually bright room and made it feel uncharacteristically gloomy.

Mother insisted the four of us gather for an elaborate and multi-course supper in the dining room every evening, where we sat around an enormous table of pure-white Jerusalem stone. The servants always set the table with Mother's finest stone utensils, which were the only tableware used by all the priestly families to ensure ritual purity, being nonporous and, therefore, impervious to contamination. The incongruity of the beautiful room, the events of the morning, and the dismal day were weighing on me.

Father had just returned from the Temple and washed and purified his hands in a bowl the servants had set out for him. When he finished, he gestured for us to be seated, with Mother across from him at the far end of the table, and Jonathan and I at the midpoint, facing each other.

"Who will go first?" Father asked as he stared at the fresh bread and olives laid out before him.

"I will," Jonathan volunteered, always happy to be done with it. He pushed his hair out of his eyes and spoke in a voice lower than usual to imitate the pompous priestly tone he had learned at Father's knee. "Thou shalt not steal is the eighth commandment, and it means exactly what God commanded—that people shall steal nothing from anyone else."

"Perfect, Jonathan. And why did God command people not to steal from each other?"

"Because He is God, and He commands. It is not our place to question why," said Jonathan with a confident smile on his face.

"Excellent, Jonathan. You are correct; we must not steal, and it is equally not our place to question God's wisdom. Daniel, what say you?"

Apparently, Father was hungry this evening and not expecting an elaborate discussion, so the conversation, so far, did not bode well for me. I sat up a little straighter and cautiously began my discourse.

"But Father," I said, "aren't there exceptions to not stealing when someone is starving?"

To my surprise, Mother stopped serving herself and said, "Just today, Daniel made an exception to the eighth commandment."

Father looked at me, cocked his eyebrow in the way only he could, and said, "What's this, Daniel?"

"He tried to reward a thief who stole bread from our kitchen," Mother said, expanding on her efforts to entangle me in trouble.

"What do you mean by 'reward'?" Father asked, shifting his attention from Mother back to me.

"Instead of handing him over to the authorities," Mother continued, "he allowed a miscreant who broke into our house to steal a loaf of bread he had taken from the kitchen. Daniel confronted the fellow but left it to me to notify the authorities, which I did, of course."

"What is this, Daniel? Why did you not take him to the authorities yourself, and who gave you permission to give away our food?"

I could not believe what I was hearing. I pushed my chair away from the table and stood, perhaps to boost my self-confidence by attaining my full height.

"But this is exactly my point, Father. Aren't there exceptions to the commandments? This poor fellow and his family hadn't eaten in days. Are we not supposed to provide *tzedakah* to the poor?" I noticed Jonathan eyeing his food and considering a bite but deciding against it.

"This is exactly how I arrived at my thinking on the sixth commandment, Father, for they are both easy to understand— don't steal and don't kill. There is nothing complicated about that. But, if that is true, why is there so much killing in our ancient stories, and why did Mother feel justified in sending this fellow to certain death by crucifixion by calling Roman troops instead of Agrippa's men?"

Mother objected in the background, but I was so focused on making my points, I could not hear her words. Father stood up and came closer as I took out a scroll I had brought from his library. I rolled it to the right place and continued. "In Deuteronomy, for example, God said to the Israelites, 'As for the towns of these people that the Lord your God is giving you as an inheritance, you must let nothing that breathes remain alive. You shall annihilate them all—the Hittites and the Amorites, the Canaanites and the Perizzites, the Hivites and the Jebusites—just as the Lord your God has commanded.' Which proves killing can be permissible, so long as God commands it."

At the edge of my attention, I heard Mother or Jonathan gasp, but I carried on. "So, then, what about the Sicarii? Aren't they trying to accomplish what God commanded in Deuteronomy; annihilating strangers in our land? Will God forgive the murders of collaborators perpetrated by the Sicarii to force the Romans from our land, even if God did not specifically command it?"

I missed all the signs of the arrival of the day's second storm. Father's face darkened, but I continued speaking. "And if someone attacks you, Father, and I were present, could I kill them to protect you? And what about accidents? What if a stonemason drops a building block on someone's head by accident and kills them? Is an accidental killing all right?"

"Stop talking."

"Does it all come down to the killer's intent? Is it ever permissible to kill, or is the commandment absolute? It couldn't be absolute because God wouldn't want you, such a venerable member of the priesthood, to be killed if I could prevent it by killing your attacker first. And God isn't unjust, so there must be special consideration if a killing is accidental. So, I think sometimes it must be permissible to kill, depending on the circumstances and the killer's intent. Actually, Father..."

The slap was so hard and so unexpected, it knocked me to the ground.

"Heretic! Stop before you infect us all with your filthy ideas! There is one God, and he delivered his commandments to Moses on Mount Sinai. The words burned onto the tablets are God's words and not open to interpretation by anyone, let alone a silly boy like you."

As I lay there, my ear ringing, the taste of blood in my mouth, and getting a close look at the beautiful mosaic on the floor, I felt, more than heard, a chair scrape, and then Jonathan was beside me, trying desperately to soothe me with kind words.

"Let me help you up, Daniel."

I started struggling to my feet, dazed, with my cheek burning, wondering to myself whether I was wrong and my brother was right. Jonathan tried to help me up, but I pushed him away, too embarrassed to accept his offer of assistance.

"Leave him, Jonathan," Father instructed.

Before Father could say another word, I got to my feet and ran from the beautiful dining room. I had no idea where I was going, but I had to get away from this family that was so obsessed with being perfect that it was beyond imperfect. I did not understand how they could be so cruel, and little did I know, as I ran out to the alleyway, I was heading straight from this awful situation right into the arms of my Sicarii abductors.

CHAPTER

3

I ran through the atrium, passed the servants who were coming from the kitchen, bringing our supper of roasted goat—a scent now ingrained in me for life; forever destined to remind me of that evening and the way Father and I left things.

I stopped for a moment at the gate to gather my thoughts and then took off running until I arrived at the Temple portico in time to witness the High Priest's assassination and to be nabbed by one of the killers.

"Hey! Take your hands off of me!" I called out as my kidnapper improved his grip on my belt and dragged me around a corner, out of sight of the Temple guards.

"Be quiet," he said, grabbing my wrist and twisting my arm high and tight against my back to make his point.

"What do you want from me?"

"Quiet. I won't tell you again."

Helplessly and clumsily, I lashed out, punching and scratching with my free hand, using the only tools available to someone raised as a scholar. I forced the fellow to lose his balance, but it was no use; he was bigger and stronger than me. He pushed me into the shadows, and another Sicarii joined us, who carried himself like a leader.

This head dagger-man turned to the one who took me and said, "Nathan, bind and gag him and bring him along quickly."

This Nathan's eyes bored into me as he assured his leader all would be well. Then, to me, he said, "You will be quiet and cooperate, or you'll walk with a dagger in your back." I glared back at him, which earned me a cuff on the head, but I nodded in assent. Then he tied my hands together with a coarse piece of rope, so snug it chafed.

"Not so tight," I said.

Not bothering to respond, he made a gag with a strip of cloth from his filthy tunic, which he shoved in my mouth, tying the ends behind my head.

"Eleazar," Nathan nodded to his leader, and with that, we began to weave through the city.

The bridge where I was taken is in the Upper City, home to the city's elites: where the priests, merchants, and members of the Sanhedrin, or the Jewish tribunal, lived. Their homes, in many instances, palaces, in other cases, luxurious villas like those found in Rome, were grouped together on the Western Hill, overlooking the Temple Mount. From where I was captured on the bridge, I could look out and see the entire Lower City, where the tradesmen and artisans lived in more humble abodes. Bisecting the Lower City, and running down the Central Valley, was a major thoroughfare, leading from the Dung Gate past the Siloam Pools and climbing to the plaza adjacent to the Temple entrance. Directly below me was the Hasmonean Palace, and off to the right in the distance was the Circus Maximus Theater, built by Herod the Great. I could also see most of the robust walls surrounding Jerusalem and the many towers and gates.

My captor dragged me down a staircase leading from the Zion Bridge and into the Lower City. He pulled me incessantly as we penetrated areas less well lit, where I stumbled more often in the darkness. We soon arrived at a part of the Lower City I was unfamiliar with. Approaching a large structure, I saw one of Eleazar's men slip away, and when we got closer, I realized he had disappeared through a tall fissure in the wall behind the building. Soon, it was my turn, and Nathan pushed me through the gap in the wall into a hidden world, where I immediately tripped and fell to my knees.

What is this place? I thought. *This is not the Jerusalem I know. Will I ever be able to go home again?*

The crack in the wall opened onto a small cave that led to an underground passageway. The tunnel floor sloped upward toward the Temple, but it was so dark, I could not see the ends in either direction. The passage was carved out of the rock, with oil lamps set in triangular slits cut into the dripping wet walls every few cubits. The lamps created small puddles of light to illuminate the way where the oil had not run out.

Residents of this underground world were sprawled everywhere, surrounded by water jugs, cooking utensils, and the personal detritus of people forced to leave their homes with little warning. Everywhere I looked, I saw people crammed into this subterranean world, accompanied by the odors of the day's cooking, which reminded me how hungry I was.

I frequently tripped with my hands still bound behind my back, and finally, Nathan decided it would be easier to remove my bindings so he wouldn't have to hold me upright. As we looked for a place to settle, I tried speaking through my gag, but my words came out so muffled they only irritated Nathan.

"Quiet. You don't need to talk."

But I tried again and again, and realizing I would not stop, he tugged the gag so it stretched over my jaw until I could clearly say, "Where are we? Who are these people?"

Enough light shone nearby for me to see Nathan's look of scorn as he answered in his low-pitched voice. "These people are Jewish patriots and freedom fighters." And snarling, he added, "These are the Sicarii, and they refuse to cooperate with Rome and give away our homeland like your family does."

Why does this man hate me so much?

"You assume a lot about my family, but what do you actually know about them?"

"I know all I need to know by looking at you," Nathan said, pointing to my tunic, which was fancier, decorated with more ornamentation, and cleaner than his. "You stink of privilege. Who's your father? A merchant, or maybe the lowest life form—a tax collector?"

My face flushed red, which he, fortunately, could not see in the poorly lit tunnel. "I work hard ten hours a day, six days a week, studying to be a Temple priest. I work with my mind, not with my hands, and there is nothing wrong with that."

"You're the son of a priest?"

"Yes," I responded without thinking, not realizing I had uttered the one word that could endanger my life even more.

"So you're the son of a collaborator?" Nathan was becoming more agitated by the moment. "*Yimakh shemo*—May his name be erased," he said as he cursed my father. Then he shoved me hard against the wall, where I tripped over some rubble and fell. "Your father and his sort collaborate with Romans and make themselves richer at our expense. Aren't you ashamed?" And then he beat me with his fists and kicked me in the ribs and stomach to punctuate his accusation.

"That's not the way it is," I managed between kicks, trying to protect myself. Then, finally, Nathan stopped his assault as if to give me a chance to explain. "The priesthood only cooperates with the Romans to preserve our traditions and our manner of worship."

"No, they do it to protect their privileges. How can a priest afford a fancy house? You have slaves working on Temple-owned land, and each priest gets a portion of the Temple tax people like me pay to worship." Warming to his subject now, he became more animated as he moved in closer, almost nose-to-nose, practically frothing at the mouth. "Priests get part of what money changers and the animal merchants charge at the Temple. It's all corrupt. That's what the priests really want. You're lucky I don't do to your family what they did to mine."

"What? The Temple priests did something to your family?"

"No, the tax collector. You're all collaborators. I lived with my parents and brothers on a farm in Galilee, and the tax collector forced us off our land. We had no place to go, and we asked the local priest if we could work on Temple land for food, but he turned us away because the priests have slaves for that."

Nathan's accusations of priestly collaboration didn't sound right to me. How could it be? Father was a senior priest, and he was always preaching to us about being good observant members of the community. But our home was luxurious, and Jonathan had mentioned Father's Roman partner. Now, seeing how these Sicarii live, I knew we were truly privileged to live the way we did. And what about that fellow in our kitchen that morning, with Mother and Father unwilling to share food with his starving family? That was not righteous of them.

Nathan had stopped talking and settled on the ground across from me to wait. These were the first quiet moments I had had to myself since supper, and it gave me a chance to think over what had happened. I sat there in the silence, thinking and nursing my wounds, certain the rebels in this rancid tunnel would kill me without hesitation.

With my ribs aching, I thought about the argument I'd had with Father. These Sicarii were genuine thugs. That must be why Father said there can be no exceptions to the commandments because some people will so quickly resort to violence and are incapable of understanding nuance. But I could never say these things out loud, for it would not end well for me.

What, then, were my options? Resist and try to escape, or go along? I needed more information before I could decide.

"Where are you taking me, Nathan? What's the plan?"

Nathan moved closer as if to not wake those sleeping on either side of us. And then he punched me so hard I held my tongue.

A wave of sound pierced my oblivion. Slowly, I pried my eyes open. The people in the cave were whispering to each other urgently.

"What is it?" I slurred.

"Be Quiet." Nathan rose to his feet and peered over the heads of those closest to us.

Eleazar and another equally tall man strode over to Nathan, and Eleazar, without prelude, said, "We're off to the caves at first light." Then, noticing me, added, "What is your name, boy, and who is your father?"

"Daniel, and where are you taking me?"

Eleazar scanned me up and down and frowned. "Who is your father, Daniel? And don't bother lying."

I had never been reluctant to announce Father's name before, but I was afraid to get caught in a lie. "Yochanan, a Temple priest."

"What luck is that? A priest's son," said the tall one, whom Eleazar addressed as Menachem.

"Yes, he'll fetch more than the son of a merchant. Nathan, when we return to Jerusalem in two days, I'll have you approach Daniel's father with a ransom note."

So they're holding me for ransom. I wish them luck with that.

Without waiting for an answer, Eleazar ordered Nathan to go with Menachem and his troops. "I'll take Daniel and a few men through the tunnel that drains into the Siloam Pool. Meet us at the caves as soon as you can. Menachem has a special surprise waiting for us."

Turning back to me, Eleazar gestured. "Come on, it's time to move."

I looked and saw him clearly for the first time. He appeared just as disheveled as I remembered from earlier when he murdered the High Priest. He was at least half a head taller than me, and he had to bend over not to bump against the roof of the tunnel. While he examined me, I noticed his eyes—cold and unfeeling, like those of a ruthless killer—and I reminded myself not to get on his wrong side.

Eleazar soon nudged me out of my thoughts, and we crawled over and around the unwashed bodies of Sicarii families. We pressed ourselves against the wall and squeezed through—rubbing against men and women alike—their foul-smelling bodies forcing me to hold my breath. Having never touched a woman before, except my mother, I flushed red in the dark as I squeezed by.

Finally, we emerged from the tunnel somewhere near the Temple and continued our progress through the back alleys of the Lower City until we came upon a water well cover hidden off a major thoroughfare. The entire time, I prayed we would meet a patrol, so I could cry out. But the thick air of the sandstorm and reduced visibility must have limited the number of patrols.

We came to a sudden halt, and Eleazar nudged me into the shadows. "Down there, Daniel." He slid the well cover aside and gestured for me to enter a dark vertical shaft. "Use the handholds. They're there, even if you can't see them. Wait for me at the bottom."

Soon, my feet found the ground, and I stood aside to allow Eleazar and the other men to descend. I was in a dark space, which opened into a larger square shaft, and I realized we were in Hezekiah's Tunnel, a water channel carved hundreds of years before to feed the Siloam Pool.

Eleazar lit a torch, and we began our trek. The tunnel zigged and occasionally zagged, heading downhill at a slight angle. Soon, another passage joined ours, and we found ourselves walking mid-shin in freshwater. After slogging along in silence, except for the squelching sound of our sandals, Eleazar stopped his men and turned to me.

"Daniel, we are leaving the tunnel in a few minutes. I don't want to hurt you, so I ask you now, will you promise to come without making a fuss?"

I nodded yes, but continued examining my surroundings, looking for any chance to escape.

Eleazar noticed my search. "Don't even try it, Daniel, unless you want to end up like the High Priest."

So appallingly warned, I was more discreet as I surveyed my surroundings.

The tunnel ends at the Siloam Pool, so Eleazar will exit the city through the Dung Gate. That's my best chance to escape. After that, I can go into the Hinnom Valley, and from there, circle back to the Essene Gate near Mother and Father's house. But will they even let me in? What choice do I have?

As we emerged from the tunnel at the Siloam Pool, moments past dawn, I spotted women filling their water jugs. This was my chance. The city gate was beyond the far side of the pool, and I hoped either my voice would carry far enough or one of the women would get the guards' attention.

How can I get away and cross the square without being recaptured? Will I be able to break away? I'll have to run as fast as I can. I have to go now before it's too late. This is it.

I jerked away from Eleazar and moved out of his reach by a few paces. Then, taking a deep breath, I shouted as loud as I could, "Help! Help me! These men are kidnapping me. My father's a Temple priest. Help me—"

Immediately, one of Eleazar's men threw his arms around me and wrestled me to the ground. I tried to break loose so I could run to the gate and attract their attention.

Some women raised their heads to see what the commotion was about, but they did not react, and it seemed the guards stationed at the gate were too far away to hear me. I had misjudged how far my voice would carry.

I should have waited until we were closer to…

Before I could finish my thought, someone hit me in the head hard enough to make me blackout.

CHAPTER

4

I awoke sometime late morning, judging by the position of the early summer sun, high in the sky and boring into my body. I was prone in a jolting mule-drawn wagon, surrounded by the Judean desert. My eyes were watering, I had a terrible pain in my head, and I was so confused about how I got to be there.

"What have you done to me?" I shouted at the cart driver. "And why do I smell like wine?" I soon stopped yelling because my head was throbbing and thought, *How did they get me past the guards and out of the city?*

The terrain changed as we moved deeper into the wilderness; the further we went, the more barren it became. Looking back to what had been my home, I could still see the massive walls of the city in the distance, the crenelations appearing like the maw of an enormous monster. With every step the beast of burden pulling the cart took, my surroundings became less familiar. How would I ever find my way home?

Finally, Eleazar yelled to the cart driver, "That rock cairn up there on the right is the turnoff from the path."

Once we turned, we climbed into the hills until we arrived at the mouths of several caves, well hidden from the main road. Eleazar gathered his men around a small clearing in front of one of the caverns.

"We'll use the caves as our base camp for a few weeks until after the Jerusalem campaign," he announced.

I looked around in wonder. *Are we going to live in these caves? Won't there be bats in there?*

"Settle in the men's cave up above tonight, and be ready to leave for Jerusalem again in the morning, where we'll join the battle against the collaborators," Eleazar said. Then, noticing me, he added, "Daniel, you'll be staying here until your father pays the ransom, and then we'll see."

The anger I had been holding in for so long spilled over. "What have you done to me? What sort of people are you? First, you grabbed me to help cover your escape, but now I find you have kidnapped me for profit."

"Settle down, Daniel." And with a cautionary tone to his voice, he added, "We'll talk later. Now, go eat something and rest."

I was exhausted, afraid, hungry, and every bone in my body hurt, so I bit my lip in silence.

"Malachi," Eleazar signaled to one of his soldiers standing nearby, "take Daniel to the men's cave and find him a pallet. Then look for a better pair of sandals than those pretty ones he's wearing and make sure he gets food and water."

"Yes, sir," the soldier replied and gave me a shove. "Get a move on."

We clambered up a goat path toward the upper caves, passing caves of all shapes and sizes along the way. As we climbed, I noticed Menachem arriving from Jerusalem with his men. Eleazar caught sight of him too and stopped him along the narrow trail directly below me to let him know a hunting party would soon return with an ibex for the evening meal.

"Good," I heard from our perch on the trail above them. Looking down, I saw Menachem for the first time since leaving the tunnels in Jerusalem. He stood just as tall as Eleazar, and there seemed to be a familial resemblance between them. I learned later that they were cousins. Both had a commanding presence, but the appearance of leadership seemed to weigh heavier on Menachem. He was a few years older and looked it, with bags under his eyes and a bald spot on his head.

Menachem resumed speaking. "We'll need a decent meal and rest tonight because it's back to Jerusalem tomorrow morning, armed with the equipment we brought from Masada."

So, the reports of a weapons cache at Masada were accurate. Every little boy in Israel has heard of the mighty stronghold, and I often played Invade the Fortress with my friends as a youngster. King Herod the Great, a convert to Judaism, built the Masada fort close to one hundred years earlier as a place of retreat if the Jewish population ever turned against him. According to lore, he had stored swords, spears, and shields for hundreds of defenders and food to last decades in massive storerooms.

Menachem pulled Eleazar aside and lowered his voice. "The sooner we get to Jerusalem, the more impact we can have."

"I'm assuming we'll go after those collaborating priests first, right?" asked Eleazar.

Do they plan to kill more priests? How will I get to Jerusalem before them to warn Father?

"You're thinking too small, Eleazar. First, we have to aid the Zealots to take care of those patricians—the old guard priests, the merchants, and other Roman supporters. Then we can help them chase the Romans out of the city."

Eleazar offered Menachem his waterskin.

Menachem thanked him, drank deeply, and then said, "With the weapons we are bringing from Masada and the two thousand men we can put in the field, we should be able to break the backs of those supporting the Romans in Judea. Then we'll take over the Temple and all of Jerusalem."

Eleazar stared at Menachem. "I didn't realize the scale of your ambitions."

Thrusting the water skin back into his cousin's hands, Menachem looked at Eleazar to see if he was being mocked. "You don't think that Ben Shimon is up to chasing the Romans out of Israel, do you?"

Eleazar put his arm around his cousin's shoulders and said, "No, he may be a Zealot leader, but he has always seemed so insignificant to me. There is no other but you who should lead the revolution. After all, you are the son of the rebel leader Judas of Galilee and learned from him more than any other."

"Good. I'm glad you agree." Then, nodding in the direction of his cave, Menachem said, "Now, come with me, and I'll show you the weapons we brought your men. The dry air left them in perfect condition and without rust."

Malachi was still climbing the path, so I bent over and fiddled with the lace of my sandal so he wouldn't think I was listening to the conversation going on below me.

They not only have the will, but with those weapons from Masada, they also have the way. How can I get back to Jerusalem before them to warn Father?

"Excellent. My men need proper equipment. Many of them are still using swords they inherited from their fathers or grandfathers."

The hunters returned with a few ibex at dusk, which they dressed and cooked over an open fire. True to his word, Eleazar had Malachi bring me to supper, and despite myself, the smell of roasting meat whetted my appetite as we waited for it to be ready.

Darkness fell, and feeling unwelcome and every bit the hostage, I sat on a flat rock in the shadows to eat and observe the warriors and their families nearer to the campfire. I noticed Nathan seated with a few other unmarried men and laughing uproariously.

"Malachi, where is Judith, that lovely sister of yours?" Nathan called out.

Once again, I could not help but notice the low pitch in Nathan's voice.

Malachi had stiffened and then responded. "Serving the food you are eating. So watch your tongue."

"Is that how you speak to your commander?"

"That's how I speak to a commander who disrespects my sister."

"Disrespect?" asked Nathan, scowling. "Why is it disrespectful to want to spend time with her?"

"So that's what you imagine will happen?" said a woman from the shadows. She stepped into the light now and poured a skin of water on his head. "You think I want to spend time with you, you presumptuous fool, when you cheapen me like this in front of the community?"

Nathan leaped to his feet. Malachi stood, and for some unknown reason, so did I, puffing myself up as if to stand by Malachi's side. I don't know what possessed me to do it, and I must have looked ridiculous, posturing as if coming to Malachi's rescue. But I soon realized I did not even come up to Malachi's chin and wondered to myself where they had found these hearty Sicarii.

"Whoa! What's this?" said Nathan. "You have an ally, Malachi? He's a good one to have on your side. He likes to get knocked about. I have it from personal experience."

"My name is Dan—"

Nathan reached over and pushed me down, hard. His friends laughed. Malachi leaned into Nathan, then, with his chest out and making fists with both hands, said, "Leave him alone."

Nathan stared intently, first at Judith and then at Malachi. "Come on, Malachi. Let's do it."

Somebody in the circle around the campfire mumbled under their breath, and a hush descended.

"What's that?" Nathan looked around the campfire, straining to see who spoke. "Who said that?"

"I did," said Judith.

"Repeat what you said."

"I said you're nothing but a bully."

Nathan launched himself at Malachi and me and tried to give us the beating I suspect he really wanted to give to Judith.

"Enough," Eleazar yelled, cupping his hands around his mouth so all would hear. "Save your energy for our adversaries. You'll have plenty of chances to fight come tomorrow."

"But I am fighting an enemy. Isn't Daniel the son of a priest?"

"End this now, Nathan. I promised Daniel his safety, and I won't have you violate my oath," Eleazar said as he moved in front of Nathan to block his way. "Break it up, everyone. It's time you all got some sleep. We have a long day heading back to Jerusalem tomorrow."

CHAPTER

5

It was dawn the following day when a kick startled me awake.

"Daniel, wake up! It's time to see the troops off to Jerusalem, and then we are going to earn our keep."

"Leave me alone. I want to finish my dream," I mumbled.

I was having a pleasant dream about how Father had invited me to eat a special meal with him. It was delicious, and... *Oh no. I fell asleep and didn't escape.*

"What's that?" my assailant asked. "Get up," he said as he kicked me again.

I opened my eyes enough to recognize Malachi. Around us, Menachem and Eleazar's men were gathering to leave for Jerusalem and were in a frenzy as they collected their belongings and ate before their departure.

"What did you mean when you said we are going to earn our keep?" I said.

Malachi rolled his eyes. "Everyone who wants to eat around here has to work, including hostages. So if you're hungry, you'd better get up."

"I will, but first, tell me where I can go to relieve myself."

"You mean take a piss?"

"Yes, among other things."

"Funny you should ask, Daniel. Today, you and I have been assigned to privy duty."

"What is privy duty?"

Laughing, Malachi said, "Come, I'll show you."

"Aren't you going to Jerusalem with the troops?"

"No, Eleazar assigned me to watch you to make sure you don't escape."

I tried lying there quietly for a few more minutes, just taking in the dark cave that had recently housed dozens of men, but Malachi was having none of it.

"Up with you" was coupled with a final, jarring kick to the foot.

The morning was uncomfortably quiet as the two of us worked side by side, digging new privy trenches and covering the old ones.

I have to learn more about these people. Malachi seems like a decent enough guy, but why is he a Sicarii?

Throughout the day, while wiping the sweat and flies from my eyes as we dug, I asked Malachi questions about the caves and the Sicarii.

"We've been using the caves for years."

"So, do you live here all the time?"

Flicking a fly from his face, Malachi mumbled an answer so he wouldn't have to open his mouth too much and risk swallowing the creature.

"No, sometimes we're here, and sometimes in the tunnels in Jerusalem; it depends whether we've been assigned a mission. But I'm not in the tunnels very often. That's only for the assassins. Eleazar had me trained as a soldier instead because I'm tall and too easy to spot and remember."

Interesting. So not everyone is an assassin. That makes sense, given the number of Sicarii Menachem mentioned yesterday. Two thousand assassins would be rather a lot.

The day grew hotter as we worked, and I spotted waves of heat shimmering up from the ground as the sun climbed higher in the summer sky. As I dug shovel after shovel of sand, the air burned my nostrils while the soil absorbed the heat and radiated it back out again, burning my feet through my sandals. I dreaded picking up the shovel to dig, for touching it felt like holding a poker used to move coals around in an oven; fine in the winter, but torture in the summer.

After a brief break in the shade of a boulder, I reached over to pick up a shovel when Malachi knocked it out of my hand without warning.

"Why did you do that?"

He pointed to where my hand had just been, and I saw a scorpion slowly backing away, its tail arched high, ready to strike.

"The yellow ones hurt the most," he explained.

After a long day of work and our evening meal, I collapsed by the campfire, my back aching and hands bloodied with broken blisters. Soon after, I moved a few paces away from the campfire to escape the heat as it made my sunburned skin feel ablaze.

"You did a good job today, Daniel," Malachi said as he took a seat next to me at the campfire. "Not bad for someone who has obviously never worked a day in his life."

I looked at him sidelong. He was a little older than me, and his well-muscled body spoke of years of soldiering. And he was a good-natured giant who freely wore a smile and was hard to dislike.

I felt conflicted. On the one hand, once we'd warmed up to each other, I enjoyed the time I spent with Malachi that day; but I could not forget he was my captor and guard.

"You are right. I have never done manual labor before," I said, deciding to act friendly and relaxed with him. That would help me escape later. "My mother always discouraged us from helping the servants, and my father thought it did not reflect well on us as future priests if we did physical labor. We could not risk being sullied as ritual purity is paramount for priests."

Malachi looked at me and nodded as if he understood, then returned to staring into the fire. I wasn't sure if he was interested, but I kept talking. "However, I see after our labors today I have missed out on the benefits of working, such as the satisfying feeling of a job well done and being exhausted from the hard work. I'm sure I'll sleep well tonight."

Malachi's eyes left the fire again and fastened themselves on me. He smiled. "It's most generous of you to recognize the many benefits those of us who have worked our entire lives have reaped." I thought I detected a note of sarcasm in what he said. "But tell me, Daniel, why do you talk like that?"

"What do you mean? What's wrong with the way I talk?" *Maybe this being friendly wasn't working out so well.*

"You sound like you are reciting a Temple prayer, so scholarly and very formal and polite."

I felt the color deepening on my face. "What are you talking about? I talk the way I talk."

Malachi shook his head and stared back into the fire. "It's all right. You just can't help yourself."

Somewhere in the distance, I heard a yipping and howling. "Jackals," Malachi explained as he stood abruptly. "I'm off to sleep now. You should come too."

We retired to the men's cave. I laid on the blanket and struggled to stay awake while Malachi fell asleep quickly. I would not fall asleep again and miss my chance to escape.

When Malachi's breathing was regular, I edged off my pallet, careful not to touch him across the small gap between our mattresses. I stood slowly, my knees creaking so loudly from the effort I thought Malachi heard the sound as he shifted in his bed. But no, he settled back down, and I took a step, and then another, and then he snorted, surfaced, and fell asleep again. The tension was unnerving, and I moved faster across the cave, figuring the stress was worse than getting caught. I could always claim I was going to visit our freshly dug latrine if he woke.

I crept my way toward the opening, encouraged by Malachi's deep snoring. Sentries no longer stood at the cave entrances since all available men were in Jerusalem now; only the elderly and convalescing remained. I made my way out of the cave and followed the goat path to a place where I could climb some rocks and head for the open desert. The going was rough, with stones of different sizes strewn everywhere, and I was afraid I would uncover a snake or scorpion every time I stumbled.

Am I heading in the right direction? The moon was behind me when I left the cave, and if I keep it behind me and walk for an hour and then make a right turn, I should eventually cross the path to Jerusalem.

Within an hour of leaving the camp, I was hopelessly lost, and not knowing in which direction to head, I hunkered down between a few rocks to wait for daybreak. Crouched in my hiding place, I heard the howling, laughing, and snarling of wild animals, and I trembled, expecting to be attacked at any moment to become some animal's repast. Then, exhausted from the long day of work and the stress of anticipating my violent death, I closed my eyes to rest.

My eyes flew open in the predawn, and I realized I had fallen asleep again, despite my fear of capture and wild animals. What woke me, though?

I heard it again—the sound of footsteps on gravel. And then Malachi's shadow fell upon me.

"You had to run, didn't you? Did you really think you could escape?"

Afraid of his wrath but relieved to be found, I was embarrassed to see I had only made it a few hundred paces from the cave. It seems my upbringing had not prepared me for a life outside the cloistered confines of the Temple, and I had walked in a circle.

"Come with me now," he said, as I stayed where I was, cowering, afraid of both the animals and the beating Malachi would now give me. "Stand up, Daniel. Do as I say, or I will have to drag you back to camp. If we leave now, I have a chance of getting us back before someone notices you are not there."

I looked up from the nook I was hiding in. "You don't intend to beat me?"

"I should. But what's the use of that?"

I was doubtful, based on my experience with these people since my kidnapping. "Nathan would beat me."

"Well, you should know by now, I'm not Nathan. But Daniel, promise me you won't try to run away again. Do you know what they will do to me if you escape? You don't want to know. So, promise me you won't try, and I'll forget this ever happened."

I'm shocked by his humanity, I thought to myself while looking up at him. *Nathan probably would have killed me. But how will I warn Father now? I don't see a way to escape. I don't know how to find my way in the desert, and I'm not a hero. I'm apparently unable to flee on my own, and if I keep trying, some wild beast will devour me.*

I promised him and thanked him for finding me. He didn't respond right away, and I noticed him staring at a spot near my left foot.

"What is it?"

"You're welcome, but before we go back to camp, I want you to crawl out of your hiding place and come toward me, making no sudden moves."

"I will, but why?"

"Just do as I say, Daniel. Now."

I slowly stood up from my crouch and moved toward him, and as I did, I caught movement out of the corner of my eye. Looking down, I saw a sand-colored snake with two horns sticking up above its eyes. It was as long and thick as my arm and slithered out from behind the rock where I had spent the night.

"Slowly. He doesn't want to bite you—he is just afraid."

"Not as afraid as I am," I said as the snake slid past me and slid away in the most mesmerizing undulating slither I have ever seen.

"That was close. A bite from that one would be a serious problem. If it didn't kill you outright, it would cause your limb to swell up to twice its usual size and produce unbearable pain. Assuming you lived, it would take at least a month to recover."

Completely frightened now and unsure how I survived the night, I put distance between myself and my nighttime hiding place. Then, on the way back to the caves, as we slipped on the loose rocks of the desert, I asked Malachi about the animal sounds I'd heard during the night.

"What sounds did you hear?"

"Snarling, howling, yelping, and laughing."

"The snarling was probably a leopard, although they are usually closer to Ein Gedi. The howling might have been a pack of wolves; the high-pitched yelping, jackals; and the laughing sound would have been a pack of hyenas. They were all attracted by the ibex we killed for dinner."

"Then thank you again for coming to find me. Now let's get out of here."

"Back to a day of work, then. Let's go."

Although exhausted from not enough sleep, Malachi and I spent an amiable time together that day, and again, we sat near each other at the campfire come sunset.

Since I had promised Malachi I would not try to escape again, I had to find a way to live with these people. So, I decided I'd try to get to know them better and tell them about my family and me to help them understand that not all priests are collaborators.

Looking intently over the fire, I tried to engage Malachi so I could watch his reactions as I shared my story.

"My parents raised me to believe Temple priests and their families were of a special class," I started, "with the High Priests more special than others. That might not be very nice, but it came about because of the injunction that priests must be pure when they sacrifice to God on behalf of the people. This sets us apart from everyone else to remain as unblemished and as pure as the sacrifices we make. This was not a choice we made, but one of God's admonishments."

Others began gathering around to listen, and I became uncomfortable speaking so openly about priestly affairs and stood to relieve my unease.

"I understand your point, Daniel, but this need for ritual purity has isolated the priests from the very people you represent," Malachi pointed out.

"That's true," I admitted. "My family members live very insular lives, obsessed as we are with both physical and familial bloodline purity. Except for our servants, I rarely come into contact with non-priestly individuals. This time I am spending with the Sicarii is an eye-opening experience for me."

"How so?" someone asked.

"Well, the only time I have heard mention of the Sicarii at home was when they kill a priest, and then my father calls them a scourge that would bring down the Romans on our heads and end the Temple rituals that make us what we are as a people. My father's position is not surprising given the Sicarii's targeting of Temple priests. He fears for his life."

"But the priests ignore the needs of the people. What about the Temple fees and collaborating with the Romans?" someone else asked from the shadows.

"I don't know about these things. Would someone tell me about them so I can better understand the perspective of the Sicarii? Malachi, can you help me understand?"

CHAPTER

6

I stood and threw more wood on the campfire, causing hundreds of insect-like orange sparks to fly into the sky. I had never experienced this before, and it became an aspect of living in the desert I came to love. We were so far from the city, the sky was black, and we could hear the absolute silence surrounding us. The stillness reminded me of being outside in Jerusalem during a heavy snowfall when the absence of people and the muffling effects of the snow amplify the silence.

I looked across the campfire to where Malachi sat, my question still hanging in the air, wondering if he would answer me.

He replied with his disarming smile. "Since you've asked so nicely, I'll tell you about myself. That way, I'll also tell you about the Sicarii. But if I hesitate, know it is because of the pain of reliving it. And you should also know, my story is my story, and every Sicarii has a different one."

Clearly wary of dredging up unpleasant memories, Malachi stood up and paced. His disembodied voice came to me from beyond the fire, accompanied by an occasional crackle as the sweet, sharp smell of a burning balsam branch permeated the air.

"My father was a stonemason who spent years working on the Temple. But that work ended a few years ago when the construction of the Temple was completed. Suddenly, my father found himself without work and in competition with hundreds of other stoneworkers for the few remaining building projects in the city."

While Malachi was speaking and pacing, a young woman came over, took his arm in hers, and put her head against his shoulder, making him stand still. Malachi brushed her forehead with a brief kiss, and as he did so, I could not help but notice how beautiful she was, with long black hair and dark eyes. But it was more than just her beauty that gripped me; there was a visible intelligence and toughness there, which I would soon experience firsthand.

"This is my sister, Judith," said Malachi, introducing her as he resumed his story. "The Roman artisans left for home, and the remaining Jewish masons starved. Not wanting to leave his beloved Jerusalem, my father pieced together what work he could, but it was never enough. All the craftsmen suffered, along with the merchants and traders. Only the priests thrived because the money to support them in the luxury they live in comes from the half-shekel levy each Jew pays to the Temple, a mandatory tithe to observe the pilgrimage festivals at the Temple. So, we pay the Roman taxes, and we pay the Temple priests. We are squeezed so hard, we cannot live."

Mistakenly thinking this might be a good time to share some of the wisdom imparted upon me growing up, I said, "My father always told us the people were happy to maintain the Temple and priesthood."

Snorting, Judith joined the conversation. "Daniel, don't you see how self-serving your father's position is, and as a result, how insulated your upbringing was? Didn't you look outside your parents' home and see the poverty and suffering of everyone else? Are you so naïve or just willfully blind?"

I remembered the thief, his stolen bread, and the death sentence Mother imposed on him, and I could hear the truth in their words.

"You are right. My parents hid the poverty you speak of from me, but they do not collaborate with the Romans."

Judith interjected again. "Daniel, there is more to our story. Let Malachi finish, and you will understand."

Malachi stood again. "Our mother was the first in our family to die of starvation. Our father lasted longer, but he couldn't face the shame of not feeding his family. By then, we were living in the tunnel under the grand staircase, the same one we Sicarii use today. The three of us slept next to each other, and one day, I awoke to see our father was missing. We waited for his return, thinking he had gone to relieve himself. Judith and I searched for him when he didn't come back, first in the tunnels, and later in the city. We still don't know what happened to him, but I think he wandered off into the desert, not able to cope with the disgrace of failing his family."

Still standing, Malachi went on as Judith took a seat on the other side of the fire. "We continued begging for food in different places around the city every day and sleeping in the tunnels every night. This period was hard for me but worse for Judith. If we separated, even for a few minutes, men would make assumptions and approach her."

Judith's eyes moved from the fire to the ground. Malachi noticed and went to her, wrapping his arm around her shoulders to soothe her. "There were so many nights we fell asleep famished, only to face the next day with more of the same. Then, finally, after several months, we met a rough-looking group of men in the tunnel, and they took us to their leader, Eleazar, and he took us in."

I stood and walked over to Malachi. Looking at him, I said, "It is unforgivable that I didn't know my family was so affluent when others were so poor. My father taught me the people wanted priests to live the way we do, and I never thought to question him."

"Well, I've about finished my story, and when I'm done, you can throw yourself at my feet and beg forgiveness," Malachi said with a small, forced chuckle.

I returned to my seat as Malachi finished.

"We've been with Eleazar and his troops for three years now, and while it hasn't always been easy, they have always taken good care of us."

I took a few moments in silent reflection to think about Malachi's and Judith's story. Their suffering had been horrific. Yet, this type of destitution and suffering had been happening right outside my family's door.

I struggled to see Malachi's and Judith's faces from my seated position. Standing to see them better, I said, "I am sorry for what you experienced and for my blindness to the plight of my fellow Jews." Then, shaking my head in disbelief at my ignorance, I added, "I don't know how I could not have known these things, but I thank you for sharing your story and helping me see through your eyes, so I can now put away my father's version of reality."

Judith stood up and had the last word. "I am glad you could see through our eyes, Daniel, but do not pity us ever, for you insult us with your newfound and easily gained insights. Instead, when you return to Jerusalem, use your privileged position to improve the lot of those less fortunate than you. Then the telling of our story will have been worth it."

Judith's harsh words caught me up, and all I could do was nod my silent acquiescence. At this rebuke, I decided to retire with Malachi to our cave, whereupon I settled down to sleep with embarrassing recriminations swirling around in my mind.

CHAPTER

7

· · · · · · · · · · ● ● ● ● **●** ● ● ● ● · · · · · ·

Weeks later, I was lying on my pallet in the already heated air before dawn. My eyes were closed, and I was considering whether to get out of bed when Malachi once again kicked my foot to wake me up. I was startled and blurted out, "Stop!" *This is becoming quite the habit.* "Don't kick me. Just call my name," I added, too energetically.

"Sorry, we're on latrine duty again today. Up you go."

I hate speaking so early in the morning. "Why? We just dug new ditches two weeks ago. Are they full already?"

"Well, you use them every day, so you should know, but that's not the reason. The warriors started arriving from Jerusalem late last night, so we're going to need more pits. Come on."

After breaking our fast, we gathered our tools and reported to the trenches. Long lines had already formed, and people looked impatient.

"Let's wait until everyone is finished with their business," Malachi suggested. Meanwhile, he spotted some friends back from Jerusalem.

"How goes it, Ephraim? How was Jerusalem?"

"We routed the Romans," mumbled Ephraim, "and took the Antonia Fortress."

"I'm sorry I wasn't there."

"Don't be. You're lucky you were here."

"Why? What happened?"

The line moved forward as Ephraim answered. "Things started out all right, but in the end, we had to leave Jerusalem in a hurry. But I'll leave it to Eleazar to tell the story. He should be back soon."

It took Eleazar another day to arrive, and it was Malachi and me who spotted him first. With hundreds of soldiers returning from Jerusalem, they had assigned us latrine duty for the second day. We were lucky, though, since we were digging new latrines, so we could situate them away from the ones in use. The soil in the new location was sandy with small rocks, so our shovels came out full each time. As we dug, an image of Father digging latrines crept into my mind, and I chuckled loud enough to be heard.

With salty sweat dripping into his eyes and beard, Malachi wiped his face on each shoulder and then said, "What's so funny, Daniel?"

"Sorry. I was imagining my father here in my place, which amused me considerably."

"Do you hate your father so much you would wish him here instead of you?" Malachi asked.

It was a good question, and I pondered it for a moment. *Father was not a loving parent, always holding Jonathan and me to exacting and unattainable standards. But did I wish him ill?*

"Daniel. Are you there?" Malachi asked, tapping on my head like he was knocking on a door.

"Sorry," I said, just as I caught movement on the path from Jerusalem out of the corner of my eye. "I don't hate him, but he makes it hard to love him." I still had told no one about my argument with Father for fear it would lead to my death. *Does he even wonder what happened to me? By now, Eleazar must have sent him a ransom note. Did he agree to pay?*

"Malachi, look," I said, pointing over the crest, "Isn't that Eleazar?" We were behind a small hill, so Eleazar could not easily see us, but we watched him while he approached the caves.

Malachi stopped digging and leaned on his shovel to watch. "He looks terrible. Things must not have gone well in Jerusalem."

The contrast in Eleazar's appearance from when he left for Jerusalem and now was alarming. Then, he stood tall; now, he appeared bent over and unkempt. I could hear him mumbling to himself, but I couldn't make out what he was saying.

As Eleazar approached the camp guards, he straightened up and ran his fingers through his hair and beard. The sentries noticed him and shouted his name, and word spread quickly through the caves, announcing his arrival. Malachi and I joined the gathering crowd, and Eleazar, overwhelmed by all the attention, thanked the throng and promised to speak with us after he got some rest.

The following morning, Malachi once again kicked my foot to wake me.

"What?" I responded peevishly.

"Sorry. I forgot not to kick. Eleazar has summoned you to his cave."

"What does he want from me?"

"I don't know, but I have learned from experience that it is always best to jump when Eleazar says jump.

"All right," I said as I stood and smoothed my hair and tunic down the best I could. I climbed the goat path to the commanders' cave, and an armed sentry stopped me as I approached.

Smirking, he managed a "What do *you* want?"

"Eleazar summoned me, so you might want to announce me. Do you know my name?"

"Everyone knows the name of the collaborator's son."

Single-mindedness must be a highly sought-after quality in killers.

"The collaborator is here," he announced, so loud the bats at the back of Eleazar's cave could hear him.

I heard Eleazar's muffled response, and the guard stepped aside to let me pass. I found Eleazar sitting partially in the shadows, one leg dangling from his pallet, eating a breakfast of olives and freshly baked bread.

My stomach growled, and I said, "Good morning," before Eleazar, his mouth still full, had a chance to.

He swallowed. "And to you, Daniel. How have you been settling in?"

"Considering I am being held for ransom by killers in the middle of the desert, I am doing well."

"I'm glad to see your sense of humor has not abandoned you," he said while rising from the bed.

"Why did you summon me?"

"You've been here for weeks now, and we must decide what to do with you."

"Did my father pay the ransom?"

"No, I sent Nathan with the ransom note, but the Upper City was in turmoil."

"So, you want me to choose between returning to my family or staying with the Sicarii without knowing whether my family will pay the ransom? That is a simple choice. I will not remain with you. How could I live with a group committed to killing people like my father?"

"You need to reconsider, Daniel."

"Why is that?" I asked. "Why not collect the payment and let me go?"

He looked at me with an expression I did not recognize and said, "I would, Daniel, but your situation has changed. Your family has been taken from you, just as mine was from me several years ago."

"What do you mean, 'taken'?" I said as the meaning of his words dawned on me. "Are they dead? What does this have to do with your family?" I asked, stepping closer as I heard the guard behind me matching my steps. "What did you do to them?"

"I did nothing, and this has nothing to do with my family, other than to signify I too understand the pain of loss. My wife and two young children were killed by a priest's security squad in retribution for the assassination of the priest's son. But I was a teacher in Jerusalem then and not part of the Sicarii, and they were murdered for being in the wrong place at the wrong time."

"I care only about my family—not yours."

"Daniel, I understand you said that from a place of pain, so I will ignore it. Let me tell you that when Nathan took the ransom note to your father, he found brigands had invaded the house. Everything of value had been stolen, and the occupants of the house lay dead. And to make matters worse, there are no longer bodies to bury, or a house for you to inherit since your parents' home caught fire later that night when the High Priest's house next door was burned to the ground."

"And Mattathias's family—what happened to his daughters?

"Mattathias's family is dead."

"No, I don't believe you. You sent Nathan to do this. You know he hates me. Why did he have to kill them? Why?"

"It was not Nathan, and I did not command it. I promise you that."

With spittle flying, I screamed, "You're a liar!" I screwed up my face to control my emotions, but nothing could stop the tears from flowing. "Why should I believe you? You are a killer. I was on the bridge and saw you murder the High Priest. I know what you're capable of. Why is violence always the way for you?"

"Because it works. There is nothing violence won't solve. The Romans and the priests have taught me this many times over." Eleazar continued. "I still suffer the consequences of the violence in Jerusalem. And last night, as I lay awake, twisting and turning, remembering how my men were killed at the Temple, and my dear cousin, Menachem, was tortured and killed in the Lower City, I realized, yet again, how effective violence can be."

I hadn't known that. So Eleazar's cousin is dead, and it sounds like Eleazar witnessed his killing.

Pacing back and forth and quite worked up now, Eleazar continued. "And because it is so effective, I will further embrace violence and single-handedly wield it to eliminate all collaborators and force our Roman enemies to give up and go home. That is why our retreat to Masada is so important. It will give us the time to rebuild our forces and prepare for the final onslaught against Rome's presence in Judea, and I, Eleazar Ben Yair, and my troops will push them out and achieve a glorious victory."

While Eleazar rambled on with his delusions about the use of violence, all I could think of was my family.

They were all dead. My dear brother, Jonathan, the better part of my soul, is gone. My mother, who could grate on me like no other person, and father, the cruel and loveless taskmaster, are both gone forever. And poor Rachel. They died without even knowing what happened to me.

What will I do? I thought Father would pay the ransom, I would return home, and everything would be the way it was. I want to tell Father I agree with him now—there can be no exceptions to the commandments. I've learned that allowing exceptions would only give the Sicarii the cover of law for their murderous activities.

But now, there is nothing for me to go home to. I have no place to live and no way of providing for myself. I have to tell Eleazar I will remain with the Sicarii, though I do not know what that means. Eleazar says they are going to Masada, but will I become a Sicarii warrior?

Snapping out of my reverie, I became mindful of Eleazar staring at me, still waiting for an answer. "I will stay with you, not because I have a choice in the matter, but because I don't. You have taken everything from me."

Ending his monologue on violence, Eleazar said, "I'm sorry for your loss, Daniel, and I understand your decision is not by choice. However, now that I no longer expect you to be ransomed, I will release you from captivity, and you can join us as an equal member of our community. In return, you will work and support the community and come to our defense if we are threatened. Do you accept these conditions?"

"Yes, but from a lack of options."

"So be it. Now go find something to eat and return to work," he said as he gestured for me to leave.

The Sicarii pooled their resources and labor, so breakfast was provided communally. I arrived as people were forming up and got into line to wait my turn. It relieved me not to see anyone I knew, so I could continue my thoughts unabated. When I finally arrived at the front of the line, I saw Judith was the server and greeted her. As I did, someone shoved me from behind.

"To the back of the line quisling. This line is for warriors only," said one of Eleazar's soldiers.

"Then why are these women and the elderly in line?" I asked unwisely.

Taken aback by my gumption and emboldened by his friend's behavior, a second soldier pushed me to the ground and stepped into my place.

"We don't answer to you. Now get out of line," he said as he turned to Judith. "Give me bread and olives," he ordered.

Once again, I am the object of their derision, I thought, hoping my cheeks weren't too red from my humiliation. *Have I made a mistake telling Eleazar I will stay? How can I live among these miscreants?*

Judith's response heartened me. She stepped out from behind the table, helped me stand up while pulling me to the side, and gave me half a loaf of bread and some olives with oil.

"Hey, why are you serving him first?" one soldier asked.

Ignoring him, Judith said, "Here, Daniel, take these and go before they cause more trouble."

"Thank you," I said as I took the items from her while grimacing because of the torn skin on my hands.

She took my free hand, and noticing the injuries, added, "Come to me after I finish serving, and I'll clean these cuts and put a balm on them."

"Thank you again," I said, as her kindness opened a floodgate of tears. Judith noticed, and I whispered to her, "Eleazar just told me my family is dead. Brigands killed my parents and twin brother when they plundered my parents' villa. I can never go home." I said nothing of Rachel.

Whispering back, she said, "I am so sorry, Daniel. I know how much it hurts to lose everything."

Her compassion hurt so much. I feared meeting her eyes, but I choked out, "My parents and I were not close, but they were my parents, after all. But my brother and I were like one. I can't believe I'll never see him again."

"You know our parents are also dead, so maybe we can be like family to each other."

I saw the empathy and need for family in her eyes and responded with understated enthusiasm. "I would like that."

CHAPTER

8

• • • • • • • • • • ● ● ● • • • • • • • • •

That night, we began our trek to Masada. We were over five hundred strong, with more children and elderly than Sicarii troops. The going was treacherous—we were hiking at night to avoid the day's harsh sun, and the terrain we walked on was rocky and prone to small landslides.

Before we began our final descent into the Asphalt Lake valley on the second day, Eleazar called a halt to the march and gathered us close to him so everyone could hear. Then, picking up one of the young children and holding her in his arms, he announced, "We will rest here so you can wash the trail dust off yourselves in Ein Gedi's pools and allow your injuries to heal."

Most of the people I'd spoken with had heard of the Ein Gedi waterfalls, but few of the Sicarii, composed as they were of people living on society's margins, had actually been to visit. Thrilled with this opportunity to enjoy the famous spot, they expressed their pleasure with smiles while Eleazar continued.

"Come sunrise, I want to send a few scouting parties in to check out the town closest to us. First, we have to know if they'll welcome us as their new neighbors or if they'll see us as a threat. We also have to see if they'll be willing to trade with us since there are so few natural resources in the area."

Someone from the crowd shouted, "But what do we have to trade with?"

"You're right. We have little, but soon, we'll have our own crops and orchards. Masada is well-suited to growing fruits and vegetables.

He didn't answer the question, I thought to myself.

"But it's in the middle of the desert. Is there enough water to raise crops?" someone else called out.

"Yes, King Herod was a smart one," Eleazar responded. "He built huge cisterns that refill every year during the rainy season, so we'll always have water to grow our crops. Enough questions now. My little friend is getting restless," Eleazar said, indicating the young girl still in his arms. "Ruben, Nathan, and all the lieutenants report to me, and we will arrange for the scouting parties. Daniel, you too."

Almost a dozen of us gathered and tried to get comfortable as we settled on the rocky ground around the campfire.

Standing so all could see him, Eleazar began the briefing. "We will dress a few of our smartest men as Essenes to visit the marketplace. Ruben will lead this group." Then, holding up a pouch, he added, "Take a few coins from this purse so you can buy some supplies. Go in small groups and take a few donkeys with you."

"How much should we take?" someone cried.

Eleazar turned to Nathan. "How much is enough to buy several bunches of dates?" he asked under his breath. Nathan whispered in his ear, then Eleazar raised his head again. "Half a shekel. And while you're negotiating with the seller, find out what you can. Then, once you've gathered the intelligence, send one man back to camp to report."

"What will my team be doing?" asked Nathan.

"Your team will go to the farms to buy agricultural supplies to grow dates, figs, wheat, barley, and other vegetables."

"What about livestock?"

"We have enough goats for cheese and yogurt, but we will also need chickens for eggs. So, buy supplies we can consume in the coming weeks, but buy seeds too."

Eleazar looked around to see where his coin purse was and went over to retrieve it. Then, throwing it to Nathan, he said, "Take two shekels, but I'll also give you surplus weapons from Masada to trade."

"What if they are not interested in trading for weapons?" Nathan asked.

"You must gather these supplies any way you can. We will die without them. Any other questions?"

I stood up so Eleazar could see me. "Do you intend to force the people of Ein Gedi to provide supplies if they are not willing to trade?"

"I didn't tell Nathan to take them by force. I told him to gather them by any means necessary, Daniel. And don't try to be my priest or my conscience. I won't have it. These people collaborate with Rome, so they are our enemies."

"So, you mean to steal them? Won't that violate the eighth commandment, not to steal?"

"What did I just say, Daniel? Didn't I tell you not to be my conscience? We have a code we live by, right, Nathan?"

"Right, sir. In Deuteronomy, God commanded we kill all our enemies, and that's what we do."

I could not believe Nathan was alluding to the same part of Deuteronomy I had quoted to Father weeks earlier. Appalled, I looked back at Eleazar and said, "Maybe you do need me to be your conscience if that's how you think we should treat our neighbors. We might have to depend on their generosity someday. Besides, Ein Gedi is a royal estate, and stealing from these people will attract Rome's attention."

Scowling, Eleazar said, "Every person here has suffered severe deprivation since the rebellion, and I can't subject them to more starvation, especially to protect a whole settlement of Roman collaborators."

"But—"

"Enough, Daniel," Eleazar cut me off. "You misunderstand. This is a military operation, and I am your commander. I don't answer to you." Then, turning in the direction of his lieutenants, Eleazar said, "Gather your men, and Nathan, come see me for weapons. We leave at dawn. You're dismissed."

Dressed in the pure white of the Essenes, our groups descended into Ein Gedi, arriving as the merchants were setting up their stalls. The market was smaller than the one in Jerusalem but not as claustrophobic since the buildings in Ein Gedi were mostly one-storied. We approached where fruits and vegetables were displayed, next to the pens where the butchers kept their goats and sheep before slaughter. The stench of rotting blood from the previous day's butchery lingered, and even the strong scents from the spice market nearby could not overcome the smell of dead animals that had seeped into the ground.

Those of us assigned to gauge Ein Gedi's willingness to have new neighbors split into smaller parties and visited the stalls in the market. We soon had our answer. Yes, the residents of Ein Gedi had heard of Masada's occupation by those killers, the Sicarii. Yes, news of the Sicarii withdrawal from Jerusalem had already reached their ears, which they shared with us with glee. They hoped the miscreants would now disperse back to where they came from so Ein Gedi could resume its profitable balsam oil trade with the Romans in Judea and Rome itself.

We left Ein Gedi walking north and soon circled back toward camp to meet Eleazar. Nathan's scout had not returned yet, so I found Judith, and we sat together while enjoying a meal.

With Judith sitting close enough to hear, Malachi asked whether I would join the men that evening if a raid was necessary.

"I don't see how I can. Eleazar granted me my freedom, but I still have to live according to Jewish law."

"I'm not sure how that will work, Daniel. We Sicarii have to make exceptions to living by the commandments all the time to accomplish our larger goal of forcing the Romans out of Israel."

"Does that include stealing from our neighbors?"

"If it's that or starve, then yes."

"But what if it causes our neighbors to starve?"

"You make things overly complicated and ask too many questions, Daniel."

"Hmm, I'm sure my brother and father would have agreed."

"Anyway, I think you should," Malachi said, and I saw Judith give a slight nod in agreement. "Eleazar is not a patient man, and if you don't show him a willingness to join us, he might decide he's done with you. I know because I have heard him say so already. And that's without considering what Nathan might be whispering in his ear to turn him against you."

Malachi's comments and Judith's nod gave me a lot to think about. The more I did, the more I realized I was in danger if I could not adapt. Ein Gedi was a desolate place, and I could easily have an accident. Would anyone notice if I vanished? Would anyone care?

Nathan's runner soon arrived with news of their only limited success. He would need our help to acquire the remaining stores and had meanwhile dispersed his troops into the fields on the outskirts of Ein Gedi to rest and wait for our arrival.

Still reluctant to break any commandments, I said, "I see I have no choice. It's a matter of *pikuach nefesh*, and in this case, the life it is preserving is mine."

We returned to Ein Gedi that night in silence, and the troops went about their tasks unmolested. I was later sickened to learn Eleazar and three of his men had slit the throats of the four village guards so they couldn't warn their neighbors of our activities.

We went from farm to farm, gathering what we needed by breaking into storage sheds, stealing seeds of every type, and praying we would not be caught. Whether the barking of dogs or the creaking of door hinges, every sound made me think someone was about to detect us. But we went the entire night without being discovered.

We stole shovels, saws, and carts to carry our cuttings in, and then we went into the orchards and used the shovels to separate date pups from the sides of the mother trees. We took cuttings from olive and pomegranate trees, causing immeasurable harm to them, and collected dozens of chicks, which we threw into sacks so they wouldn't run away. Come morning, the people of Ein Gedi would wake up to the utter devastation we had wreaked upon their farms.

When we finished, a large group of us readied ourselves to set out, but the guilt of the damage we did overwhelmed me. Unable to control myself, I went to where Eleazar was issuing orders to his men and, interrupting his instructions, I grabbed his arm and said, "How can you do this to fellow Jews?"

Eleazar looked up at me, shocked I had grabbed him and spun him toward me.

"They will—," I started to say when Eleazar backhanded me across the face so hard that he knocked me to the ground. Again, my ear was ringing, and I could taste the blood seeping into my mouth. This was the second time someone had slapped me hard enough to drop me in a heap. That my own father did it was unforgivable but ultimately forgiven. That Eleazar did it was unforgivable and would never be forgiven.

"Silence Daniel! Don't say another word! I won't tolerate any more of your Ten Commandments speeches." Then, turning to Nathan, he said, "Bind him until I tell you to release him. Now, let's go." And cruel Nathan once again tied my arms behind my back as tight as he could, securing my ankles for good measure.

Why couldn't I learn to keep my mouth shut? Did I have a need to always be right, or was it because I genuinely believed in the obligation to follow the Ten Commandments and the other six-hundred-thirteen rules in the *Tanakh*? I could obey the laws myself and not insist others do so, but not confronting others condones their actions, which is the same as me choosing to disobey God's laws.

Nathan threw me into a cart and had one of his soldiers drive it back to the Ein Gedi camp. People gathered around to see who was trussed up like an animal and didn't seem surprised to see me. Many of the children had fun poking me with sticks until Judith saw me bound and put an end to it.

"What happened to you? Why are you tied up, and why is your face swollen?" Then, looking at Nathan, she ordered him to "Come over here and cut these ropes."

Nathan ignored her.

Refocusing her attention on me, she asked again, "Why are you tied up?"

Stretching my jaw to relieve the pain, I said, "I asked Eleazar why we were stealing from our fellow Jews, and he hit me. I don't think he liked my question."

"Be quiet," Nathan shouted at me. "Judith, you shouldn't get too close to this one."

"Thanks for the advice, Nathan." And facing me, she whispered, "No, he doesn't like having his authority challenged. You'd better be more careful around him. Stay right here, and I'll get something to help the swelling." She walked to her belongings and brought back a water skin, three longish green leaves, and a mortar and pestle from her pack. She sat down next to me where I still laid, bound with the rough ropes chafing my wrists and ankles.

"Judith, I told you to leave him be. What are you doing?"

"Stop trying to tell me what to do, Nathan. You are not my brother or my husband. I do not have to, and will not, abide by you."

Turning to me, Judith said, "These leaves will make a poultice to keep the swelling down." She tore the leaves into smaller pieces, put them into her mortar, and added water. Then, slowly, she ground them together. After she's made a paste, she surreptitiously loosened my bindings. Finally, she applied the unguent to the swollen side of my face—touching me again—and causing my breath to catch. I pretended it was due to pain, but admit it was the pleasure of feeling her fingers on me.

"This should ease the abrasion, and the balm should help the healing," she said close to my ear so Nathan could not hear, and again caused my breath to catch.

"You are really quite good at healing."

Judith stopped what she was doing and looked at me. "Thank you for seeing me, Daniel. I enjoy healing and want to learn more. Hopefully, there will be someone at Masada I can study with. Maybe Dorit, the midwife, will accept me as an apprentice, and I will learn to deliver babies too. I can't think of anything better than helping mothers give birth and being able to heal people."

At that moment, I realized how dear Judith was becoming to me, and it pained me to think I would leave her behind when I escaped that evening. For I'd decided I could not stay with the Sicarii. Just then, the cart jolted, and we resumed our trek, with me still loosely bound in the back of the mule-driven cart, shaking my way to Masada.

Darkness descended, and the moon had not yet risen when I attempted my escape. I was well-rested, having slept most of the day, and Nathan was no longer walking next to me, giving me time to loosen my bindings even more. I shifted my head to watch the cart driver and noticed his head bobbing as he fought off sleep. The family walking behind us had slowed down and opened a wide gap, so there was no one close by to see me escape the ropes, stretch my legs, and drop off the cart when I saw an outcropping of rocks I could use to slip into the shadows and wait for the caravan to pass me by.

I waited for the cart to hit a rock and timed my jump off to coincide with the bump. My feet hit the ground in a perfectly timed maneuver, and as they did, I fell on my face as the forward motion of the cart and my numb legs executed a flawless attack on my balance. Struggling to get up, I took long enough for the family behind me to close the gap, see me, and sound the alarm. Nathan, of course, appeared out of nowhere, and began to beat me with enthusiasm.

"Thought you'd escape, did you?" he asked, panting from exertion.

"Stop, you brute," Judith yelled as she tried first to grab Nathan's arm, and when that didn't work, to get between Nathan and me to protect me with her body. "You're going to kill him. Stop it!"

"So what?"

"You'll have to go through me to do it," she said.

I suppose he must have called upon his tiny bit of remaining humanity because Nathan restrained himself. Instead, he retied my bindings and, once again, threw me into the cart while admonishing the cart driver to pay better attention.

CHAPTER

9

We arrived at the base of Masada at dawn and with the sun at our backs. Eleazar was walking the length of the human caravan when he came to my cart.

"Where is Nathan?" he asked no one in particular. "And why is Daniel still tied up?" Then, as he untied the ropes binding me, he explained, "This was not my intention, Daniel. I told Nathan to release you when you got back to camp yesterday, not to leave you tied up overnight."

I collapsed as I tried to stand, my wrists and ankles in agony from the chafing of the ropes, and my arms wouldn't move since Nathan had bound them even more tightly behind my back after my escape attempt. Then, still prone, I rolled around and sat facing the rear of the cart, letting my legs dangle. A thousand daggers stabbed me from my knees to toes.

"Daniel, I will not tolerate a repeat of you lecturing me. Never do that again."

He reminds me of Father scolding me for something requiring no further explanation, but I better not argue with him. So, I let him run on, just like I would Father, as the daggers completed their work.

Judith broke through the crowd, carrying her mortar and pestle, and I watched in delight as she prepared another concoction and set about touching me and healing me again. When she finished and rejoined Malachi, I craned my neck around to get my first look at Masada.

The approach to the fortress had been a strenuous affair and required hours of careful walking across a plain of rocky sediment washed down from the Judean hills above. Crossing this plain is difficult because of the jagged rockiness of the deposits. It slows people and animals and is especially torturous for those still recovering from being bound and thrown into carts.

Masada is the highest landmass in its immediate environs. Still, its presence can sneak up on you because the terrain is uniform in color for as far as one can see, disguising the height of the sprawling plateaus. Once across the rocky plain, we still had to wend our way between and over the crisscrossing foothills. Craning my neck from where I was, I could see the infamous Snake Path, so named because the white trail resembles a serpent ascending the mountain, twisting back and forth on itself at least a dozen times to moderate the steepness of the ascent.

"Daniel!"

I turned to see Malachi and Judith approaching from the front of the procession of marchers.

Are these people my friends? I'm not sure I know the answer, but they are two of the friendliest people I have met since being taken as a hostage. But I can't ever allow myself to forget they are Sicarii. If I met them under different circumstances, I would call them friends, even though we come from disparate backgrounds. But I will have to decide soon, since I'm developing feelings for Judith, and I think she might be doing the same for me.

"How are you?" Malachi asked when they joined us.

"Better."

"I just heard Eleazar yelling at Nathan for what he did to you." Malachi looked me in the eye and said, "My friend, acts of violence brought you here, but I know you have no place to go now, so I hope you can find it in your heart to stay with us.

They have been awfully nice to me, but I'm not sure I can get too close to them. It's too soon.

By now, the marchers had come to a standstill and were uncertain how to proceed without clear direction. As we stood waiting, we heard shouts from the lieutenants for us to come closer to hear Eleazar's words.

"The first group to climb the Snake Path will be my troops and the young and healthy. We will depart in a few minutes," Eleazar announced.

Climbing a little higher on the path, I suppose so he could be better seen and heard, he added, "It's a short but intense climb, and carrying our belongings should take us about two hours to ascend. Be sure to stay on the path, so you won't cause rock falls for those behind you."

Using a mantle he had wrapped around his shoulders, Eleazar illustrated how everyone should cover their eyes, noses, and mouths to protect themselves from the dust those in front would inadvertently kick up. "Once at the top, you will be free to explore. Before resting, find open rooms in the casemate walls so we can move everyone into temporary shelters by tomorrow."

Calling to his lieutenants to gather round, Eleazar added, "As soon as we finish the climb and everyone finds a place to sleep and a bite to eat, we'll descend the Snake Path again and help the rest of the community to the top. If you can volunteer to help, let one of the lieutenants know. All right, let's move."

Judith asked how my legs were feeling, and Malachi slapped me on the back, almost knocking me over. "Daniel, will you join us during the climb?"

"I would enjoy that," I said. "Let's go. And don't leave this poor city dweller behind."

For an urbanite like me, raised to be a priest, the climb was intimidating. The Snake Path is insidious. It starts out as a slow incline, but your leg muscles are soon screaming from exertion, and that's before the steeper part of the climb begins. The gradient is more arduous than it appears, although the direction switching back and forth helps reduce the angle of ascent, at least. With the first zig in the path, I realized its cruel joke: we had covered the same hundred paces, only a little higher up. Within minutes, I had soaked through my tunic and tried to make light of it to Judith, who was close by.

"I think my waterskin is leaking."

"Really? I didn't know a waterskin on your right hip could leak under both arms and down the middle of your back."

"I am an exuberant climber, and those are splashes," I said but then gave up the banter so I could catch my breath and continue the relentless climb.

As we approached the steeper gradients, I heard shouting from ahead and looked up to see someone swept off their feet by a minor landslide. They stood up right away, shook themselves off, and continued their ascent, but I noticed they were now climbing with a pronounced limp.

"Being such an accomplished climber, you should have given us all a lesson in avoiding avalanches before we started on our way," Judith teased.

"Don't laugh," I said, trying to breathe. "It is a difficult skill to learn, but an important one on a hill like this," I added, trying to catch my breath and struggling to finish the sentence.

That earned me another little grin.

We continued to climb as the sun rose with us, mocking us and making each step harder. As the gradient increased, I bent over to compensate, and my breathing became shallower. I was desperate to stop and rest, but couldn't, because I didn't want Judith to leave me behind. And the path was so narrow that if I stopped, it would hold everyone up. So, we continued to climb, more than halfway up the facade now, and as we approached the next zig in the path, someone twenty paces above us staggered and stepped off the trail, releasing a salvo of large rocks in our direction. I dropped my baggage and jumped for Judith. Grabbing her around the waist, I pulled her to the side, only to trip and have her land on me as we slid down the hill in a tight embrace.

Again with the touching, but this time, our bodies are in full contact. Judith's ribs and waist are narrow, and her hair has a sweet smell, with just a hint of dust from the climb. As I recovered and remembered the embrace, I noticed a slight bulge where there shouldn't be one and bent myself at the waist so others wouldn't see.

This is a breach of Jewish law. Even though a prohibition on touching a woman who is not my wife is not specified in the Ten Commandments, it is mentioned in Leviticus. Like with killing, there can be no exceptions. How can I accept that touching a woman by accident is all right but not admit that killing someone by accident is all right? I'm not such a hypocrite.

Once the rocks had stopped sliding down the hill, others scurried from below and above us to make sure we were uninjured. We did our best to rise with our dignity intact, dust ourselves off, and assure them we had survived the ordeal. This time, I caught Malachi's expression, and it contained a look of concern.

Looking at the ground, embarrassed but warmed by the physical contact, I said, "Judith, we should find a *mikvah* once we reach the summit to purify ourselves."

Standing there on the trail, with hundreds of people waiting for us to continue climbing, she cocked her head, gave me a stern look, and said, "I may not be as exact in my observance as you, Daniel, but I am not soiled by what happened. It was an accident."

"How or why it happened doesn't change that it happened," I said, "so we must purify ourselves."

"Then please do so, Daniel. Just don't tell me what to do."

After an uncomfortable silence, we struggled back onto the path, careful not to cause our own landslide, and continued climbing for another hour. Within minutes of our fall, we arrived at what I now know was the most challenging part of the ascent. The Snake Path ends before the top in a vertical climb, which slows everyone to a crawl. Those of us further back in line put our belongings down so we could rest, and before long, it was our turn.

Hand-over-hand, we climbed the last section, with the sun bearing down on us relentlessly—sweat pouring down our faces. Here and there, someone had carved steps into the rock. But as I climbed, I wondered how we would get the elderly and injured up this steep incline.

After a few more paces, I arrived at the casemate wall. Judith was waiting but looked away when I came to stand near her. Eventually, she turned to me and said, "Daniel, don't ever take that sort of liberty with me again."

"I'm sorry, Judith, I was just trying to save you from being overcome by the landslide."

"I'm not talking about saving me from the rocks. I'm talking about presuming you can tell me I need to be ritually purified. I've had enough of men telling me what to do in my life, and I won't tolerate it from you. Especially since I thought we were becoming friends."

I had never heard a woman talk to a man like this before, and the concept of men and women being friends was a foreign one to me, even though I now realized that's what Judith and I had become. In Jerusalem, every woman I knew deferred to their fathers, husbands, and brothers, and I thought that was the way it was supposed to be. My betrothed, Rachel, whom I had not thought about once since being abducted, never spoke to a man unless spoken to and would never reveal her thoughts to a man. I much preferred Judith's way, but how to tell her without sounding like it was my place to approve or disapprove of her actions, which would be just as bad as my original offense?

All I could think of saying was, "Thanks for being honest with me, Judith. I didn't mean to overstep, but I see I did. So, please forgive my presumptuousness, and I promise not to do it again. I hope you'll forgive me."

Judith looked at me, tilted her head a little as if seeing me for the first time, and gave me a brief smile in return. From this, I surmised it was the right thing to say.

Still standing close, but not together, we looked back down at the climb we had made. I was awestruck by the beauty at our feet. It was late morning, and the sun was climbing high above the red-drenched Nabatean mountains to the east, the sky was a brilliant cobalt blue and streaked with a few puffy white clouds, and resplendent in its varying shades from deep indigo to cerulean, was the Asphalt Lake—the dead sea, so-called because it supports no life. This was to be our new home, and I enjoyed sharing the view with Malachi and Judith. Overwhelmed by the beauty, I smiled, turned, and passed through the Snake Path gate to our future.

CHAPTER

10

I had heard of Masada and its fortress since I was a boy. King Herod the Great had built it as a retreat in case the Jewish population of Judea ever turned against him. Herod lived in constant fear of revolt, since he was an Idumaean whose family had converted to Judaism, and there were large portions of the population that never accepted him as a fit leader for the Jewish people.

Passing through the Snake Path gate, I came to understand the level of Herod's paranoia. The casemate wall is, in fact, a double wall comprising an outer wall made of stones, an arm span deep, and an inner wall half as thick. Between the inner and outer walls, there is a gap three arm spans wide, which Herod's soldiers and workers had used as windowless living quarters. It was these same spaces that would become our new homes.

"Daniel, come with me. Let's explore," Malachi said as he headed off to an entrance to one of the towers closest to the gate.

I looked at Judith to see what she thought, and she nodded, so I took off after him. Then, from behind me, I heard her say, almost to herself, "You two go. I'll look for rooms for us while you're away."

The casemate wall encompasses the entire mesa, which is roughly diamond-shaped, with its points in each of the cardinal directions. The wall has a battlement with twenty-seven guard towers interspersed along its length. Each tower is twice the height of the casemate wall and is reached by stairs from the ground or by ladders from the parapet.

We climbed the stairs and ladder to the top of the tower and didn't know which incredible view to take in first. To the east was the breathtaking vista of the red Nabatean Mountains and the Asphalt Lake. Behind us was Masada's plateau, which is not as level as it appears. Instead, it slopes up from the side with the Snake Path, with the highest points being near what I later learned was the storeroom complex to our right and another gate straight ahead of us. Seeing that we were in the desert, I had expected the soil to be dust and rocks, but it appeared a rich brown loam, with small areas of lush plantings near the palaces and small oases of palm trees off to the left.

Looking directly ahead, we saw a building composed of a series of arches opening onto a courtyard, where many of Eleazar's troops had assembled. Then, looking further left and entirely across the plateau, we saw an extravagant complex that must have been Herod's Palace.

The majority of Masada's buildings seemed to be to our right, so that's the direction we headed next. We could see a guard tower and a dovecote in the near distance, and further to the north, we saw a vast complex of ten or more long and narrow buildings and numerous other structures. Following the parapet for a few minutes, we soon found ourselves above the long buildings, which had openings on one of their long ends. We surmised these were the infamous storage facilities Herod had filled to bursting over a hundred years before.

Continuing to the northwest corner of Masada, we were surprised to look back and see another sumptuous three-tiered palace built on the side of the northernmost façade of the promontory, which had been hidden from view when we stood above it. The uppermost level housed King Herod's living quarters and a semicircular balcony, which had afforded the king views of the Asphalt Lake, the northern plains, and the Judean desert to the west. The middle tier was circular, and its use was inscrutable from where we stood. Finally, the lower terrace was surrounded by colonnades on three sides, and we assumed it was a festive hall where Herod would have entertained his guests.

We continued walking on the western casemate wall, passing the same palace we had already seen in the middle of the plateau, arriving finally at the southern fort, where some Sicarii troops were already stationed. The views looking out from Masada were striking in all directions. From the southernmost tip of Masada, we looked out across a jagged ravine onto a plateau in the distance. Further on, looking down from the Snake Path casemate wall, we were able to look north and east into an abyss-like rift leading from the Masada plateau to the Asphalt Lake and the Nabatean Mountains directly beyond.

We had entered on the eastern side of the plateau through one of Masada's three gates, and when we arrived back at our starting point, Eleazar was waiting for us inside on a slight rise, surrounded by those who preceded us.

"Gather round," we heard Eleazar's lieutenants saying as they corralled us into a group at the bottom of the rise where Eleazar was standing. "Eleazar will address the community."

Standing above us all on a small crest and waving his arms to highlight what he was saying, Eleazar began his remarks. "Welcome to Masada, your new home. Isn't it as beautiful as I promised?" I saw bobbing heads of consent throughout the crowd. "This is a new beginning, and I encourage you all to find a space to call your own and settle in. The casemate wall contains room enough for most of our families. Once the wall is at capacity, the remaining families will overflow into the visitors' quarters right behind me. We'll reconvene tomorrow evening, and I'll tell you what life will be like in Masada. Go now, find your new homes, and rest."

As the crowd dispersed, I started moving away when Judith said, "I found two shaded rooms near each other with a fresh breeze. Let's put our belongings in them, and then we can eat," she added, apparently having set aside her earlier annoyance with me. "Soon, families will be everywhere, so we should go quickly."

"An excellent idea," said Malachi, and with that, Judith settled it; we were to become neighbors and live near each other for all our years at Masada.

"Come, Daniel. You heard Judith. Let's go," Malachi said with a smile.

Ever competent, Judith pointed across the plateau and said, "Malachi, breezes will come from the left of the Northern Palace, so that's where I found rooms."

"Good idea," said Malachi. "Besides, Eleazar and his lieutenants will be in the palaces. So, we'll be close, but not too close."

We continued to climb beyond where Eleazar stood and passed what he called the visitor's quarters, which we later learned is where visiting guests would have stayed in Herod's day. Judith informed us she had entered a room in the casemate wall directly behind them, but soon realized a few of Menachem's men, who had been at Masada since liberating it from the Roman garrison, were already living there.

Nearby, Judith led us to two adjacent rooms with separate entrances close by the Western Palace. Our new quarters were small compared to what I was used to, but I soon realized they were the nicest rooms on Masada because of the prevailing breezes that cooled them.

We weren't the only ones to appreciate how nice the rooms were. As we stood by the entrance to the rooms we had selected, one of the more boorish Sicarii, Simon, walked by, still looking for accommodations. Seeing the three of us standing outside such pleasant rooms and realizing I was not Sicarii, he decided to take my quarters.

Simon came near, standing close enough for me to smell his sour breath. "You can't have this room. These rooms are for Sicarii only."

With as straight a face as possible, I responded: "I must have missed the inscription over the door. How do you know?"

"What?" he asked. "What are you talking about? There are no inscriptions."

"Then how do you know these rooms are only for Sicarii?"

Puzzled by my question, he called a friend over for help. "Amos, who should have this room, us or the collaborator?"

"Us, of course."

Expecting no less from Amos, I almost said something foolish when Malachi intervened and saved me from a likely thrashing. He took them aside, whispered something, and they left without a word. I was relieved since the constant attacks by ignorant Sicarii were wearing on me.

Amazed by their departure, I asked Malachi what he said to make them leave.

"I told them Eleazar wanted you near him because he didn't trust you not to stir up trouble."

I couldn't help but admire his creativity, and I smiled my thanks.

As the sun continued to climb in the sky, we moved closer to the casemate wall to find some shade and resumed discussing our living arrangements.

"We'll need to build cooking stoves in each room. I've never built anything before, but I'll help you, Malachi," I said.

"No need for two stoves," said Judith. "I can cook for you sometimes, and other times you can fetch food from the communal kitchen."

"Thank you," I said to Judith with sincere gratitude. "I don't know what I would have done otherwise. I've never cooked anything before either."

"By your own admission, you can't build or cook anything. So, what are you good for?" And there it was again, Judith's grin that accompanies her teasing.

"I can tell you everything you ever wanted to know, or not know, about the Ten Commandments."

"God, help us," the siblings replied in unison.

"Well, it's settled," said Malachi. "I like this location. We can see the whole plateau from here, and we'll be right in the middle of things."

We all agreed.

"I don't know about you two," I said, "but I am famished after that climb. Let's see what we have in our packs we can eat now. I don't think I can wait to prepare food."

"I have two pomegranates and a few handfuls of olives," Judith said.

"I have a few figs," Malachi said.

"And I have two handfuls of dates," I said. "Yet another Judean feast."

Then we heard one of the lieutenants shouting outside. "If you've already found shelter, go to the storage rooms for food."

"What food could they have prepared so fast?" I asked, looking at Malachi.

"Who knows, but let's find out."

Our rooms were close to the storerooms, so we followed the gathering crowds. As we rounded the hill near the Northern Palace, we could see cisterns to the left and the storeroom complex to the right. It was vast and comprised multiple chambers, each so long, we couldn't see the back wall from their doorways. We followed the crowds until we came to a narrow gate between the wall and a large building in front of the storehouse complex. I couldn't detect any food smells in the air, likely because the scorched air of the desert overwhelmed everything.

Many of the doors were open, and Malachi and I peeked in, where we saw a wealth of stored food. Herod had laid in supplies to outlast any siege, including corn and assorted legumes in clay storage vessels, dates, dried fig cakes, barley, walnuts, and endless jars of olive oil and wine. It amazed me these stores had lasted so long, as if a miracle had saved them for the day the Sicarii would need them.

Malachi and I joined a line, and a lieutenant gave us handfuls of dates and a fig cake to add to our veritable feast. Back at our rooms, we cleansed our hands, thanked God for the food, and sat with Judith for our first meal together.

This is starting to feel like a family.

Malachi and I descended the incline from our room to the Snake Path gate to join the others in bringing up the elderly from below. We were late, and Eleazar was pacing aggressively, glowering as he waited for us stragglers to reach the gate. Standing around him were his lieutenants, armed with swords and shields as before, which I thought odd since he was inside the walls of an isolated desert fortress, surrounded by his own people.

With the sun getting lower in the sky, the eastern side of Masada, including the Snake Path, was now in complete shade, even while the top of Masada remained in sunlight, and the air was cooling quickly.

Eleazar stopped his pacing long enough to ask Nathan a question. "Were you able to find ropes?"

"Yes."

"Good. We'll need the ropes for the elderly and injured. Leave them right outside of the Snake Path gate. All right, let's get going."

Last night's beating and the first climb of Masada earlier in the day had not yet depleted my enthusiasm, and as the day advanced, I still had excess energy to expend, perhaps due to the excitement of my budding friendship with Judith. Feeling thus endowed, I said to Malachi, "I'll race you to the bottom."

"Wait," he shouted as he grabbed my arm. "This is dangerous. You don't want to cause another avalanche."

"He's right," someone chimed in.

"Daniel, trust me, or you'll be sorry."

"How do you know it's dangerous? You've never gone down before."

"Yes, I have. I was here last month with Menachem's men when we defeated the Roman garrison. One of the men caused a landslide."

"I didn't know that."

"It is just one of many things you don't know about me, Daniel. Now, listen. Climbing up Masada, you took one step at a time. But going down, you can cause a rockslide, with you sliding on your backside in the middle of it, or you can tumble head-over-heels. So, to prevent yourself from rolling like a stone, turn your feet parallel to the mountaintop and sidle your way down while bending at the knees like this."

He showed me what he meant, and I followed Malachi's example, and we arrived uninjured at the bottom in one-quarter of the time it took us to ascend.

"Malachi, let's find your friend, Aaron the stonemason, with the broken leg and help him to the top. He'll need the extra help."

"That's very generous of you, Daniel."

"If I am to live among you, I have to show people I am not the spoiled son of a priest, and I can do that by working hard and making myself indispensable."

"Well, if you want to help Aaron, let's go find him," Malachi said as we wandered around the base camp, and after a quick tour of the elderly and injured, found Aaron and offered him our help.

"I don't know. Are you sure your helper's strong enough not to drop me?" Aaron asked Malachi, only half in jest.

"I've worked with Daniel for a month now, and there is nothing to fear. He is determined and reliable."

And with Malachi's endorsement, we began our climb of Masada for the second time that day, with Aaron's right arm over Malachi's shoulder, his left arm perched on the top of my head, and his crutch from his broken leg banging against my knees with every step.

We had only gotten as far as the first switchback when I noticed a small cloud of dust in the foothills, near where the second group of climbers had gathered.

"What is that?" I asked my companions. "It looks like a group of riders on horseback." We were fascinated, mainly because horses were a rarity in Israel, so these riders must have been foreign or very wealthy.

As we stood watching, the cloud resolved itself into three riders on horseback approaching at a gallop.

"Who leads here?" the one outfitted in a fine green Roman-style tunic asked, glaring down at the crowd as the riders came to a sudden halt, causing a cloud of dust to envelop the gathering.

"I do," said Eleazar in his most haughty manner. "And who are you, and what do you mean by charging at us like cavalry?"

"We are Joseph, Ezra, and Benjamin, representatives from Ein Gedi, and you and your people are despicable. It will take us years to recover from the damage and thievery of your thugs. Ein Gedi is a royal estate and valued by the Romans, so we will report your actions to the Roman general in Caesarea Maritima."

"A royal estate, you say, and valued by the Romans? So, you are close to the Romans, would you say?"

"Of course, we are close. Ein Gedi is the only place in the world where the *afarsemon* balsam grows, which is valued by the Romans and Egyptians for the perfume it makes. Queen Cleopatra herself would often send for our balsam oil, and we have a thriving business of exporting it to Rome."

Eleazar turned to his followers, and with a knowing tone, asked, "So then, is it accurate to say you have an accommodation with Rome?"

It was then that this Joseph of Ein Gedi realized the people gathered before him were Sicarii who kill collaborators, and that he, in his quickness to accuse us of wanton destruction, had condemned himself.

Trying to extricate himself, he said, "We are not collaborators, but business partners. We export our goods to their markets, but there is no collaboration."

"I think we will have to agree that we shall never agree on that point. But for now, I say, go report our actions to your Roman friends. Tell them Eleazar Ben Yair, supreme commander of the Sicarii, looks forward to the day we'll send the Roman general and his troops back to Rome with their tails between their legs, or else scatter their bones to be parched by our desert sun. Tell them where to find us." And with that gratuitous provocation, Eleazar turned his back on our visitors and began his ascent of Masada while I stood on the path a few paces above him, shocked by his imprudent challenge to Rome.

CHAPTER

11

The next day, a Friday, was treated like Shabbat. Many of us, exhausted by the trek from the caves, lazed around to replenish our strength. It was a welcome reprieve, and shortly after the evening meal, one of the lieutenants walked the grounds and called everyone to assemble.

"Gather round! Gather round! Meet at the crest to hear Eleazar's remarks," he intoned.

The heat of the day was already dissipating, and we gathered, somewhat refreshed, for Eleazar's assembly. Everyone congregated around the same crest we did when we'd arrived the day before, and Eleazar stood against the dramatic backdrop of a large moon, flanked by fires on tripods, with his armed lieutenants on either side. He appeared very much the supreme commander. The community arrayed themselves around him in all directions. Some sat, and others stood, and all but the closest struggled to hear.

Eleazar paced back and forth on the crest as he prepared to share his thoughts and then stopped in front of a small group of soldiers I didn't recognize. Addressing the leader of these troops, Eleazar began.

"I want to start by thanking Samuel and his men for holding Masada for us after taking it from the Roman garrison. I know Menachem was proud of your leadership when you liberated Masada, Samuel. Thank you for your service, and I will now incorporate you and your men into my forces."

Turning back to the larger audience, Eleazar continued. "To the rest of you, I am so proud of you. You have endured the hardships of Jerusalem, a difficult march from the caves to Masada, and then climbed the treacherous Snake Path. We lost a few of our elderly and injured along the way, and for them, I say, 'Blessed are you, Lord, our God, king of the universe. Please bless our friends and family who have joined you in the heavenly host and know we will remember and honor them always.'"

The assembly mumbled, "Amen."

"We have overcome a lot and will overcome more still as we settle into our new lives. But, unfortunately, we left the caves so quickly, I never had the chance to share with you the grand success of our Jerusalem campaign."

Was that groaning I just heard?

"Jerusalem was an important milestone in our battle to force the Romans from our land and punish the priests who collaborate with them. We have spent years assassinating priests to convince them to stop supporting Rome, but their forces are still here. So, this campaign was a direct action against the Romans and their allies among the Jews."

"Where's Menachem?" someone shouted from the crowd.

With narrow eyes, Eleazar responded, "I'll get to that soon. Have patience, my friends." Eleazar descended from the crest and moved through the gathering as he spoke. "After we left the caves a few weeks ago, our troops went to the Lower City, where we joined up with Zealot forces. The weapons we brought from Masada were much needed, so they invited us to join them in the hopes we'd help turn the tide in battle.

"The night we arrived, we had great success. Led by Menachem's troops, we defeated King Agrippa's army, and the next night we burned the High Priest's house."

So, the Sicarii forces were responsible for burning down my parents' home.

Eleazar continued. "And you'll be happy to know we burned the money-lender bonds in the city records office, so they can't prove who owes what to whom." Many in the crowd cheered for their good fortune as they had left debts behind.

Eleazar motioned for everyone to quiet down and then continued. "Our men were at the front of every action. Using strategies developed by Menachem, we attacked the Antonia Fortress and the Royal Palace the night after and won every battle."

I looked to the front, where many of Eleazar's troops were gathered, and noticed them shuffling their feet and speaking to each other in low tones.

"Malachi," I said, "according to Eleazar, the Sicarii forces had a grand success, so why aren't his men celebrating?"

"Good question. Maybe Eleazar's just trying to put a good face on it. But we never heard the full story from Ephriam," he responded.

Eleazar hesitated as he looked at his troops and then back to the audience. "After a few days, we noticed the other insurgency leaders becoming jealous of Menachem's successes and his popularity with the troops. We didn't think it was a serious problem until our men captured the former High Priest, Ananias, whom we found hiding in his palace. Menachem wanted to execute him right away for collaborating with Rome, but the other leaders refused, and so Menachem ordered his men to execute the priest at night after the Zealots had gone to sleep.

"The following morning, Menachem and I went with our men to worship at the Temple. Menachem appeared in royal blue garments his men had found when they ransacked the Royal Palace, and his men wore the armor brought from Masada. As we approached the Nicanor Gate, the other rebel leaders confronted him, furious that Menachem's men had executed the priest. We were all gathered in the Women's Court, and they accused him of being a tyrant, and just as they weren't willing to let the Romans rule them, they told Menachem they wouldn't let him rule them either.

"Words were exchanged, and Menachem declared himself to be the Messiah Israel had been waiting for, just as his grandfather, Judas the Galilean, had done years before. He also claimed leadership of the resistance movement, but the other rebel leaders refused to cede leadership to him because they had their own ambitions."

Eleazar's voice was becoming louder as he became more animated. "While this confrontation was happening, more residents of the city streamed into the Women's Court and joined the fray. At first, they just shouted at us, but within minutes, the crowds climbed the stairs to the balconies above the colonnades and pelted us with rocks.

"It was frightening," Eleazar admitted, and all around us, the men who had been with him nodded in agreement. "The rebel leaders backed us up against the Nicanor Gate, where they beat many of our men, breaking their bones and leaving them to scream out into the plaza in pain. There was so much blood, it obscured the pattern in the stones of the courtyard, and about half my men didn't make it out alive. I fought with the rearguard, and the projectiles thrown on to us by the public injured many of my men before we reached the gate to escape. It was terrible what they did to the ones we had to leave behind. We heard they stoned them and beat them with logs they found in the Chamber of Wood. I still cannot understand what triggered such hatred. They revolted against us, even though we came to liberate them.

"Menachem ordered me to take all my men and return to Masada, so I sent messengers to our brothers who were not with us at the Temple and told them to meet us back at the caves. I know not everyone made it out alive, but I'm confident many who didn't get out remained behind to continue fighting the Romans, just as we will do from Masada.

"Menachem had already started his retreat, and I saw him running down the grand staircase with his personal guard, so I headed into the back alleys with as many men as I could. We reached the underground tunnels and hid down there for two days, hunted like animals the whole time. Later, I heard Menachem and his guards made it as far as the City of David, but the rebels captured him and his men and tortured them to death. Menachem died on a stake, eviscerated from belly to breastbone."

That's horrible. So, with all those men lost, and Menachem killed, the Sicarii made no gains and were chased from Jerusalem.

Malachi turned to me and seemed to have the same thought, although neither of us expressed it aloud.

"So, while the Jerusalem campaign ended in defeat for Menachem and his men, my troops were largely able to escape, and we will continue the fight against Rome and her collaborators from here.

"Going forward, we will live free of the Roman yoke, and together, we'll create a military community to strike against our enemies. But know this, the Romans will not forgive us for besting them at the Antonia Fortress, and one day, they will come looking for us. But before that, we'll build a Sicarii army and continue attacking the collaborators and Romans wherever we find them. And so, Masada must remain a community under military command. Therefore, we will share the work and the decision-making, with one exception. The military command structure will decide all defense matters, and we will overrule any decision made by the group if we think it conflicts with military requirements."

After the last sentence, I heard muttering from the crowd. Eleazar ignored the murmuring, but the grumbling surprised me, so I looked to Malachi and Judith beside me for insight.

"I thought Masada would be a community ruled by its members as the Roman threat subsided."

"So did I," said Judith.

"And I thought there would be less need for killers and soldiers now because of our distance from Jerusalem," Malachi added.

"Why do you think there was grumbling when Eleazar said he could overrule community decisions?"

"His troops support him, but only about one-quarter of the people here are combatants—the rest are family members or other refugees," said Malachi.

Eleazar had released me from being a hostage just a short ten days before, so I don't know what possessed me as I said, loud enough to be heard by Eleazar and those around me, "Who decided the military could veto community decisions? Who are the leaders here?"

For the first few minutes, my words echoed as the front rows repeated them for those at the back, and then absolute silence descended, and my questions hung in the air. The Sicarii still saw me as an outsider, so I think it shocked everyone when I spoke up—Eleazar most of all. But, it seems, I had asked the questions in many people's minds, as heads nodded and voices agreed. So, I waited, expecting an answer to my questions. But Eleazar's reply shocked me.

"Who are you, Daniel, to be asking questions? You are the son of a collaborator, brought here as a hostage. I have shown you mercy because thieves murdered your family, and I have allowed you to remain with us. But you are not a member of the Sicarii and have no rights among us. Therefore, you will be silent."

Silence fell, and the crowd members exchanged looks.

Continuing as if I had not interrupted, Eleazar resumed. "I won't pretend our situation isn't grim. We have a lot of hard work ahead of us to achieve self-sufficiency. But we have ample supplies to meet our needs for the next several months for those who did not see the storerooms earlier. That will give us time to plant and harvest crops of vegetables and cereals. Unlike Jerusalem, the growing season here is longer, from August to April, and I am told we have excellent soil to work with. We also traded with Ein Gedi for agricultural supplies, including seed and farming tools."

"What do you mean by 'traded'?" someone from the audience asked. "I was down below when the riders came from Ein Gedi. They accused us of stealing, and you did not deny it."

"Tomorrow morning, we will designate what land will be agricultural fields, and the farmers among you will plant our first crops," said Eleazar, ignoring the outburst.

"Our first mission is to build a free and viable community here. Each of you will have to contribute your absolute maximum every day. The conditions are harsh, and we can't afford to fall behind in our labors. We will not tolerate idlers, and I will exile shirkers."

Again, quiet murmuring.

"I will expect each of you to contribute to your areas of expertise. I will now read off a list of specialized labor. Tonight, think about your skills and where you can make the most meaningful contribution. My lieutenants will meet you here tomorrow morning at dawn, and you will divide yourselves into groups according to your skills. If a group has more than it needs, we'll move people around based on a lottery. Those with none of the skills I list should report to the farmers' group as unskilled labor.

"Here is the list: farmers with knowledge of row crops and orchard management, shepherds, poultrymen, butchers, cooks and bakers, laundresses, spinners and weavers, tanners, armorers, stonemasons and carpenters, and dove keepers. Military personnel will remain under their existing chains of command, and any man wanting to enlist in military service may do so tomorrow. Males older than fifteen will train as part of an auxiliary unit and have periodic guard duty and patrol responsibilities for one month out of every four. That's all for tonight. You are all dismissed to your quarters."

And with that preemption of power and dismissal, our new lives began, as a free community, under military rule. We returned to our rooms accompanied by the murmurings of our neighbors, many of whom whispered so Eleazar's men would not overhear them.

• • • • • • • • • ● ● ● • • • • • • • •

We gathered at first light for work assignments, where I was cheerily greeted by Nathan.

"The collaborator is here, and my day has already been ruined."

"Good morning to you, as well, Nathan," I said with the smallest of bows. *Your day is not ruined nearly as much as mine. Can I not get away from this monster?*

Judith, Malachi, and I had walked together to the assembly point to volunteer for work duties. It was already a dazzling day, with the Nabatean mountains appearing aglow from behind.

When we arrived, Malachi reported to the officers' quarters, and Judith, having decided she preferred cooking to spinning or weaving, joined the kitchen staff. Having no skills other than studying our ancestral laws and rituals, I found the farmers' group and volunteered as unskilled labor, only to discover a few minutes later that Nathan was responsible for the farming team.

The farming volunteers were abundant, and Nathan quickly divided the group into their specialties. Those with crop experience stood on the right, and orchard workers stood in a smaller group on the left. He intended to assign unskilled workers daily.

"Which of you field workers have the most experience?" asked Nathan. Then, after a brief discussion among themselves, a raisin-skinned man with a flowing gray beard came forward.

"That would be me."

"And what is your name?"

"Yoav, sir."

"Yoav, you are now the civilian head of the farmers. We will work together to ensure you have the supplies and resources you need to make our crops flourish. I'm sure I don't have to tell you how critical your job is, and I expect everyone to answer Yoav as though he were Eleazar himself. Now, let's do the same for orchard workers."

A few minutes later, a big burly fellow with no hair on his head stepped forward and said, "My name is Benjamin, sir."

"You heard my comments to Yoav, and the same applies to you, Benjamin. Every evening after supper, I expect both of you to report to me at my quarters, and we'll review our plans for the upcoming days and weeks. I will get you what you need to succeed—and succeed, you will."

Then, turning to the larger group, Nathan issued his orders. "We'll walk down to the southern gate where you will take a quick break while I consult with Yoav and Benjamin on where to plant crops and orchards. Then we'll mark the location of the fields."

I knew few people at the time, so I walked behind Yoav and Benjamin and listened to them talk about the soil quality. Next, we headed to an oasis of date palms someone might have planted in Herod's day and settled down to wait for Nathan and his chiefs to finish their discussions. While waiting, I plucked fruit from the date palm and handed them to others, taking a few for myself. Out of curiosity, I sat down close enough to hear Nathan, Yoav, and Benjamin speaking.

"Most of the open space is available for farming, so the first thing we'll do is to delineate the land for agriculture and calculate how many yokes we have. However, I'm still not sure there is enough land to support us. So, we might need to supplement from other sources."

"Where can we supplement from, and where will our tools come from?" asked Benjamin, rubbing his bald head. "We're in the middle of nowhere."

"Don't worry. God will provide," Nathan replied while noticing me and winking in my direction, intending to goad me. Then, pointing with his chin, he added, "Over there by the wall are piles of supplies Eleazar had us bring from Ein Gedi. We should get the seed into the shade before it gets too hot. We have stakes and mallets here we can use to mark everything out.

"All right," Yoav replied. "Once we clearly understand the boundaries, we can calculate the size of the fields. From there, we can divide up the land by crop and orchard type."

I observed him more closely as he spoke. While Yoav was certainly older than most, he appeared vigorous, with a combination of intelligence apparent in his eyes and taut muscles, which indicated a lifetime of hard work. He looked like he could outlast me in a day of physical labor, although most people could.

Benjamin added, "Once we finish laying out the fields, we should build a few huts to store the tools and seed."

"Good idea," Nathan said, nodding approvingly as he stood up. "Enough talk. Let's divide into workgroups and get started."

Climbing on a rock nearby, Nathan called for everyone's attention. "Quiet everyone. We're going to divide into three crews, one each under Benjamin, Yoav, and me. Skilled labor will be divided into two groups. Farmers will gather around Yoav, and orchard workers will go over there by Benjamin. Unskilled workers will gather here next to me."

This group was the largest by far and comprised approximately fifty city dwellers with few of the practical skills needed at Masada. As we gathered, Nathan recognized me and called me over.

"So, we have the son of a collaborator here," he announced, loud enough so everyone could hear. I didn't understand why he called me out. Perhaps it was to turn everyone against me from the beginning, or just to satisfy his vicious need to hurt me. I intuitively understood I should not cross him and responded the only way I could in the situation.

I reminded him, "Eleazar himself has seen fit to release me from my captivity. That should be good enough for you. And besides, you know I have nowhere else to go."

"You have nowhere to go because your parents were killed for being collaborators."

I looked at him with suspicion. "According to Eleazar, my parents were the victims of robbers. Do you know something different?"

Seemingly flustered, he said, "No. That's what happened." Then, turning away from me and toward the crowd, he said, "Now, let's get to work. I want everyone to stand in single file from here to that tower over there, with an arm's length between you. We'll walk in a straight line from here to that crest, clearing rocks as we go. We'll pick up the largest rocks during our first pass and drop them in carts that will be ahead of us. Then we'll walk back in the opposite direction, collecting smaller rocks and dropping them in the cart. All right, everyone, line up."

And that is how we spent the morning until the kitchen workers brought us a light breakfast of bread and corn mush to eat.

Nathan called out to get everyone's attention. "You are free for a few hours after you finish eating. Make sure you come back when you hear me calling for you."

Judith was among the kitchen workers, and I went to where she was serving. None of the men had bowls, so they doled the corn mush out onto the bread, and we ate that way. A few men fetched water from a nearby cistern, and it was fresh and cold.

"They are turning me into a farmer," I said to Judith.

"Really?" she said, again grinning. "You still look like a city boy to me, but now with blisters on your hands."

As I struggled to think of a clever retort, Judith knocked a stone loose with her foot, and a large yellow scorpion appeared with its tail up high, ready to strike. Before I could warn her with words, I grabbed her by her hand and pulled her toward me as the scorpion skittered away and disappeared under a nearby rock.

"Daniel, what are you doing?"

"You kicked a rock, and there was a scorpion."

She jumped away, shaken by how close she had come to being stung. "That is twice you've saved me. Thank you."

I blushed and managed to blurt out, "I'm happy to help."

Later that day, we returned to work and laid out the fields. While we cleared the rocks in the morning, Nathan, Yoav, and

Benjamin measured the area available for planting and arrived at a rough plan for how much of each crop to plant. Next, we divided the land into smaller plots for our orchards, which we planned to plant with dates, figs, pomegranates, olives, and carob. Earlier residents of Masada had planted many fruit trees, which were already producing.

We had enough corn to last for months. So, we just planted barley, chickpeas, lentils, kidney beans, and onions for now. This would make up our entire diet, along with cheese from the goats, eggs, and the occasional meat from the goats, sheep, and chickens.

Our crops were in the ground within the month, and the plan was to harvest them, beginning after Hanukkah and through Passover. The shepherds spent those months strengthening their flocks, and the poultrymen increased their broods many times over. In their free time, people improved their accommodations by building divider walls to make smaller, more private rooms between the casemate walls and also stoves for baking and heating in the cold months. And, of course, the soldiers guarded, trained, and improved our defenses.

Over the next several months, I made myself indispensable to Yoav. Since the other workers didn't mind me giving directions and willingly followed my example, I became the nominal leader of the unskilled laborers, and Yoav started inviting me to dinner to help him organize the work.

Dinner with Yoav and his wife, Dorit, the midwife, was like I had always imagined dinner with parents should be but never was. They were both down-to-earth and loving people who didn't have children of their own, so I often felt I filled that role for them, just as they filled the role of parents for me. It was such a relief to have elderly friends I could speak with and seek advice from, and they filled a gap in my life I had yearned for but had not realized was there until they occupied it.

Dorit had prepared part of a small roasted goat for dinner. Fortunately, I had overcome my aversion to the smell by now, which still reminded me of that last meal with my parents. Yoav passed me the platter of meat, and I asked Dorit a question I had planned to ask her for several weeks.

"Do you mind me bringing Judith with me to supper sometimes?"

"Please bring her as often as you'd like. I enjoy her company." Dorit looked at me with her piercing dark eyes, surrounded by a halo of graying hair, and hesitated before she added, "Are you two becoming close?"

I turned red, and Yoav lightheartedly admonished Dorit. "Goodness, woman, leave the boy alone. Can't you see you're making him uncomfortable?"

Trying to change the topic, I asked Dorit to pass me the onions.

We spent the remainder of the meal in joyful conversation, and after helping to clean up, Yoav invited me to stroll with him.

Once out of Dorit's earshot, he said, "You have genuine feelings for Judith, don't you?"

What could I say? I hadn't often let myself think in those terms, but the truth was, we were spending most of our free time together and we enjoyed each other's company immensely. But according to our traditions, it was unheard of for young single people to spend unchaperoned time together as we did.

"I admire Judith," I sputtered.

Yoav gave me a knowing smile. "I've seen the way you are with her, Daniel, and so have others. I see how you burn brighter when she is near you, and Dorit tells me Judith talks about you all the time. Have you ever discussed your feelings with her?"

"No, I haven't."

"Well, you should."

"Why the hurry?"

"Because people are gossiping. All right, enough of that. Now let's plan how we will allocate the pickers for the harvests."

We sat near the campfire and quietly discussed the plans.

"It is becoming hot enough during the day that we can't push people too hard," I said. "They'll want to work straight through, but many will faint if they do. That will hurt our chances of getting everything picked. So, we should insist on a break from late morning to late afternoon."

"Agreed, but with the crops ripening at the same time, we will need to draft other groups to help."

"Do you want to speak with Nathan, or should I?" I asked.

Yoav said he preferred to do it. "He has something against you, but whatever it is, I prefer it stay between you two, so nobody gets hurt."

"I've never understood it," I said. "Most people think I am the aggrieved party since he beat me, but in Nathan's world, that somehow gives him the right to be angry with me."

"Well, whatever it is, you stay away from him."

"I think we'll be fine. He doesn't have time to bother with me."

"Let's hope so," Yoav said.

But of course, we were wrong.

CHAPTER

13

A few days later, we were in the fields in the early morning, with the sun just a finger or two above the mountaintops. We began harvesting the onion and barley crops at dawn, and there was a festive mood in the air. Not only were we bringing in our first crops, but we also had dozens of women working with us, adding their arms and backs to the effort. The men worked hard to impress the women, bent over all day to pull the onions from the ground, and all were enjoying themselves. Harvesting creates a rhythm of its own, whether it is the bending and cutting of crops or the lifting and swinging of baskets onto carts.

Nathan appeared at a distance as I was releasing everyone for the morning break. At first, I didn't see it, but I began feeling Nathan's fury as he got closer. His face was crimson, body rigid, and feet stomping as he stormed straight at me. Yoav must have caught his demeanor, too, because he started toward us from the other side of the field, hoping to intercept Nathan, and blunt his rage. Yoav didn't stand a chance, though, since Nathan was faster, closer to me, and going downhill.

Surrounded by the released workers heading back to their rooms, Nathan forced his way through the crowd until he stood one foot away from me. Then, leaning in, his nose almost touching mine, he shouted, "Where are all these people going?"

"They're going home for their midday break," I said, my ears aching.

"What do you mean, midday break? Who said they could have a break? We have crops to bring in."

As I opened my mouth to answer, I could hear Yoav shouting in the background, trying to get Nathan's attention. "Yoav and I agreed the pickers should have a rest period. They'll be well-rested and pick more in the afternoon. I thought he discussed this with you."

"You and Yoav agreed?" he said, seething. As he yelled, his spittle sprayed my face. "Who are you to agree to anything? When did you become an expert? How many times have you done this in your life, city boy?" And with this, he pushed me in the chest and knocked me to the ground. However, this time, I sprung to my feet and launched myself at him; all those months of working in the fields had made me much stronger. But Nathan, the street fighter he was, stepped aside and tripped me, and I sailed past him. Then, before I could get up, Nathan attacked me from behind and pummeled me with his enormous fists. The pickers jeered at him, but hesitated to intervene; no doubt afraid of any cruel reprisals.

"Nathan, stop this right now." Yoav grabbed Nathan's arms and tried to pin them behind his back. Others jumped into the fray now and came between Nathan and me while he continued to struggle against Yoav. "What is wrong with you? Why did you attack Daniel?"

"Hands off me, old man."

"Not until you've calmed down."

"I'll see you punished for this."

"Punished?" said Yoav in disbelief. "By whom? Since when do we punish people?"

By then, Nathan's burst of anger was spent, and Yoav released him, only to have Nathan stomp off as he yelled over his shoulder, "You'll see, you two. Now, get these people back to work."

The workers were still standing around, murmuring between themselves and looking embarrassed because they had not stepped in when Nathan attacked me.

"What should we do now? Do we stay or go?" someone asked.

Another said, "You heard Nathan. Let's get back to work. Daniel, where should we start?"

I sent them back to work while still on the ground and in pain from the beating.

"Yoav, I think we need to see Eleazar." I struggled to my feet, feeling every hit I had taken. "We need to report this incident. Eleazar's reaction will tell us whether he thinks Nathan has the authority to override our planning. For now, I suggest everyone return to work while Yoav and I go to Eleazar."

"I'm concerned we'll get an answer we don't like," said Yoav.

"Understood, but," I said, turning toward the crowd, "I think it is important to know whether this is a free community, as was promised, or a community controlled by bullies. I know my preference. I want to have freedom from the Romans and anyone else who would tell us how to live our lives."

"Be careful what you say," someone said. "I don't think that crowd likes to be challenged."

"All the more reason to ask where we stand."

Weeks had passed since I last saw Eleazar, but I knew he had established himself in the Western Palace, the most elaborate of Herod's palaces at Masada. Yoav and I wanted to approach him immediately, so we took a quick break, then climbed the hill to the palace.

I couldn't help but notice the number of Eleazar's men surrounding the building as we approached. They did not appear to be on duty, and I could see many loafing around or practicing their swordsmanship. I thought their lolling around was odd, given how hard the civilians were working to harvest food for all of us to eat, soldiers included.

Two guards with shields and spears stopped us at the main entrance to the palace.

"Who are you, and what do you want?" asked a guard.

"My name is Yoav, and this is Daniel. I oversee our field crops, and I have a question for Eleazar."

"What do you want from him?"

"We have a question about the harvest we need to discuss."

"You don't need Eleazar for that. I'll get you one of his lieutenants. Isn't Nathan responsible for agriculture?" he said, turning to the other guard. And before Yoav or I could stop him, he went inside to get Nathan. Luckily for us, he brought Ruben back instead.

Approaching with a smile, Ruben said, "Yoav, Daniel, Nathan isn't here now. How can I help you?"

Ruben had always been the least belligerent of Eleazar's lieutenants, and I always felt safest with him, even when he was a member of the team that abducted me. Today was no exception.

Standing on the Western Palace's portico in the glaring midday sun, I explained, "I had just had a run-in with Nathan, and we would like to report it to Eleazar and ask him a few questions."

"What kind of run-in?"

Trying to find a spot of shade for us to stand in, we moved closer to the palace as Yoav told him what had happened with Nathan.

"I don't understand why he treats Daniel this way," said Yoav. "And how does his violence solve anything?"

Ruben gathered us loosely in his arms and pointed to a spot a few feet away with his chin. Then, speaking very quietly, so the sentries could not hear, he said, "Nathan thrives on violence, and Eleazar knows that and uses him as an enforcer. You don't think Nathan would be this violent without Eleazar condoning his actions, do you?"

"That never really occurred to me, but all the more reason for our community to be ruled by civilians," I added.

Aghast, Ruben said, "Don't say that to him," his eyes widening as he shook his head from side to side.

But before I could ask why, I noticed the guards coming to attention, and from the darkened corridor behind Ruben, I heard a shuffling of feet as Eleazar said, "What can't they say, and by *him*, I assume you mean me?" And with that, Eleazar emerged from the entranceway and greeted us. "Yoav, good to see you, my friend. Daniel." He nodded toward me. "What is happening that has Ruben riled up?"

"There was an incident in the fields just now," said Yoav, preempting me.

"And what was this incident?" Eleazar asked, raising an eyebrow while looking at me.

"Your man Nathan laid into Daniel and beat him."

"What did Daniel say to provoke him this time?"

Really? Is it always my fault?

"Nothing. Nathan asked why we were sending people home before he pounced on Daniel and thrashed him."

"Which people were being sent home?" asked Eleazar.

"The pickers," I said, trying hard but not succeeding, to control my mouth. "Yoav and I agreed we should give the pickers a midday break during the harvest, so they can come back rested in the afternoon and work harder."

"You and Yoav agreed? But Nathan oversees agriculture. Why are you two making these decisions?" he said with rising irritation in his voice.

Yoav jumped in again before I could say anything else and answered. "Nathan has had night guard duty, so we haven't seen him much lately. In his absence, we continued planning for the harvest."

"Nathan is in charge of the harvest. He will make these decisions, not you two."

"Why not?" I said, sounding exasperated. "Is there something special about his decisions? Are they better than Yoav's decisions; Yoav, a farmer of thirty years?"

I saw fear in Ruben's eyes, and then the storm hit.

"Yes, there is something special about Nathan's decisions," Eleazar said, becoming more animated now. "They are military decisions made by my lieutenant, and his decisions are an extension of mine, and that makes them special."

Stepping back to avoid being hit by Eleazar's gesticulating arms, I said, "Thank you for clarifying. So, you see Masada as a military base, whereas I think of it as a village of civilian farmers," again speaking before thinking through the consequences of my words.

"This was never up for discussion," Eleazar said, incensed and leaning in close. "What do you mean by calling this a civilian settlement? This is a Sicarii base, and the Sicarii are warriors. The civilians are here because they are the families of my soldiers, and they are here to support the troops."

"But not all of us are warriors. Half of us are children, and half again are women. The Sicarii mission, as I learned it, is to create the conditions to live in freedom. How do we live in freedom if we're just trading Rome for another military ruler?"

"Yoav, take him away. Quickly, before I have him arrested for sedition. Hurry before I hurt him."

"Daniel, don't say another word," Yoav said as he grabbed my face and forced me to look into his eyes.

As he dragged me away, we heard Eleazar screaming at Ruben, "Why were you warning them not to say these things to me? What were you afraid of? I should know what he is thinking so I can protect the community from him."

As we left the palace and began our walk back to the fields, I said to Yoav, "This is not right. Eleazar and his men think violence will solve everything, but we will lose our souls if we go down this path. Don't they understand?"

"I agree, Daniel, but let's discuss it tonight, away from inquisitive ears, and see what we can do."

Nathan's orders to get back to work meant the pickers finished earlier than planned but much the worse for wear. Nevertheless, the extra time allowed Judith and me an opportunity to gather much-needed firewood, so we set off a few hours before dusk down the shallow ramp near the cisterns.

There is an area below the plateau where the tamarisk tree is plentiful with its lovely pale pink flowers. We were always careful not to trim the tamarisk trees themselves because they are slow-growing, and their flowers attract the bees that produce our sole source of honey. Instead, we only took branches that had already fallen to the ground, and we broke them into smaller pieces, which we then bundled together to carry up the ramp.

Today, we had to go farther afield than usual to find fallen branches. I had never been so far out before and noticed a cave not far from where we were gathering wood. I enjoyed my time with Judith immensely away from the gossipmongers' eyes and was not in a hurry to go home.

"Let's explore that cave," I suggested.

"Haven't you had enough yet today, Daniel?"

"I'm just curious. I've never noticed it before, and we won't be out this way again for a long time."

It was an inviting cave, bleached white by the intense sun. The opening was wide, and the cave was shallow, so it was well lit inside.

"Look, Judith, there are no signs of animals. That's surprising. And the floor is smooth, so there are very few places for scorpions and snakes to hide."

"Yes, Daniel. It's a delightful cave. Can we go home now?"

"Of course, Judith. But I like this cave. Maybe if Eleazar and his men become too unbearable, we can come here and live."

CHAPTER

14

That evening, Yoav, Judith, and I sat in silence around a small campfire near the entrance to our rooms while Dorit was off helping bring another child into the world. Judith threw more wood on the fire, and hundreds of sparks flew into the sky, reminding me of other campfires since my abduction. The past few months of working with Yoav and getting closer to Judith were dear to me, and the sparks flying to heaven and the periodic popping from the salts of the tamarisk tree reminded me how wondrous it can be to live in the desert.

"I've been with the Sicarii for three years now, and Eleazar's reaction doesn't surprise me," said Judith, opening the discussion. "He always behaved this way, only controlling himself around Menachem."

"I've noticed it, too, but his behavior is more extreme since the retreat from Jerusalem," Yoav added while pouring us watered wine. "I don't know if it's because he is out from under Menachem or because he thinks, given Menachem's experience, he must rule with a tighter fist."

Offering up my stone cup in a toasting motion, I added, "Or maybe being hunted like an animal for two days in Jerusalem changed him. I saw him from afar when he returned from Jerusalem. He looked like the walking wounded and appeared disheveled and was bent over like a broken old man. Yet, when he approached the caves, he straightened up and tried to appear his usual self."

"But he doesn't behave like a broken man now," Yoav said.

"Like what?" we heard from the shadows. My heart skipped a beat until I realized it was Malachi returning from guard duty.

I recounted our day to him, including Nathan's explosive behavior and Eleazar's thoughts on managing the community. Then he shared his more informed perspective of someone who interacts with Eleazar and Nathan every day.

"Nathan's violence doesn't surprise me. As Eleazar's temper frays, Nathan takes it as permission to do the same. And Eleazar lets him."

Judith threw another tamarisk branch on the fire, and we all shied away a little in anticipation of the initial pops it would make as the salt residues on the bark ignited.

"They both have a lot of responsibility," said Malachi. "I'm not surprised they yell sometimes."

Yoav looked incredulous. "This wasn't just yelling. Nathan attacked and beat Daniel, and I'm still not sure what set him off."

"It was because of the perception you were usurping his authority," added Judith.

Malachi stood as he spoke again. "But it was an actual challenge to his authority. You made a major decision about deploying the pickers without consulting him."

Yoav also stood, and becoming more excited, he added, "I don't think that's the point."

"That is exactly the point," Malachi said a little too loudly. "You can't expect to go against Eleazar's vision of this community and not get burned. His vision is what binds the community together and gives it direction."

"I can't believe these words are coming from my brother's mouth," Judith said, looking at Malachi quizzically. "What are they teaching you over there? You're starting to sound like one of them."

"Before, we were almost exclusively a military organization," said Malachi, now sounding offended. "Still, since coming here, the need for an agricultural enterprise to ensure our survival has become evident to Eleazar. He worries it will give rise to a parallel civilian authority that will challenge his leadership. He already thinks people are positioning themselves to compete with him for the governance of the community. And he is convinced civilians shouldn't rule this place since we still need protection from the Romans, and he is still building his offensive capabilities so he can attack them."

Signaling to Malachi to come and sit by me, I said, "But of course, Masada should be a civilian community. Most of us are civilians, and the people are changing now that there is no direct confrontation with the Romans. They are settling down and becoming farmers. That's the primary reason I don't think the military should rule us."

Judith brought her brother a plate of food, as she always does when he comes home from guard duty. But, not willing to let Malachi off the hook, she served up her opinion together with the food. "We can protect ourselves, even if we have civilian leaders, as long as we have a military force too. Why does he think he has to rule over every aspect of the community? Besides, his troops are only about a quarter of the people here, so why should he be able to impose his will on everyone?"

Not giving Malachi a chance to answer, I jumped in and asked why the soldiers were not helping during the harvest. "We are not here to support 'his' troops like Eleazar said today."

"Daniel, be careful what you say," Malachi warned, as an unseen soldier listening from the ramparts heard Daniel's comments and left immediately, probably to report them. "Eleazar has ears everywhere, and what you said is exactly what has him worried."

I dismissed Malachi's comments as overly dramatic. Sure, there was always the chance Nathan might beat me again, but they would never go beyond that.

"In fact," Malachi continued, "right before I came to eat, Ruben told me to warn you to be careful. Nathan showed up after you and Yoav left, and Eleazar had a full-blown tirade against you after Nathan told his side of the story. Eleazar called you a menace and said they must put you in your place."

"What does that mean, Malachi?" asked Judith. "Are they threatening to silence Daniel and anyone else who thinks a man with authoritarian tendencies should not rule us? Isn't that why the rebels in Jerusalem rejected Menachem? They didn't want to fight against the Romans if it meant an autocratic Menachem would take over once the foreign occupiers were forced out. Why trade one Godless ruler for another?"

"I don't know what it means. I see Eleazar and a few of his lieutenants staking out more extreme positions, and I fear for you, Daniel, and anyone else they think opposes them."

As the fire dwindled to embers, I said, "Thank you for the warning, Malachi. I will take it to heart, but we must raise these issues at the next assembly and discuss them as a community."

"Are there any questions?" Eleazar said.

He had been speaking for an hour, sharing his thoughts on our defenses and agriculture and issuing instructions for the coming month. I was surprised he asked for questions since he is the only one allowed to address the community as a whole during the monthly assemblies. On the other hand, maybe he thought he had us well enough trained that we would not dare pose questions.

After a contentious disagreement with Judith and Yoav, we finally agreed I would ask the question at assembly. As I stood to pose the question, I saw Eleazar notice me standing there, and then I saw him decide to ignore me. Not wanting to miss my chance but afraid of the consequences, I took a deep breath and spoke as loudly and as clearly as I could, hoping they could hear me all the way in the back rows.

"Eleazar," I said, "I have a question for you about the future of our community."

"I will not take questions from you, Daniel. Sit down."

Not to be deterred, I posed my question anyway. "I think this is an excellent forum for the community to discuss the future nature of our settlement. We are all gathered together, and I'm sure everyone wants to know the plans for transforming the community into a civilian-governed farming settlement."

"We have discussed this, Daniel, and you know there are no such plans. Masada is a Sicarii base and governed by military leadership. Therefore, this is not open for discussion."

"Why not?" shouted someone from behind me.

"Yes, why not?" shouted another.

"We should at least discuss it," said a third, which was accompanied by a chorus of others agreeing.

"I think we should also discuss why the troops are not helping to harvest the crops we all eat. The civilians could really use the help, so they don't have to work dawn to dusk for five months of the year."

"My troops are busy defending the community. They don't have time to pick fruits and vegetables. That is why we have the civilians."

"So, you are saying Masada is a military community, and the civilian residents are here to feed the military, and this will never change?" I said, as I sensed some agitation among Eleazar's lieutenants, and saw Nathan and a few of his men moving toward me from their place in the front.

After receiving whispered orders from Eleazar, other lieutenants signaled their men, who were now moving between seated audience members.

Nathan had cut through the crowd, kicking them out of the way, to find his way to me. *Not again,* I thought. But yes, again, I realized, as Nathan stopped before me and commanded me to sit down and be quiet. I could not let him intimidate me and have our assembly end this way.

Trying to look around Nathan, I said, "Eleazar, will you—"

But Nathan was having none of it and shoved me so that I fell over Yoav, who was sitting nearby.

"Stay down," he commanded me, as two of his troopers stood on either side of me, swords drawn, ready to back up Nathan's order.

The audience witnessed this naked abuse of power against me and expressed their displeasure through gasps and shouted objections. Eleazar's response was simple yet effective.

"Daniel summarized the situation neatly, and anyone who objects can find their way to the Snake Path and leave. Therefore, there is no more to say, and you are all dismissed."

As the audience members stood to disperse, I noticed Nathan returning to his spot by Eleazar's side and Eleazar whispering into his ear. As he whispered, Nathan glanced back at me and gave a brief nod, as if sealing my fate.

Walking back to our rooms, Yoav shared his concerns about my safety.

"Daniel, I was wrong. It is too dangerous to confront Eleazar this way. I never thought he would use force in public like that or openly declare that the military rules this community. I understand your deeply-held convictions, but if you continue to challenge him, I believe he will eliminate you like an annoying thorn in his sandal."

I noticed Judith was silent, which was unusual. When I looked at her to ask her thoughts, I saw a glistening in her eyes and did not ask my question since her answer was so plainly inscribed on her face. It was then I decided to do something about these constant threats. We would have to work toward changing the leadership of the community, or we would have to leave.

The following day, I sought out Malachi and asked for his help.

"Will you train me on the use of swords and daggers?"

"Why? You're a farmer now. What use do you have for weapons?"

A reasonable question, but isn't it obvious? "To defend myself from Nathan."

In all the time I have known Malachi, I have never known him to laugh so hard or for so long.

"You've hurt my feelings," I said.

"That's not the only thing that will get hurt if I agree to this madness. What makes you think you can learn enough to protect yourself from Nathan? He has four qualities you lack, so any contest between you would most likely end in your death.

First, he's a good swordsman. Second, he's strong. Third, he's fast. And fourth, he's ruthless. Can you match any of that?"

I had been guiding Malachi into the date orchards all this time so no one could overhear our conversation.

"What choice do I have? You saw him last night. He was ready to kill me. All he needed was the order from Eleazar."

"You're right about that. All right. I'm off-duty tonight. We'll come down here after supper and get started. What excuse will you give Judith?"

"I won't need to make anything up."

"Why not?"

"It was her idea."

We met at dusk, well away from curious eyes. Starting with wooden practice swords, Malachi taught me a few of the fundamental defensive skills of retreating, parrying, blocking, and so on and some basic offensive maneuvers, like stabbing, lunging, and slashing. By the time we were finished for the evening, my right arm was so tired I could no longer lift it.

"Well met, my friend. Not too bad for your first time. Let's reconvene again tomorrow at the same time to start putting into practice some of what you've learned."

On our way back to our rooms, I suggested we meet a little earlier the next day. Unfortunately, since it was so dark, I could no longer see Malachi; nor could I see Nathan slinking along, well hidden by the shadows of the trees.

The next evening, we spent an hour practicing.

"Show me that maneuver again, Malachi."

"Which one?"

"The one I can use to protect myself from overhead slashing attacks. Nathan is so aggressive; that's how he'll probably attack me."

"You mean like this?" I suddenly heard from behind me as I jumped sideways just in time to feel Nathan's blade whoosh by my ear and nick my shoulder lightly as it passed by.

"Nathan, what are you doing?" screamed Malachi as I scrambled behind the closest date palm.

Turning his head right and left while looking for me, Nathan spit, "I would ask the same of you, Malachi. Why are you training this collaborator?"

I could see Nathan assuming an attack stance. Sensing he was preparing to attack Malachi, I emerged from my hiding place.

"Isn't accusing me of being a collaborator getting a bit old, Nathan? You know it's not true, and besides, why do you hate me so much?"

"Your father was a collaborator, and so you are a collaborator."

"That is ridiculous. How can I be held responsible for what my father might or might not have done?"

"How can you have been studying to be a priest and not know it says in the Ten Commandments that 'God will visit the iniquities of the fathers on the children?'"

"That is the second commandment, and it concerns idol worshiping. The full text is in Exodus, chapter twenty, verses four to six, and reads:

"'Thou shalt not make unto thee any graven image or any likeness that is in heaven above, or that is in the earth beneath, or that is in the water under the earth: Thou shalt not bow down thyself to them, nor serve them: for I the Lord thy God am a jealous God, visiting the iniquity of the fathers upon the children unto the third and fourth generation of them that hate me; And showing mercy unto thousands of them that love me, and keep my commandments.'

"Don't ever think you can outquote me when it comes to God's commandments," I finished.

Nathan, no longer able to contain his mounting fury, lunged at Malachi. But Nathan didn't realize Benjamin had been experimenting with a new way to harvest dates. First, they laid nets on the ground below the dates, and then they shook the date clusters, loosening the fruit and collecting it in the nets. As Nathan lunged at Malachi, I grabbed the net he was standing on and raised it quickly, causing it to foul his feet. Nathan tripped, and as he fell, his sword reversed in his hand as he landed at Malachi's feet. The tip of Nathan's sword entered his own waist, and passing through, now protruded from his back, with only a blade's width of skin holding it in place.

Nathan writhed in pain but stood and pulled the sword out by the pommel; only a tiny amount of blood emerged.

"You'll both pay for this," was all he managed to say as he limped away.

Once again, I was injured because Nathan was so quick to resort to violence. Luckily for me, it was only a minor cut on my shoulder this time. Malachi walked me back to our rooms and delivered me into the hands of Judith, who had been sitting quietly by the campfire.

"What happened?" Judith asked urgently as she ran to me. I hadn't realized there was so much blood, which made the wound look worse than it actually was.

"Nathan and I had another disagreement," I answered, throwing my sword to the ground. Judith ran to the nearest cistern to draw fresh water and then cleaned my left shoulder and arm of the quickly drying blood that covered them.

Once she'd washed the wound and found the source of the bleeding, she said, "This looks like a sword gash. How did you get this?"

"As I said, it was from Nathan. He attacked me from behind while Malachi and I were training. I can only surmise he takes issue with me being trained to defend myself."

"This needs to be sewn. Let me fetch and boil some white linen thread, and I must borrow a needle from someone. Stay here, and I'll be back soon."

Judith returned sooner than soon, and after setting the water to boil the thread, reexamined the wound. "It's not too deep but will require at least seven stitches. It's going to hurt." Which it did.

After sewing the wound closed, Judith picked a few leaves from the plants by her front door. She had planted the garden, which contained medicinal herbs, soon after arriving at Masada, in keeping with her desire to learn more about curing plants and becoming the community's healer. And since I was injury-prone, she also likely grew it in anticipation of the next time Nathan wounded me.

After the long workday, sword practice, and the excitement of being injured, I was woozy. Sitting right outside the door to Judith's room, I gathered up my courage and said, "Sometimes I wonder if I get injured often because I enjoy your ministrations so much." I thought to bring a smile to her face with my words, but Judith surprised me as in all things.

"Then you are a fool, Daniel. I might be familiar with the healing arts, but I cannot bring you back from death. Is this worth it? Can't you accept this is the way it is going to be with Eleazar in charge?"

"No, I can't because it's not right for the community. Why should we have to live under an authoritarian who sees violence and theft as legitimate ways to solve every problem? How can our friends and neighbors live as moral members of the Jewish community if our leaders are so corrupt and willing to violate Jewish law?"

"Then maybe you should leave Masada and find a more righteous place to live," Judith said.

Her comment stung. "Would you dispense with me that easily?"

"Not easily at all, Daniel. But I don't want to see you hurt anymore. If you're not careful, I believe Eleazar will order your death, and I'm certain Nathan will be happy to oblige."

Of course, Judith was correct in her assessment of the situation. I could not leave Masada because of my feelings for her. But I also could not go because so many of our men were tired of dying, and their families were tired of their men being killed. Furthermore, almost all my friends and neighbors agreed that Masada should transition from an armed rebel camp into an agricultural settlement. Personally, I would be happy if it did, and knowing these people as I had come to over the years, I knew they also wanted to live moral lives according to Jewish law.

Several weeks passed in quiet since my most recent altercation with Nathan, and I could not believe I had escaped reprisals for his injury. However, when the payback finally did come, it came in a way I would never have expected but was intended to inflict the most pain on me, Malachi, and innocent Judith.

With my shoulder almost completely healed, I invited Judith and Malachi to join me for breakfast one morning. They agreed, and we walked to the communal dining room together.

The dining hall was on the lowest level of the Northern Palace and was the largest open space in Masada. We think it was initially Herod's banquet hall, and before or after meals, Herod likely invited his guests to the outer terraces on the northern, eastern, and western sides to enjoy the views of the desert and the Asphalt Lake.

We descended the stairs from the upper levels of the palace and arrived at the southern veranda where food had been arrayed on tables by the kitchen staff. It is an elegant room, surrounded by balconies on all sides. The hall itself is an enclosed space with a high ceiling and columns every ten paces, with frescoes painted on the plaster walls between the columns, which give the appearance the walls are of multi-colored marble.

"We're late," said Judith. "There's not much left."

"But I had my heart set on boiled eggs," I said.

Judith, who worked in the kitchen, told us to find a table while she went to see if there were any eggs left in the kitchen.

As we sat, waiting for her return, I noticed Nathan and some friends sitting at a table on the far side of the hall, close to the staircase Judith had just descended. This was the first time I had seen him since our most recent confrontation, and I looked away, not wanting him to see me noticing him. However, when I turned back a moment later, I saw he was no longer with his friends and didn't see him anywhere else in the hall.

Concerned, I said to Malachi, "Wait here. I think Nathan might have followed Judith downstairs. I'm going to see if everything is all right."

I got to the top of the kitchen stairs when I heard Judith shouting, "No, stop it!" I looked back and noticed Malachi and Nathan's friends had also heard the shouting. Everyone started moving at once, with me being the closest and reaching the staircase leading to the storerooms and kitchens first. "Leave me alone, Nathan. Get away from me."

I descended the stairs and stopped at the landing at the bottom but couldn't see clearly in the low light.

Where is she?

"You should stay away from him," I heard Nathan say from the shadows several feet in front of me.

There. There's movement in the door of the storeroom. He's leaning in toward her. Is he kissing her?

"You heard her. Move away," I yelled as I launched myself at Nathan, striking him with my good shoulder in the spot where his own sword had penetrated his waist.

He screamed and staggered, then fell to his knees. But he recovered quickly and attacked me with surprising speed, and this time, Judith joined the fray, jumping on his back and clawing his face.

Meanwhile, Nathan's friends, Malachi, the kitchen staff, and other diners had joined us from the dining room, wanting but unable to participate in the fray due to insufficient space in the passageway. I noticed Malachi had pushed his way through the crowd, drawn his dagger, and was approaching us quickly in the narrow hallway.

Still on Nathan's back and choking him now, Judith screamed, "Stop it, Nathan. Enough!"

Once again, his iota of humanity got the best of him, and rather than hit Judith, Nathan staggered away, his back to Malachi while he screamed, "You'll pay for this with your life, Daniel."

Then Judith and I, seeing Malachi approaching, simultaneously yelled, "No, Malachi," as one of Nathan's friends hit Malachi in the back of his head, knocking him out before he was able to reach Nathan.

"What is happening here?" asked one of the cooks.

I remained quiet, uncertain whether Judith wanted me to share with others what Nathan had tried to do, but then Judith, turning to Nathan, said, "I've always called you a thug, and this morning you have truly proven yourself to be one. Now, we'll see what Eleazar thinks of your behavior." And with those parting words, my friend, Judith, turned her back on us all and climbed the stairs like a queen.

I checked on Malachi, then followed closely behind Judith, and when I caught up, we walked back to our rooms in silence. As we arrived at Judith's door, she pulled me inside and broke my heart as she sobbed for several minutes, her head on my shoulder and arms draped around me. I could not protect Judith in this manner, and there was only one thing I could think to do that might.

· · · · · · · · · ● · ● · ● · · · · · · ·

Because of the confrontation with Nathan, I expected to be called before Eleazar. That he didn't summon me was surprising and suggested Nathan was embarrassed by his behavior. For the next several days, Nathan avoided both Judith and me, although I noticed an increase in petty encounters with Nathan's men.

After a few days had passed since the upsetting events in the storeroom, Judith and I spent a quiet evening sitting on the tree stumps by the campfire in friendly silence. My thoughts were floating aimlessly as I sat there, and Judith knew me well enough to let my mind wander with only the occasional question or comment. Most consuming, as always, were my thoughts of Judith and how to protect her from Nathan and gossipmongers.

I really didn't understand why it had taken me so long, but quite suddenly, I croaked, "Judith, will you marry me?"

"I'm sorry, did you say something?" she asked with that infuriating grin on her face. "You swallowed some of your words, so I didn't quite hear you. Did you ask me to go hiking with you?"

She was going to make this difficult. Finally, I cleared my throat and looked at my beloved with gentle yet intent eyes.

"Judith, my dear. I love you with all my heart, and I hope you will consider spending the rest of your life with me in marriage."

"That's more like it. Daniel, my dear. I, too, love you with all my heart, and there is nothing I would like more than to spend the rest of my life with you. But tell me, what took you so long?"

Unable to speak, I walked over to her and brushed the hair from her face with a husband's familiar gesture. She smiled and sighed a much-contented sigh, and I smiled back, took her face in my hands, and kissed her gently on the lips. Then, with blurring eyes, I sat next to her—closer than was appropriate for two unwed people—and said, "You know I am a man of my convictions. It might take me a little longer than some to arrive at decisions, but once there, nothing will steer me from my course."

"That's one of the reasons I love you, Daniel, because of your tenacious dedication to what is right and your willingness to stand by your beliefs. So yes, Daniel, I look forward to a long life with you."

I want to share our news with Yoav and Dorit. They'll be so excited for us and relieved, and Yoav won't have to worry anymore that our situation is becoming ever more untenable.

"I'm going to tell Yoav and Dorit. Will you come with me?"

"Yes, of course, Daniel. But why the hurry? Stay here with me for a few minutes, and let's enjoy this moment together."

We continued to sit outside our rooms while deriving great pleasure from each other's company and the thousands and thousands of pinpricks of light in the heavens. I told Judith about Yoav's concern, and she acknowledged it was becoming a problem for her as well.

"The gossipmongers I work with are becoming more vocal. Earlier today, one called me a whore," Judith explained, with a look of consternation on her face.

"How did you respond?"

Laughing, she said, "I told her it was true, and that shut her up."

"You did not."

"But I did."

Worried and pacing now, I said, "That's no solution. You've given her permission to spread ugly lies about you."

"What was I supposed to do, Daniel? We are living here in unusual circumstances. With Malachi away so much, we are alone like a married couple but not living in the same room."

"Not quite like a married couple," I said, blushing.

Judith agreed. "You're right—not quite, but we spend a lot of unchaperoned time together. And another thing about married couples; they know their feelings for each other. I have been close to you for almost a year, but I've never known for certain how you feel about me, Daniel. But I will tell you how I feel about you." She paused then, struggling to gain control of her emotions. "Every night, I go to sleep and toss and turn all night, hoping someday we'll be together. Does that make me a whore?"

Wrapping my arms around her tightly, I answered in the only way I could. "No, my dear. You are not a whore. On the contrary, you are my beloved."

Given our living conditions and that we were both orphaned, Judith and I agreed we should marry sooner rather than later and dispense with a few of the formalities of a typical wedding. But, not having forgotten the purification traditions of our forefathers, we both wanted to come to our wedding after ritual immersion. While Herod had built many luxurious baths and pools on Masada, none of them met the requirements of a *mikvah,* and so I planned to recruit other newly engaged men to construct one. We estimated a month for construction, so we settled on May for our wedding. Since we are both poor, we also agreed Malachi should not have to provide a dowry and that Malachi and I would simply switch rooms once the wedding ceremony took place.

Two nights before our wedding, Malachi visited us in our rooms. After dinner, he informed us he had guard duty the night of the wedding and would miss the ceremony.

I could see Judith struggling to gain control of her temper, and she managed a restrained "Absolutely not. You can't miss the wedding. You are my only living relative."

Malachi, having been on the receiving end of his sister's ire before, knew there was no point in arguing, so said only, "I'm sorry I'll miss it, but there's nothing I can do."

"Of course, there's something you can do," I said, hoping to mollify Judith's anger. "Have you told Ruben about the wedding?"

"He knows about the wedding, but he said the orders came from Nathan."

And I suppose they came to Nathan from Eleazar. This is about punishing me for challenging Eleazar and punishing Judith for rebuffing Nathan's advances. He has not forgiven her for that.

"I think nothing we say will change Nathan's mind. This isn't about when you do guard duty, Malachi. Besides, you know

Nathan is Eleazar's sycophant, and he takes great pleasure in lashing out at us," I concluded.

"Can you try reasoning with him?" Judith asked Malachi, trying to find a workable solution. "If not, we'll change the day to one when you are available."

Looking miserable, Malachi explained: "You don't understand the chain of command. I could never approach Nathan or Eleazar about this directly. I will have to ask Ruben, and he will have to ask Nathan. But I don't think Ruben will do it. And you can change the day of the wedding, but they will change my guard duty to whichever day you choose."

"Let me speak to Eleazar." Both Judith and Malachi looked at me like I was out of my mind.

"You can't," said Malachi. "Please don't interfere with this—it will only make matters worse. Promise me you won't."

I was quiet, but Judith broke the silence. "I have a suggestion. We can move the ceremony to wherever you are doing your guard duty. At least that way you can hear the ceremony, even if you can't see us. Is that an acceptable compromise?"

We all agreed it was, and I was proud of my ingenious wife-to-be.

On the day of the wedding, Yoav and I meandered through the orchards toward the casemate wall on our way to the newly constructed *mikvah* so I could immerse myself in its purifying waters as the sun rose.

The pool was small and could only seat a few at a time. Stepping inside, I sat on the bench on the men's side to remove my sandals and tunic and then descended the few steps into the immersion pool. The pool was well lit by a window facing the east, and the beautiful colors of sunrise over the mountains illuminated the interior in a swath of reds. I laid back with my head in the water, closed my eyes and slowed my breathing, and felt the morning light on my face.

I spent my few minutes in the *mikvah* saying the traditional prayers and contemplating how I had arrived at this wondrous moment.

Because of the adversity I have encountered, I am changing. I am a different person than I was in Jerusalem, and I am about to marry the most wonderful woman in the world. Judith is my soulmate, and I am so fortunate to have met her. Her smile gives me endless pleasure, and her laugh gives me so much joy. Just seeing her makes my heart beat faster.

Oh no, just thinking about her now is leading to impure thoughts. I must begin the purification prayers all over again.

Our wedding took place later that day, within earshot of Malachi by the southern fort. Looking around while waiting for Judith to arrive with her attendants, I saw hundreds of my friends, neighbors, and fellow farmers but no evidence of Eleazar's troops, for which I was grateful. Fortunately, Nathan had not shown himself in weeks, although he occasionally met with Yoav to discuss farming matters. Yoav tells me that Nathan's recovery is slow, both from the initial run-in with his own sword and the follow-up injury when I collided full force with his still-healing wound.

Yoav was to perform the ceremony, so he and Dorit were at the front, readying the items for the service. As I watched them, I heard Judith and her friends approaching through the orchards and could tell it was them by their joyous singing. They arrived just in time; we had planned to observe the wedding rites just before sunset.

I saw the crowd part to let Judith's entourage through. She had dressed in a pure-white tunic, with her black hair intertwined with pink flowers and arranged in a way I had never seen before, but in a way in which I would ask her to arrange it again. She beamed as she walked through the crowd, and her face lit up when she saw me. I remember thinking to myself, *No man has ever felt as loved as me.*

We stood before Yoav as he started the rites. Judith looked across at me, taking my hands in hers. Her eyes sparkled as she continued smiling at me.

"I am so honored Daniel and Judith asked me to perform the wedding ceremony. I've known them for a year, and Dorit and I love them like the children we could not have. Daniel came to us as a hostage. But since being freed, he has captured our hearts through his commitment to the community, hard work, and good nature. Judith has grown into the generous and spirited young woman we love so much. These two are fortunate they found each other through so much adversity. Join with me in wishing them a wonderful and fruitful life together."

The sun fell behind the wall as Yoav uttered the words our people had intoned for millennia to consecrate marriages, and Judith and I shared our promises to each other as the day's light disappeared.

While the ceremony was drawing to an end, Yoav again addressed all present. "Since Jerusalem's occupation by the Romans, we can't observe many of our traditions, dependent as they are on access to the Temple. So let me propose this. The groom will break a glass to mark these hard times instead." And with that, Dorit placed a small cup wrapped in cloth close to my right foot while Yoav whispered, "Stomp on it and break it. Judith, hold his arm so he won't slip."

I stomped for all I was worth, sensing that an inability to shatter the cup might herald bad luck. The crowd erupted in shouts of joy and well wishes when they heard the smashing of the goblet.

As the community dispersed, I heard a soldier barking something over the shuffling sounds of the crowd. Unfortunately, the fire bowls Dorit had placed for the ceremony were blinding me, so I couldn't see who was shouting.

The crowd went silent, and we heard a soldier issue an order.

"Stay where you are. Eleazar will address the crowd."

Around me, I heard grumblings of "What's this about?" and "Why is he going to speak?"

"Our supreme commander," shouted the same soldier, providing an introduction for a man who didn't need one. Then we heard the disembodied voice of Eleazar from the battlement.

"Welcome everyone to this blessed event. It's gratifying to see our community growing and maturing to become the best place to live anywhere, as I predicted. I have accomplished so much since we arrived and will continue to build our exceptional home. May we see many more marriages. And Judith looks wonderful, doesn't she?"

After he finished, he disappeared into the shadows, and we did not hear from him again at our blessed event.

As Judith and I wandered homeward, we heard people muttering all around, "So, he thinks he built this by himself," and "What's wrong with him, not blessing the bride and the groom?"

But that wasn't the worst of it. The next day, we learned Nathan had reassigned Malachi, so while we thought he had been close enough to hear the ceremony, he had actually been guarding the Northern Palace at the opposite end of Masada.

The pettiness and vindictive behavior concerned me, and hearing people speak against Eleazar openly and defiantly increased my concern for our isolated community.

17

About a year later, I woke up, snuggled close to Judith, and took in the scent of her sleeping. It was so early; the birds had yet to start their incessant chatter. The moon lit up the room enough for me to see my beloved's dark hair spilling across her face, single strands loosened by her tossing and arched like miniature, colorless rainbows. Her lips were parted, and her face was relaxed. I held her tight with all my love, thinking drowsy thoughts to myself while drifting in and out of sleep.

When the birds finally started their morning songs, Judith stirred.

"What are you doing awake so early?" she said in a whisper.

"How did you know?" I asked.

"You weren't snoring."

I kissed her hair. "Is it that bad?"

"No, it's endearing. So, what were you doing besides watching me sleep and adoring me?" *How well she knows me.*

"I was thinking about what we've built here in such a short time." Imagining the scene outside our door, I continued,

"When we came here, there were buildings, but not much else. Now, we have a vibrant community, and everywhere is lush. Trees and wildflowers are growing outside every room, and the people are changing too. We arrived as a band of killers and rebels, and we're evolving into an agricultural community."

"Living in a fortress," Judith said, casually but not lightly.

Most of the people are becoming less militant. But, of course, having to weed our crops all day long does that to people.

Judith turned to me, more awake now, and said, "But I do like how the men are spending more time with their families instead of planning assassinations. You can't imagine what it was like when we lived in the tunnels. And the women worry much less now about whether a Roman patrol will kill their husbands."

Still hugging Judith tightly, I agreed. "People are more relaxed, and families are growing. We are five hundred and ninety-five people now. Eighty-nine children have been born since we arrived, and another thirty-seven families are expecting children right now."

"Thirty-eight," said Judith.

"No, thirty-seven. Where did you hear thirty-eight?"

"You are the first to hear it's thirty-eight."

"What do you mean?"

"I mean, you can be slow for such a smart man," Judith said, with a smile I heard rather than saw.

I disentangled myself, jumped from our pallet, and turned to kneel beside my wife. "Are we number thirty-eight?" I said with a most eager look on my face.

"Yes, my love, we are," is all she needed to say.

I looked at her through misting eyes, pulled her close, and said, "Thank you, my dear."

Nine months later, little Hannah came into our lives and changed them forever.

"Daniel, it's time."

It was the middle of the night when Judith nudged me awake with those gentle words and her elbow.

"Time for what?" I said, still asleep.

"Time for you to get out of bed, get the midwife, and start a fire to heat water."

"In the morning," I said and fell asleep again until a much sharper nudge into my side startled me awake.

"Daniel, either you wake up now and get Dorit, or you'll have to deliver our baby yourself." Of course, all I heard was baby, but it was enough to penetrate my stupor.

"Huh? What?" I said.

"The baby is coming. Go get Dorit."

"The baby?"

"Yes, right now. Go find Dorit."

And with that, I was off.

By the time I returned with Dorit, Judith was in full-blown labor, and her screams had alerted the neighborhood to the imminent arrival of our little blessing. I built a fire while Dorit sat comforting Judith. Hearing the groaning from our room pained me, and as I entered to check on the situation, Judith told me to leave in a tone I had never heard before. Ever compliant to my wife's wishes, I sought Yoav's companionship by the campfire, and he and I spent the rest of the night in occasional conversation, punctuated by nodding heads and Judith's screams.

"So, what do you think is happening?" I asked Yoav at one point.

"You're asking the wrong man, my friend. I've never had the privilege of having to wait outside while my wife gives birth to our child. I envy you."

"The magnitude of this hasn't hit me yet," I said.

"When your baby is born, you will feel the same responsibility I feel to the six hundred people of Masada," someone said. Yoav and I turned to see Eleazar approaching in the twilight from the nearby administration building.

"I didn't know you were there," I said.

Stopping several feet away and standing perched above us on the hill, Eleazar said, "I heard the good news and came by to congratulate you myself. And I'm glad to find you both here and alone because I've wanted to talk to you for several days now."

"About what?" Yoav asked before I had a chance to say something that might antagonize Eleazar.

Coming a little closer but still standing above us, Eleazar continued. "Nathan is concerned about the yield from the upcoming harvest. He thinks it won't be enough to keep us from starving."

"We agree. So, what do you propose?" I asked. "Are you willing to split the community and send people away? We have more people than food and no way to grow more."

"No, we won't send Sicarii away. We'll have to get food another way."

"Which method do you prefer: prayer or magic? If neither of those, what other ways are there? Unless, of course, you mean to steal it from our neighbors," I said, my antagonism now entirely on display.

"You tell me, Daniel," Eleazar said, annoyed with me as usual. "What other choice is there? Do we just let people die?"

"It's not that simple," I said. "Every time we raid a neighboring community, we condemn them to death. Who are we to say we live and they die? Is it ever acceptable for a stronger community to take advantage of a weaker one, to thrive at their expense?"

"You have all the right questions but no answers," Eleazar said.

Standing now, I added, "Whatever happened to living according to our laws? Who are we to take a life? And it makes little sense as a strategy. How long can we do this? There are only a few settlements within striking distance. Once we pillage them, then what do we do? And isn't this type of high-handedness exactly why we are resisting the Romans?"

Exasperated by me yet again, Eleazar erupted. "You have so many questions, Daniel, and I wish you were with me and not against me, but you have chosen your side. Meanwhile, I will do everything to save these people, as you will do for your family. And, if you continue resisting the efforts I make to feed this community, your family will be the first to suffer if we cut rations." With that, he turned and receded back into the twilight shadows.

Suddenly, I heard louder moans of pain and then primal screams, so Yoav and I didn't have time to reflect on Eleazar's comments. My Judith was in extreme pain, and I could not help her. Then there was more screaming, followed by a sudden deafening silence, which scared me even more.

"Do you think she's all right?" I asked Yoav. "Why did she stop screaming?"

"Because your baby is here," said Dorit, as she stuck her head out of Judith's room and motioned for me to come over. "You can come in and see them now."

What transpired in that room was a mystery, but now I saw an exhausted-looking Judith beaming at me, her hair plastered to her head with sweat, holding our baby in her arms.

"Come and meet your daughter," she said.

"A daughter? I've always wanted a daughter," I said, sounding like a babbling fool.

She smiled at me and said, "That's good," and closed her eyes and fell asleep.

"What now?" I asked.

"Why don't you pick up your daughter and put her in her cradle?" said Dorit. "Let me show you how, and then you can sit here and not make a sound until Judith wakes. Then I'll go to the kitchen and get you both breakfast."

As she left me alone with my sleeping family, I glanced at my beautiful wife and then bent down to look at my daughter with her scrunched-up forehead, and my heart swelled. I began an impromptu dance, humming a prayer to welcome *the new* while spinning first this way, then that, eyes closed, with my arms extended over my head and fingers snapping. I danced, overwhelmed with love, joy, and hope for the future.

Sometime after we found out Judith was pregnant with our firstborn, Nathan reappeared to take up his role as military manager of the farming team.

Yoav and I were mustering the farmers in front of the tool sheds when Nathan strutted up and spoke.

"Good morning, everyone. Today, we will weed the onion patch."

I looked over to see the expression on Yoav's face, which, as expected, appeared bewildered. *What is Nathan thinking, just marching in here and issuing instructions without coordinating with us?*

"All right, everyone, gather buckets, find partners, and let's get started."

"But Nathan," I said, "we were planning to weed the peppers, which we must finish today to prevent the weeds from choking the plants."

The crowd nodded and murmured their agreement, and Yoav began to say something when Nathan cut him off.

"Daniel, I don't know what role you think you play here, but I confirmed with Eleazar this morning that you are a general laborer. Why you act like a supervisor is beyond me. Now get down from here and join the other workers."

Absolute silence descended as everyone absorbed Nathan's words.

Welcome back, Nathan. I see we are playing a new game. What shall we call it? Perhaps, "Put Daniel in his place"? But it was a much more insidious game than that, and both Yoav and I decided not to engage immediately without first exchanging a word. So instead, I joined the farmworkers in silence, and Nathan's face lit up with the only smile I have ever seen him give since first encountering him in Jerusalem all those years ago.

I paced around the campfire that evening while Yoav shared his thoughts. "If he has conspired with Eleazar on this, there is no point objecting. That will just cause Eleazar to get his back up."

"You're right, but what can we do about it? I'm assuming you want me to continue assisting you as I have."

"Absolutely. You have been a godsend to me. I could not manage the entire operation on my own. I'm getting a little too old for that."

I love you too, old man.

"So, what do we do?" I said. "I can continue to be your assistant when Nathan isn't around, but you will have to be the one to issue all instructions to the workers. We can do our planning here at the campfire in the evenings."

Dorit and Judith had joined us now, and Judith passed around a plate of stuffed dates she'd made in the kitchen that day.

"That should work," said Judith, who had been listening in. "But Daniel, you know the workers will continue to look to you for decisions. They will not stop just because Nathan said so."

"You're right. That's just something we'll have to watch for," I said as I ate a stuffed date and hugged my wife.

The following day, Nathan did not appear for the morning muster, thankfully, giving us an opportunity to explain to the workers that I was no longer formally Yoav's assistant and that I would work alongside them. However, nothing had really changed in that. Then, as we walked to the fields to weed the peppers, one worker pulled me aside and told me quietly that his son, one of Nathan's soldiers, overheard Nathan talking to Eleazar about me. We walked side by side, and he leaned in close so no one else would hear.

"Nathan was talking about how he wants to pressure you to leave Masada, and Eleazar agreed, saying you are a thorn in his side. Nathan added he would never forgive you for stabbing him."

This is not good. I thought their goal was to torture me, not to get rid of me.

Then, a few weeks later, the workers and I were in the pepper fields, adjusting the irrigation ditches from a nearby cistern, when one worker asked me a question. As I answered, Nathan burst into view from between the date palms behind us.

"Why are you asking him?" he yelled. "He is just a laborer like you. If you have a question, ask Yoav."

"But Nathan," I said in as reasonable a tone as I could, "Yoav is in the onion fields, and I am here. And the workers know I know the answer to their questions, so why shouldn't I answer when you or Yoav are not here?"

Surely, he can't take issue with that, can he? I thought. *I am being so polite and reasonable.* But this was Nathan, and he took issue.

In a manner that was now predictable, Nathan exploded. "I have had it with you, Daniel. You will follow the orders of the military command, like everyone else at Masada, or I will have you punished. You are not special, and we will not make exceptions for you. And since you have proved you cannot obey the simplest orders, I am transferring you out of farming, beginning tomorrow. So, you are dismissed and will leave the fields immediately."

That evening, Eleazar paid a visit to our room to inform me I must serve nighttime guard duty in the auxiliary unit and make up for the months I had not served until now. Since every male over fifteen must volunteer for one month of every four, I was in arrears of six months, which I must begin serving immediately.

"There will be no leniency in this, Daniel, since you wrongfully got an exemption based on your claim you were the assistant head of the farming team when no such position exists," explained Eleazar to justify the onerous nature of the punishment. And, of course, I had no recourse since the military governance structure of Masada prevented an appeal.

Judith burst into tears at Eleazar's pronouncement. With us expecting our first child only a few weeks later, we both came to understand the insidiousness of the punishment. With me doing nighttime guard duty, I could not help Judith with the baby at night or when I'd be sleeping during the day. I did my best, but it was an exhausting period for us both, meant to drive a wedge in our marriage or force us to leave Masada together.

Hannah was born a month later, and a few months of exhausting child-rearing and guard duty had already passed when two strangers arrived at Masada's gate one night.

"Who goes there?" I challenged as we heard shuffling sounds on the Snake Path, close to where we sat, guarding Masada's main entranceway. Being an outcast, I was not engaged in banter with the other soldiers, so I had not been sitting around the campfire and was not night-blinded when I discerned two bodies approaching on the path.

"We have escaped from Jerusalem," a woman shouted out.

We were so surprised to be approached in the middle of the night, and by this woman's comment, no one responded immediately. The night guards' greatest challenge was not falling asleep out of sheer boredom during the long nights in the middle of the desert. If we were lucky enough, we sometimes experienced the occasional star shower to help overcome the monotony, but since coming to Masada, it was unheard of to encounter a stranger at night.

But now, two people were approaching, seemingly from nowhere and in the middle of the night, claiming to have escaped from Jerusalem.

"Stop where you are," I finally replied. "Identify yourselves."

Again, the disembodied voice called out. "My name is Sarah, and my husband is Jacob. The Romans have destroyed Jerusalem, but we escaped. We seek refuge. Please let us in. My husband was injured by an enemy soldier and needs care."

"Don't let them in," one soldier whispered from behind. "They lie. The Romans cannot have destroyed Jerusalem."

Although living in the desert, we knew of the Roman siege of Jerusalem from the occasional passerby. *Could the situation have gotten this bad?*

"I will go down to them and learn more. Be evermore alert in the event it is a trick meant to make us lower our guard. I'll be back soon and tell you what I learn."

Not being well-loved by my fellow watchmen thanks to Nathan having poisoned their minds against me, they were more than happy to have me put my life at risk in the event of an ambush. I took a torch and a water skin and descended to where I thought the voices were located and found two bedraggled individuals who appeared precisely as if they had just spent the past week making their way from Jerusalem to Masada by foot.

Approaching with one hand on my sword and the other holding the torch high, I noticed the woman named Sarah cowering before me, with her husband in a heap behind her. The man was in terrible shape and had a bloody mantle wrapped around his neck, obviously covering a neck wound. Looking around furtively to make sure this was not an ambush, I asked Sarah why she cowers so before me.

"It is the torch, sir. We were caught in a conflagration in Jerusalem, and ever since the burning of the Lower City, I am wary of fire."

"And what of your husband?" I asked as I gestured for Sarah to sit on a rock near her husband and offered them the water skin.

"He was injured on the last day of fighting for Herod's Palace before we descended into the tunnels. A Roman sword nicked his throat and caused him to lose his voice."

"Will he live?"

Sarah looked at her husband wistfully, and turning back to me, said, "If God wills it, sir."

"Amen," I added. "There is no need to call me sir. My name is Daniel, and I'm here to question you before allowing you entry into Masada. Perhaps we wouldn't be so suspicious if you had arrived during the day and were not carrying such inauspicious news."

Turning once again to her husband to check on his welfare, she continued. "I understand, and I will gladly answer your questions. My sole desire is to find a place for us to live in safety so my husband can fully heal."

"What made you think to come to Masada?"

"Everyone knows of the Sicarii stronghold here, one of the last remaining Jewish fortresses."

Very interesting. Did I just notice Jacob becoming uncomfortable at the mention of the Sicarii? This is not good.

I moved the torch closer to Jacob and asked, "Who is your husband, Sarah? And which forces did he fight with?" *And there it is again, that fear in his eyes.* "And why is he so afraid? Tell me the truth, Sarah. It is the only way to gain entrance to Masada, and with me, you'll get the most sympathetic audience. If you remain with us here, you will learn that not all residents of Masada are Sicarii, and you have little to fear from me."

"Tuhl mm," Jacob managed to say.

"What did he say?"

"He wants me to tell you, so he must trust you, and his instincts are usually right." Taking his hand in hers, Sarah continued. "We knew it might be dangerous for us to seek refuge among the Sicarii. Jacob was a lieutenant of Yochanan of Gush, one of the Zealot leaders. He fought alongside Yochanan until near the end, when Yochanan ordered him to facilitate my escape through the tunnels. I am Yochanan's niece and only living relative, you see."

"Where is your uncle now?"

"Likely on a Roman galley on the Great Sea. The Romans captured him two days before we emerged from the tunnels, and we heard they are taking him to Rome to be tried for rebelling against the empire."

All of my instincts were screaming trouble. I knew Eleazar would not take kindly to a Zealot leader. I wanted to help them but had to learn more first.

"Tell me more about the fate of Jerusalem."

Jacob nodded, and Sarah continued. "We arrived in Jerusalem after the success of the Roman campaign in the north. My uncle was an olive oil merchant in Gush, and he led the uprising against the Romans. After the Romans crushed the rebellion, Yochanan fled, bringing a large group of refugees with him to Jerusalem."

"Wait. That's almost a year after the Zealots killed Menachem."

They both looked at me inquisitively, and Sarah asked, "Who is Menachem?"

"The Sicarii leader. The Zealots killed him the year before you arrived in Jerusalem. That's good news for you." *That's excellent news. Maybe Eleazar won't make them pay for his cousin's torture and death.* "Continue, please."

"Once Yochanan arrived in Jerusalem, he helped the Zealots wrest control of the city from the old guard of priests and the wealthy classes. But factional fighting for leadership between the various Jewish rebel parties meant we were not ready when the Romans arrived on Passover. Many attacks and counterattacks occurred during the five-month siege, but the Romans finally broke through to the Temple Mount and burned the Temple. The Roman general could not control his troops, who pillaged and burned the Lower City and killed thousands. After that, the Romans completed their conquest of Jerusalem by taking the Upper City. The Roman general then ordered his men to level the entire city, leaving only the three towers of Herod's Palace standing and some of the wall on the west side of the Temple."

"Then where are the rest of the escapees? Why are we not seeing a flood of refugees?"

"Some people escaped during the siege and later fighting, but most are dead. Those hiding in the tunnels were the last to be captured, but Jacob knew of a place deep in the tunnels where we and a few others hid undetected. We heard the Romans killed over one hundred thousand people. After we escaped, we met people along the way who told us the Romans also took seven hundred Zealot warriors to Rome for Titus's triumph parade, and they sent all the other men to the mines in Egypt."

"What of the women and children?"

"Taken to the slave markets to be sold."

I looked at them incredulously. "Are you telling me you are the only two people to have escaped Jerusalem alive?"

"We saw some others during our travels, but very few, and they told us that a large group of refugees was headed north, whereas we chose the south. We came to Masada because it is the closest community with a healer. Jerusalem proves the Romans will seek to root out and destroy all pockets of Jewish resistance to their rule. They have succeeded in the north, and now Jerusalem. There are few remaining holdouts, but we thought Masada would be the most fortified and safest of all."

Overwhelmed by their telling of the fate of Jerusalem and sympathetic to their plight, I turned to climb back up the path. "Stay here and wait for someone to return for you. I must report what I have learned to my commanders. I request you wait patiently. Someone will be down for you in a while."

CHAPTER

19

"Ruben, wake up. We need your help."

Like any good commander, Ruben sat up immediately, rubbed his eyes, and transitioned from being asleep to awake without the usual moment of confusion most people experience.

In the predawn light of the shift commander's tent, he said, "What is it, Daniel? What's wrong?"

"Refugees from Jerusalem are waiting below the Snake Path gate. They claim Jerusalem has been destroyed." I provided Ruben with more details of my interactions with Sarah and Jacob, and he woke Eleazar and briefed him.

Eleazar, also skilled in waking immediately, ran past us and out the Snake Path gate to interview the new arrivals. I later heard it didn't go well for Sarah and Jacob. As I'd suspected might happen, Eleazar imprisoned them for complicity in the murder of Menachem.

Later that day, a large group of Jerusalem refugees arrived at our gates. After extensive interrogations conducted first by

Nathan and then by Eleazar, they determined sixty of these new arrivals were part of a large group of Sicarii left behind four years earlier. Amazingly, they had been hiding in the tunnels and fighting all this time. Then, after we observed *Tisha B'Av*, which marked the destruction of the First Temple, a flood of a few hundred more bedraggled refugees from the second destruction of Jerusalem appeared at our gates.

Apparently, the Romans had rousted the Sicarii refugees from their hiding places in the tunnels, using dogs to locate them. They then broke through the stone stairs above the tunnels, using massive hammers and levers, and extracted or killed as many Sicarii as possible. I can only imagine how frightening that must have been, having spent just a few hours in those cramped and dark tunnels myself. The arriving refugees were the lucky ones who escaped. They tore their mantles and covered themselves in dust during their journey to Masada because the Romans had destroyed our beautiful Temple. How ironic was it when we learned the Romans had destroyed our Second Temple on the same date as the Greeks had destroyed our First Temple, six hundred and fifty-six years earlier?

Within a month, a total of three hundred new civilian refugees had joined us at Masada, increasing our population to over nine hundred men, women, and children. Unlike the earlier refugees, this group had experienced four additional years of war in Jerusalem and brought their own kind of severe suffering and distress with them to Masada.

The new refugees were heartily welcomed by Eleazar and his men, but raised grave concerns for those of us who understood the food limitations of Masada.

Midmorning, a few days after the last of the arrivals had been welcomed inside the fortress, I was using our only two oxen to plow the fields to turn over the remnants of this year's crops when a small group approached from up the hill. Not recognizing them but seeing their emaciated state, I realized they were new arrivals from Jerusalem. I halted the oxen and set down the plow while waiting for them to come closer.

"Welcome. You look lost, friends. How can I direct you?"

Coming closer, one said, "Nathan sent us to work in the fields."

"Well met. We only have one plow, but I'm sure I can take turns with one or two of you. Honestly, I'd be happy for the help. Do any of you have experience plowing?"

They shook their heads, and a tall one volunteered that no, they didn't have experience plowing.

"Odd that Nathan sent you down then. He knows we only need highly skilled labor for the next few days. Well, two of you can stay here and help me. The rest of you should find Yoav further down the hill. He'll have work for you."

The towering one, who seemed to be their leader, said, "Don't give us made-up work. I have plenty of my own work to do. For starters, I have to build a decent room for my family to live in—like the pleasant room you have."

"What's wrong with your room?" I asked.

"Is your room in the casemate wall?" the tall one asked, with a sharp edge.

"Yes."

"Well, ours isn't. So instead, we'll have to cobble our shelter together from rocks strewn about on the ground. We are city dwellers, and most of us have never built anything in our lives, so we'll be lucky if our shelters don't collapse on our families during the first winter storm."

Not giving it much thought, I said, "Our storms are not intense. I'm sure it will be fine."

The tall one raised his voice and responded with an intensity that startled me. "Don't patronize me. What's wrong with you veterans? Why do you think you're so special? Just because you got here first? I stayed behind to command the Sicarii left in Jerusalem, and we were fighting the same enemy as you, but we stayed and fought longer. And for that, you make us feel like a burden?"

The tall fellow was towering over me now, every bit the commander he claimed to be, so I took a step back and said, "I'm sorry. I didn't mean to belittle your concerns. I've been plowing for days, and I didn't realize things weren't going well for you. Come to my campfire tonight and tell me about it. My room is immediately to the right of where the synagogue is being built. Will you please join me?"

Slightly taken aback, he said he would and introduced himself as Yitzhak.

"Excellent. I'm Daniel, and my wife, Judith, and I look forward to you joining us. I'll finish this plowing and see you tonight."

Every evening, campfires dotted the landscape all over our mountaintop retreat, flickering and throwing sparks to the sky, twinkling like the heavens above. Sitting around the fire was a now recurring event in front of our room whereby we entertained a regular stream of guests who came to share their thoughts and concerns. Without trying, our evening gatherings became a locus of the community, at least for the like-minded.

I related my encounter with Yitzhak to Yoav and Judith as we settled in. The unrest of the newcomers surprised them both, just as it had me. Everyone expected the absorption of this wave of refugees from Jerusalem to be easy since the two groups had once been united before splitting years before. It hadn't occurred to the veterans or the new arrivals that Masada's limitations would become a source of tension.

We expected Yitzhak soon, and I wanted to discuss the housing situation with Yoav and Judith before he arrived. "Yoav, will you be able to find someone else to plow for a week or two while I help the newcomers build their homes?"

"That's a good idea, Daniel. I'd hate to lose you for that long since you are the best plowman we have, but I'm sure we can find someone else to do the work for a while. I'll find someone to replace you as soon as we finish here."

"Good. I think it's important to help absorb the Jerusalemites. We don't need any unrest."

"You're right," said Judith, "But who else can help? How about Aaron, Malachi's friend? Wasn't he a stonemason in Jerusalem?"

"That's perfect," I said. "I'll speak with him this evening. We should also recruit some of our field hands to help collect and move rocks to where they are building their shelters. They can start with the piles of rocks we gathered when we prepared the fields."

Now we had a plan, we each pondered how to best implement it while sitting quietly by the fire when we heard someone from the shadows say, "Good evening." It was Yitzhak and his wife, Yael, whom I had not yet met. I invited them to sit on any of the remaining tree stumps we used as seats and introduced Yitzhak to everyone. He then introduced Yael, and Judith immediately signaled for her to come and sit nearby, so she could learn of any unique problems the refugee women might be experiencing.

"Welcome to you both. We're glad you could join us. Your troubles have me worried, and I wanted to see what we could do to help," I said.

"Thank you, Daniel. I have to say, your invitation was one of the first pleasant things to happen since we arrived. You can imagine what it was like to have such a narrow escape from Jerusalem, then a seven-day trek to Masada, only to be met with indifference or worse. Eleazar greeted us warmly when we arrived, but after learning how many of us there were, his enthusiasm cooled, making many of us feel like we were a burden on the settlement. It surprised us that we're being made to feel like we were imposing since we thought we were rejoining our brothers in arms."

"Well, there will be no more indifference. We have developed a plan to solve the housing problem within the week, and the three of us will try to get you integrated into the community as quickly as possible."

"Thank you," said Yael in her soft-spoken voice. "I can't tell you what a relief that is to hear. We worried we might have to make our way to the Sicarii community in Alexandria if we could not find a place here."

Judith inched closer to Yael on the seat they were sharing, put an arm around her, and said, "You're home now, Yael. No need to make the long journey to Alexandria."

I then shared our ideas with them, and as I did so, I noticed the stiffness in Yael's body leave her. Tears rolled freely down her cheeks, and she embraced Judith in return.

"Thank you," offered Yitzhak. "The housing situation provoked a lot of resentment since you veterans are so comfortable and didn't have to build your own dwellings. And then when no one extended an offer of help, it made it worse."

"That ends tonight. We will do everything we can to make you all feel welcome."

Yitzhak and Yael both smiled for the first time, and I was relieved we could make a difference in their lives after their horrific experiences in Jerusalem.

"Other than the debacle with housing, are there other issues?" Yoav asked Yitzhak. "If yes, we must address them. We can't have half the community feeling slighted."

"We hear whispers there will not be enough food or work now that we have arrived, and we worry about it too. But when we ask the work supervisor where we can help, we are told all work teams are full. So, we're feeling bored and blamed for the problems we're trying to help solve."

"I understand why this is happening," said Yoav. "Farming is a perfect example. There is only so much we can grow on the plateau, so there's a limit to the labor we can put into raising crops and the expected yield. Only by expanding the land area can we change the situation—and we have no way of doing that."

"It's an interesting problem," I said, "but something we must solve quickly because it's true, four hundred more mouths will put a severe strain on food supplies. We are already producing less than we need, and living on less food than we should. We've all gotten used to partial starvation. Does anyone know a way to increase yields in the existing fields?" I asked.

"Why not build upward, like in the cities when they run out of space?" Yitzhak said. "If you've used all available land already, why not plant on top of the casemate wall? The wall is about three arm spans wide, and who knows how many long. Soldiers don't need the entire width to patrol, so why not build raised beds on top of the wall and plant more crops up there?"

"That's brilliant," said Yoav, as Yitzhak's eyes lit up. "The wall is almost two thousand paces around, and if we make planting beds an arm span wide, that gives us more than half an additional yoke. If we cut back on food allotments, we should be able to manage."

"I like this plan," I said. "Not only will it give us more food, but it will also create the need for more labor. Let's take the idea to Eleazar in the morning."

After everyone left, Yoav returned, and as I extinguished the fire, he stroked his beard and said to me, "You know, it's not enough, don't you?"

"I know. But I prefer our solution to Eleazar's. At least our solution doesn't involve stealing or killing."

CHAPTER

20

• • • • • • • • • ● ● ● • • • • • •

Together with Yitzhak, Yoav and I went to the Western Palace the following day to present the idea to Eleazar. Beforehand, we met outside my room to coordinate our thoughts and warn Yitzhak about the difficulties of speaking with Eleazar. Unfortunately, after arriving at the Western Palace, we were again stopped by the guards and had to explain our presence there.

I wasn't looking forward to this meeting since every interaction with Eleazar was fraught with the possibility of confrontation. However, this time was not as tense as usual; perhaps Eleazar chose to be on his best behavior in front of Yitzhak. He rightfully challenged us on whether the effort would produce enough food to warrant the labor and whether we could make the raised beds narrow enough not to interfere with the defense of the battlements. Once we assured him on both counts, he approved the plan with the stipulation that Nathan oversee the construction, to our great surprise. Eleazar sent a guard from the palace to find Nathan, and we planned to start building the beds the following day.

Once the raised bed project was well underway, there was enough work for everyone, at least for the foreseeable future. It was an enormous undertaking, requiring wood for the beds to be gathered, worked, and cobbled together in place, and then good soil dug, hauled up the walls, and dumped into the beds. During the first week, Nathan recruited the field hands to work on the project. To Nathan's credit, his crews finished construction of the beds and their filling with soil in time for the late planting season in October.

Before joining in, Yitzhak, Aaron, and I gathered all the second-wave Jerusalemites for some very gratifying work. First, Aaron taught them to work with stone and mortar by building a demonstration dwelling near the southern casemate wall. He then had them break into family units, and I supplemented their ranks with the many field hands who had volunteered to help. We also filled cartloads with the same rocks we had cleared from the fields over two years before and dumped them where each new shelter would be built, and dug earth to be used as mortar. It was exhausting work, but the Jerusalemites and I were pleased to see many new homes rising.

Building their homes and the raised beds occupied the community's newest members for two months, but once they finished those two projects, there was little for them to do, and I began to worry again. Eleazar tried to address the problem by recruiting many of the men into his forces and finding meaningless tasks for the others. We were back to making work for the Jerusalemites, and we all knew it.

Yitzhak came to our campfire every evening, and Yael often came with him, as she and Judith had become close friends. One evening, after the big projects were completed and there was little work to occupy hundreds of people, Yitzhak shared his concerns.

"Eleazar has not given up his goal of expelling the Romans from Israel, and he is insisting a majority of my men join his forces to increase their offensive capabilities. But most of my men are tired of fighting after our years of struggle in Jerusalem. They just want to settle down."

"I understand," I said, similarly worried myself. Then, gazing into the fire, I added, "The same thing happened with the first wave from Jerusalem. They were tired of killing and just wanted to be with their families. They were happy to become farmers."

"But we're worried because there isn't enough work," said Yitzhak with a concerned look on his face, "so soldiering seems like a welcome option. At least it will keep them occupied. The men, especially, are getting restless without enough to keep them busy, and Eleazar's makeshift work of gathering firewood and digging latrines isn't helping. There is talk of my people leaving to establish a new settlement of our own nearby, so they can be farmers instead of fighters."

Here it is, an opportunity to solve Masada's constraint problems of too little food production and too much labor.

Excitedly, I responded, "Yitzhak, what a wonderful idea. I'd like to discuss it with you at length. Many old-timers have mentioned the opportunity to leave Masada and start a new settlement, myself included. Have you given any thought to where you would build this community?"

"What new community?" my lovely Judith asked with some reticence as she rejoined the conversation after singing Hannah to sleep.

"There has been some discussion among my people of leaving Masada and establishing a new settlement," Yitzhak explained as he added two large logs to the fire. Hundreds of sparks flew into the air as Judith pursued her line of thought.

"Daniel, I know we have discussed leaving too, but what about Malachi? I could never leave if he were to stay here," said Judith.

While this discussion was happening, Malachi, who had been on guard duty nearby, later told me he saw Nathan leaving the shadows of the battlement above our campfire. Malachi was curious to know what Nathan intended to do with this new information, so he followed him and loitered under Eleazar's window in the palace to hear what he could. He was not surprised that Nathan reported our plans to establish a new settlement to Eleazar as an established fact, which incensed Eleazar, which was Nathan's intention all along.

Malachi came to see Judith and me afterward. "Nathan told Eleazar he has to do something about you," Malachi reported. "He told Eleazar you were planning to take more than half the community with you, at which point Eleazar exploded and said you can't; that he needs the civilians to take care of the soldiers. He said the soldiers couldn't defend Masada and attack the Romans if they had to feed themselves and that it was critical to build a strong military force to go on the offensive against Rome."

We were in our room and speaking quietly so no one could overhear us.

"So, that is why Eleazar doesn't want us to leave when I suggest it," I said. "I always thought the soldiers were here to protect the civilians—that we were the settlement—but it turns out, in Eleazar's view, the settlement comprises soldiers to expel the Romans from Israel, and the civilians are just here to feed them and wash their tunics. Very interesting. We'll see how the civilians feel about this when I tell them." Which was something I planned to do at the next assembly.

Through quiet discussions over the next several weeks, I was thrilled to learn that hundreds of members of the Masada settlement wanted to leave. Still, we could not figure out how to do so without resorting to thievery of the sort Eleazar embraced so readily. Because we were members of a communal settlement, we, as individuals, possessed nothing of value we could use to purchase or trade for the supplies we needed. The only path we could think of was the same one Eleazar had chosen, but could we condone stealing what we needed when that was the one path we objected to most at Masada. And besides, we had no desire to hurt those we left behind as we had hurt the people of Ein Gedi a few years earlier. I was becoming increasingly concerned that we wouldn't find a solution to our conundrum.

While our most recent harvest had been successful, the arrival of the Jerusalemites was causing severe shortages of all foodstuffs. Even with the raised bed plantings, there wouldn't be enough seed to grow sufficient food to prevent starvation in the future. Eleazar's solution was to send a trading mission to the nearby settlement of Ein Bokek to acquire the supplies we needed for the coming season, and I suspected he intended to steal what we couldn't buy or trade for.

We later learned Eleazar's strategy was, in fact, the same as at Ein Gedi a few years before. First, he sent Nathan to trade for the seed, but the farmers at Ein Bokek refused to part with it, since they only had enough for their own planting needs. Returning empty-handed was not an option, so Eleazar ordered

Nathan to take a commando team and return to Ein Bokek the next night.

Scouting missions were a common occurrence, so no one thought anything of it when Nathan led a group of twenty soldiers down the Snake Path at sunset the next day. When they returned with tools and food goods that were impossible to produce or grow on our own, I wondered how they had gotten their hands on these items, but the soldiers were tight-lipped about their mission.

Malachi joined Judith and me for supper the evening after returning from the reconnaissance mission, and I noticed him avoiding eye contact.

"Are you well, brother? You don't seem your usual light-hearted self this evening," I said.

After minimal prompting by Judith and me, he confessed. "The patrol last night was a raid on Ein Bokek, and it was a disaster. Eleazar had intended for us to take the seed since they would not trade with us. But instead of going in by stealth, Nathan swaggered around the village and demanded the supplies. Some townspeople alerted the Roman guards at the nearby fortress, who then surrounded our patrol. We had to fight our way out and killed several Roman guards and farmers to escape. We got what we went for, but they wounded several of our men during the hostilities."

I was only mildly surprised Eleazar had resorted to raiding another settlement, but when I looked at Malachi, I realized there was more.

"What is it you're not telling us?" Judith said, voicing my thoughts. "I can tell you're leaving something out. What is it?"

Looking closely, I saw Malachi's eyes tearing.

"What is it, brother?" Judith asked again, more gently. "What happened out there?"

Staring out and not seeing us at all, he whispered, "I killed someone—a farmer. I didn't mean to," he said, wracked with sobs, "but he attacked me with a pickaxe and forced me to defend myself."

"Brother, I'm so sorry," Judith said as she put her arms around him to calm him. "I know you didn't go to Ein Bokek intending to kill. You're too good a soul for that." Then, stepping back to look him in the eyes, she added, "And I think it's time for you to resign from Eleazar's army."

"He won't let anyone resign. He's too afraid everyone will go except a few. You remember what he said when he heard civilians want to leave. He considers departing to be a betrayal and will never let soldiers go."

Judith and I looked at each other with profound sadness for Malachi, the gentlest soul I know. *Unfortunately, he will live with this for the rest of his life.*

"At what cost?" I asked.

Malachi looked up. "At what cost what?" he asked.

"At what cost will we continue taking the easy path instead of the righteous path? We are killing others so we can survive, but what is this so-called freedom worth if we steal it from others?"

"Daniel's right," said Judith. "And he's right about leaving too. But, Malachi, if we were to leave Masada, would you come with us?"

"I want to. I just don't know how I could."

"For now, it's enough to know you want to leave with us," I said. "We'll figure the rest out later."

Eleazar gave many of us yet another reason to want to leave Masada the very next day when he announced he would put "The Zealots," Sarah and Jacob, on trial for crimes against the Sicarii. This sent a chill through the community, for not every resident of Masada was Sicarii, and some other Zealots had arrived with the second wave of refugees from Jerusalem.

That evening, sitting at our campfire, Yitzhak shared his objections with me. He knew this Jacob, a key lieutenant of one of the Zealot leaders, Yochanan of Gush. Yitzhak had served with him in Jerusalem, and moreover, he knew firsthand that Jacob was a hero of the rebellion against Rome.

"Jacob led the Jewish forces responsible for defending the Antonia Fortress that abutted the Temple," Yitzhak told us. "He led a team of sappers who dug a tunnel under one of the Antonia Fortress towers. The team burrowed under the fortress walls, emerged in the middle of the Roman camp, and burned all of the siege engines gathered there, thus delaying the Roman attack on the Temple until the siege equipment was rebuilt. He is a true hero."

"Then why does Eleazar want to put him on trial?" someone asked.

Looking around to see who was listening before I answered, I said, "You remember the Zealots killed Menachem at the beginning of the rebellion? Eleazar probably sees this as an opportunity to exact revenge for his cousin from a high-level Zealot."

"But Jacob is Yochanan of Gush's lieutenant? They were still in Galilee fighting the Romans when Menachem was killed. It must have been a Zealot leader from Jerusalem who killed Menachem. Does Eleazar know this?" Yitzhak asked.

"I don't know, but honestly, I don't know if it would matter. Menachem's death is unavenged, and I think that is reason enough in Eleazar's mind," I explained.

CHAPTER

21

· · · · · · · · · · ● ● ● ● ● ● ● · · · · · · · ·

Two years passed in relative quiet, and the Jerusalem refugees had mostly been absorbed into the community. Still, a listlessness had settled over us, probably due to insufficient food and a lack of activities to engage our minds. Nevertheless, people did the best they could to overcome the lethargy by learning new crafts. As a result, we now had large groups of leather workers, fletchers, armorers, and blacksmiths.

One cool evening, little Hannah and I had just finished our meager supper. Unfortunately, Judith was unable to eat as Ari, our new son, only six weeks old, suckled and whined irritably throughout. There was no comforting the child; Judith simply didn't have enough milk, and she looked at me with worried eyes.

"I don't know what to do, Daniel," she said. "Dorit told me this is happening to many other mothers. Their milk is drying up, and the babies are starving."

I gazed at my tiny new son, struggling to get enough milk, and my heart broke. Hundreds of us had been watching as our settlement began to collapse around the edges; there wasn't enough food to sustain us—not without raids. We knew we couldn't go on like this much longer. Something had to change.

"I'll talk to Dorit," I said, kissing Judith on top of her head.

I found Dorit and sat down wearily next to her in the flickering firelight of her campfire. She looked tired and thin. "Forty-six babies born in the past six months," she said, without greeting me, her voice dull. "And most of their mothers can't feed them, so they are feeding them goat's milk." Dorit's eyes never left mine. "We must increase the food rations for new mothers."

I stared into the fire. I didn't know how to tell Dorit that it was impossible to increase rations for new mothers; we were all on starvation rations already.

"We're expecting thirty-eight more babies, and there won't be enough goat's milk for all of them," Dorit said, interrupting my thoughts. "What will we do then? People are scared. I am scared."

"Have you taken this matter to Eleazar?" I asked.

"Not yet," Dorit said.

"What matter?" Judith asked as she joined us. She was looking at me with concern in her eyes because she knew anything to do with Eleazar entailed danger.

Ari, meanwhile, had launched into a severe bout of crying, and I offered to get him.

"It won't help unless you can feed him," Judith said. "I didn't have enough milk, and he's still hungry. I'll have to get him some goat milk. I'll be back soon."

Dorit looked at me and said with her eyes, see, it is happening to everyone.

"This is exactly what we were just discussing," said Dorit. "Judith, dear, I have a better idea for tonight. Let's take Ari to

Gila and ask her to feed him. Her boy is not nursing as often, and she still has surplus milk. It won't last forever, but it will solve your problem tonight. Let's go, dear. It breaks my heart to hear him crying like this."

Judith and Dorit went to find Gila, and I sat in quiet contemplation. There is nothing as heart-rending as a crying baby, to whom you cannot explain why there isn't enough food to fill their tummy.

We will have to go to Eleazar when Judith returns from Gila and impress upon him the need to split the community, I thought. *It is the only way to solve this problem.*

It was getting late, and the palace guards were not happy to see us. But Dorit had known Eleazar for a long time and told the young fellow guarding the entrance to fetch Eleazar immediately. Nathan came out instead, and Dorit gave him an earful until he led us down the hall to Eleazar's office.

"Dorit is here," Nathan said as he stuck his head in. "She's with Daniel and Judith, and she wants to see you. She says it's urgent."

"Send her in."

"Get out of my way, you oaf. Can't you see a woman old enough to be your mother is trying to get through?" she said as she berated a soldier in the hallway. "Eleazar," she called, "Where are you?"

"In here, Dorit. To your right."

She stuck her head into the office, and we heard her say, "Very fancy palace you have here."

"Thank you, Dorit. It's not my palace, though. It's the people's palace."

"Really. I don't see many of the *people* here. Just you and your men."

"I see you've brought Daniel and his lovely wife, Judith, too. And how is the baby? Ari, isn't it?"

"Now that's exactly the problem," Dorit said, jumping right in. "The babies. We've had forty-six babies born in the past year, and another thirty-seven are due in the next six months. And the babies are starving because their mothers are not getting enough to eat, so they can't nurse their children. So, what are you going to do about it? The parents are anxious and becoming more vocal."

"What do you mean, 'becoming more vocal'? Tell me who they are, and I'll tell them to stop. We can't have that," he said.

"So typical of you to focus on the wrong problem," Dorit said as Judith and I watched in awe.

"Well, if they're so concerned, they should stop making babies," Eleazar said, unhelpfully. "But Daniel, although I'm not sure why you are here with Dorit, I'm sure you have opinions on how to solve this intractable problem. Please enlighten us."

"People are anxious, and they know this can't go on much longer," I said.

"What can't go on much longer?"

"People are talking about leaving for someplace with more opportunities," I said.

"That will not happen," Eleazar said. "Although if you and your family want to leave, please, don't let me hold you back. But right now, we have to figure out how to increase our food, especially for the young ones. And there's only one way to get food right away. We will have to take it from a neighboring settlement."

"Violence is always your first recourse. If we had split the community two years ago when the refugees arrived from

Jerusalem, we would not have this problem today. But you think thievery and violence will always work. You are a hammer, so every problem looks like a nail to you."

Exasperated with me, Eleazar came out from behind his desk to express himself more forcefully. Getting close to me, he said, "I'm so tired of you, Daniel, and your holier-than-thou attitude. You cannot solve today's problem with tomorrow's solution, so we have no choice but to raid Ein Gedi and take the food we need for the babies to survive. I've decided and will announce it tomorrow."

Eleazar called for an emergency assembly to be held at sunset the next day. After consulting with Judith, I called for an urgent meeting of my own beforehand. Yoav, Benjamin, Judith, Yitzhak, and other leaders of the various civilian groups met me deep in the date orchards to avoid being observed by Eleazar's troops. It was midday as we stood under the shade of the date palms, with a pleasant breeze blowing the fronds above our heads and causing dappled sunlight.

"Thank you all for coming," I began quietly, so as not to be overheard. "I believe we have to demand that Eleazar support the establishment of a second settlement on the large plain immediately southeast of Masada." Silent nods of agreement encouraged me to continue. "It should be open to anyone who wants to come, and I would expect about half the civilian population will want to join us. The several hundred remaining civilians should be more than enough to support the soldiers. Any thoughts?"

Yitzhak added, "We should request permission to continue living at Masada until we build our shelters and ask for enough seed, tools, and animals to start a viable agricultural community of our own."

I put it to a vote, and everyone agreed. We left the date orchard afterward, with each leader pledging to spend the rest of the day speaking to their constituencies to build support for the new settlement.

We had been planning for this moment for two years and had worked out many details of how to break away from Masada and what we would need to be successful. The only remaining question was whether Eleazar would allow it and whether we could break away, even if he objected. We were about to find out.

CHAPTER

22

W e often held community meetings on the evening of the full moon, so people were surprised when Eleazar called an assembly two weeks after the last one. All day, there was speculation about the unplanned meeting. Many thought Eleazar was about to cut food rations again. People's tempers flared whenever the conversation turned to food and the never-ending debate about how to solve our food shortage. I had never seen it this bad, and all around me, I heard people sounding desperate.

We assembled in the usual spot, and conversations ended as Eleazar came to the stage. He stood, as always, with a fire bowl on either side, and a partial moon hung behind him.

"We are aware of the difficult food situation, and it's time to take action," Eleazar said. "Mothers cannot feed their babies because they are not getting enough to eat. So, they substitute goats' milk, but there isn't enough to go around. We're increasing the goat herds as fast as we can, but we can't make goats faster than you can make babies."

There were chuckles here and there among the men.

"Our young children aren't thriving, and all of us are becoming lethargic and having trouble doing our work. Even our soldiers are becoming weaker, which poses a serious security risk.

"I know many of you think my approach to acquiring food for the settlement has been heavy-handed in the past. It pains me to pilfer food from other communities instead of providing for ourselves. But I've only done what was necessary, and I will continue to do so."

Cheers went up from his troops.

"I have given the naysayers a chance to show us an alternative path, and they came up with several creative solutions, such as building planting beds on the battlements. But even with all their wonderful ideas, we find ourselves in an impossible situation. We must solve this problem fast, or people will die, starting with the babies."

Eleazar stopped and let that settle in, giving the crowd a chance to become riled up, first murmuring among themselves and then raising their voices in indignation. I had to give him credit. He not only co-opted the position of his opposition, but he also damned our ideas while appearing to praise them. It amazed me how he undercut us, posing the argument as for or against starvation, instead of for or against stealing from our neighbors.

He interrupted the din and said, "Our only chance for immediate relief is to take what we need. We tried trading, and it didn't work. So, now, we must take what we need or die. That is the choice before you. We can take the moral high ground and starve, or you can come with my men and me when we raid Ein Gedi and take what we need from those Roman collaborators. What do you say? Who's with me?"

A roar went up from the crowd that hurt my heart.

When things quieted down, I shouted, "Eleazar, you know that only solves the problem in the short term. What happens when there are no more settlements left to raid?"

"We have a fundamental problem here of too many people for the food we can produce," Eleazar said.

I agreed and said, "The only solution is to match the number of people to the amount of food we can grow, so I propose we split the community and that a portion of us leave to create a new settlement."

"Does that solve the problem of today's starving babies?" Eleazar asked.

"Not right away. It will take us several months to find a new location and prepare. Are you willing to let us build a second settlement nearby?"

"Who is this 'us' you speak of, Daniel? Who appointed you to represent the community, and for which group do you speak? I lead us here, not you. Now sit down and stop talking."

"This is not about who leads," I said. "It is about what we value: freedom at any cost or our very souls? The manner of our survival is as important as our lives. If we break the commandment not to steal, what will stop us from breaking other commandments? I worry about this community's soul, and I'm not the only one."

"Pretty words," Eleazar said. "But I am responsible for these people, not you."

"But they should have the right to decide whether we split the community so we can all survive. Let the people decide."

Calls of "He's right" and "Let the people decide" rang out as several of Eleazar's men spread themselves throughout the audience. When I realized what was happening, I saw Nathan coming at me with his dagger cupped in his right hand by his side, but before he could reach me, a protective wall of men surrounded Judith and me.

"Is this what it has come to?" I shouted over the men protecting me. "You will use violence against those same people whose survival you told us you are committed to protecting? You've proved my point."

"No, Daniel, to answer your question, I am not willing to let you split the community. We are stronger together. And even if I did, by the time you could build a self-sustaining settlement, too many people would have died." Then, turning back to the crowd, Eleazar asked, "Who is in favor of Daniel's plan instead of conducting the raid on Ein Gedi?"

Shouts for the raid far outweighed the cries for my plan, and with that, our community members committed themselves to expediency over morality.

"All right," said Eleazar, "In four days, after Shabbat, we'll leave at dusk and march to the outskirts of Ein Gedi, where we'll rest until the middle of the night. Every man in the community will go, and if someone chooses not to, we will no longer feed him and his family. Is that clear?"

That night, concerned for our safety, Judith and I stayed with Yoav and Dorit. Unable to sleep, I sat in their darkened doorway from where I could see the entrance to our room. Toward dawn, after all the campfires had died out, I saw a shadow enter our room in silence and exit again a moment later. I shuddered from the understanding our lives were in danger and went to seek the comfort of my wife.

Several people approached me over the next few days, both in the fields and at our evening campfire. Everyone was eager to share their opinions out of earshot of Eleazar's men. They supported me, with only the occasional dissenter who thought our defense and survival were paramount. Those with families supported my position more than those without.

Few of Eleazar's troops spoke to me, so I had little insight into their thoughts outside the occasional comment from Malachi. Still, two of Eleazar's lieutenants, Nathan and Ruben, did happen to come to me.

Ruben's visit took place late one evening when only the embers remained from our campfire.

He whispered down to Judith and me from the shadows of the battlement, "I only have a minute, but I wanted to warn you to stop, Daniel. I hear things, and I want to alert you to the danger you face if you don't stop challenging Eleazar. There are already murmurings."

"What murmurings?" asked Judith. "What can they do to him? Daniel is a valued leader of the community, and I don't think even Eleazar is crazy enough to have him killed, is he? No matter how much he might want to."

"There are ways to eliminate someone other than outright murder," said Ruben. "I have heard talk of accidents. So, Daniel, stay alert. Be careful during training or when you are on guard duty. It is too easy to push someone from the wall and claim he slipped. That's all. I have to go. Beware."

This warning proved all too prescient, as, the next day, I entered a shed near the onion fields to find a shovel, only to be followed inside a moment later by Nathan.

Surprised by the sudden darkness when he closed the door behind him, I turned to hear his disembodied voice say, "Stop challenging Eleazar, or I'll kill you. Then your beautiful children will grow up without a father." He then pushed me hard and said, "Try me and see if I'm lying."

With Nathan's threat still echoing in my mind, we played with the children in the evening for a while, and then Judith fed Ari until he fell asleep. I so enjoyed this time with our children, and I held Hannah tight in my arms and stroked her hair and cheeks, kissing her eyes and nose while singing her favorite lullaby. Hannah finally calmed down enough to settle in for the night, and Judith and I got into bed.

After tossing and turning for what felt like hours, Judith asked, "What are you going to do about the raid?"

Surprised she was still awake, I said, "I haven't decided yet. I agree with Eleazar. I don't think the Romans have forgotten us, and he is right to worry about whether our troops can defend us. And people will die from hunger—our family first if I don't go—so I don't see I have a choice."

In anticipation of the raid, the people of Masada were sub-
dued on Shabbat. Then, after darkness fell, all the able-bodied
men of Masada gathered near the Snake Path gate, where we
mustered into five restless groups of fifty men each. The four
lieutenants led their units, and Eleazar led the fifth. The groups
were composed mainly of Eleazar's regular troops, with trained
auxiliaries supplementing their numbers.

To avoid the light of the crescent moon exposing our approach upon the mountaintops, we walked close to the Asphalt
Lake and its feeders from the many wadis cutting through the
Judean hills, which spread out like fans to the lake's shore. Once
we had descended Masada, we had hoped for a quick march to
Ein Gedi, but as we walked across the treacherous rocky terrain,
there was a sustained clamor from men cursing as they slipped
and fell, and shushing from their comrades and commanders.
The racket was loud, and I feared we'd lose the element of surprise long before we arrived.

We reached our destination undetected despite the arduous
journey, albeit later than planned, and more tired and crankier
than expected. We hunkered down in a palm grove for a brief
rest, serenaded by male cicadas singing their incessant love song.

Eleazar used the time to whisper a briefing to the troops.
"While some of you have objected to this raid, we embark on
a critical mission for our community. For those of you with
families, remember that we will be home with enough food
to feed them for the foreseeable future by tomorrow. We will
have increased our herds, and your wives will nurse your infants
themselves for years to come. When we finish the deed, we will
have eliminated the constant gnawing hunger we feel. Listen,
now, as your leaders issue detailed instructions for the mission."

The lieutenants gathered their men into smaller groups, and
it was my great misfortune to be assigned to Nathan.

"Except for the ten guards spread throughout the village," Nathan said, beginning his briefing, "all the people of Ein Gedi should be asleep. Our path to success is to eliminate the men first. We have a numerical advantage, and killing the men will pacify the village. If any of the women interfere, we will eliminate them too."

"No!" someone from another group said too loudly. And then another "No," and another. I heard a sustained murmuring from all five squads as the lieutenants shared the details of the plan. While the grumbling increased in volume, Nathan ordered his regular troops into position, surrounding the auxiliaries in his squad, and, soon after, the other lieutenants did the same.

"Silence!" Nathan hissed. "Do you want to set off an alarm and cause your families to starve? These people are Roman collaborators and our enemies."

Seeing Eleazar on the periphery of Nathan's troops, I asked, "Does that justify killing every person who interferes while we steal the food they need to survive? What sort of people are we?"

Eleazar answered for Nathan. "I will not argue this with you again, Daniel. If it is a choice between our survival and theirs, I will choose ours every time."

Nathan continued his instructions. "Once we eliminate the men, you will gather all the food from each home and load it onto any available cart or mule you find. Then another squad will take the storage areas and load the larger carts with what they find there. Remember, the primary goal is to collect food we can eat now, so olives, dates, figs, corn, and barley, and goats and lambs to increase our herds. Questions? No? Good, then off to your assignments. Let's go."

Nathan's regular troops prodded the auxiliaries to get us moving, and as we passed Eleazar, I saw him gesture to Nathan and whisper something in his ear.

Ein Gedi was a densely populated community of interconnected one- and two-story stone houses. The village was divided into four quadrants with two principal thoroughfares bisecting the settlement top to bottom and across the middle, with many cross-cutting alleyways and a central square large enough for the entire population to gather. Our squad moved to the outskirts of our assigned quarter, and then the scout team found the two guards and made quick work of them, slitting their throats and pulling them into the shadows to die.

Nathan gathered his squad at the end of one of the major roads to prepare for the attack. Our orders were to station ourselves outside the door of every home before simultaneously bursting through the doors, making noise, and creating chaos to disorient those inside. Then, entering the bedroom, we were to find the husband and execute him in his bed.

So, I am to become a thief and a murderer, but if I don't kill the husband, the husband will kill me.

"Quietly now," Nathan said. "Walk behind me in pairs with as little noise as possible. Daniel and Malachi, take the rear."

We moved down the road in silence, leaving a soldier at each door. Soon, we reached the end of the road, having run out of men before running out of doorways. Then, with a few more entryways remaining, Nathan ordered Malachi to one door and said to me, "Daniel, cover this house, and I'll take the last two." Notwithstanding Nathan's facility with violence, I did not believe he could single-handedly pacify two households by himself. This seemed like a terrible plan, but I said nothing.

I stood by the doors in absolute silence, anticipating Nathan's signal. Struggling to catch my breath, and with my heart racing so fast and so loud I could hear the pounding in my ears, I awaited the whistle that would mark my descent into violence.

"Coward!" I was startled by Nathan's shout and realized the attack had begun. Rather than entering the house he had pointed toward a moment earlier, Nathan was running in my direction, his sword drawn and pointed at me.

I turned to my assigned door, undid the latch, and burst in, forgetting to shout. As I fumbled in the dark, I heard a mounting uproar outside as clashes broke out everywhere. I moved in the bedroom's direction but tripped over a pallet full of children, startling them awake. I landed on my knees at the opening of what appeared to be the parents' sleeping area. As I regained my feet, the children achieved a full-throated state of alarm and made my presence known to their parents. The father was startled awake and reached for his sword. Moving as fast as I could, I lunged at him, but I wasn't fast enough, and he batted my sword away before I landed the strike. This gave him an opening to counterattack. God must have been with me because the father slipped while launching himself out of bed, and his blow missed me as he fell to the floor. I raised my sword above my head to strike at him as his wife and children screamed, and without forewarning, I felt a sharp pain in my left thigh. Turning, I saw a boy with a look of horror on his face and a spear in his hands. The son regathered his determination and attacked again with an intensity not expected from one so young. This time, he ran at me as fast as his short legs could carry him with his brow furrowed and mouth twisted.

What should I do?

Without thinking, I raised my sword, batted away the boy's spear, and saw his momentum impale him on my sword, which was as sharp as the day Herod's men had brought it to Masada over one hundred years before.

The father stabbed at me with his sword, attacking with a ferocity that forced me out the door, no doubt to distance me from his other children. Then, without warning, I caught movement out of the corner of my eye and saw Nathan, his sword drawn over his head, coming at me for the attack. As the father and I parried, I moved to position him between Nathan and me. Hoping to end it with the father, I attacked again, but the father was a better swordsman than me, and he dropped below my blade, forcing me to spin around, putting Nathan behind me again. Then, sensing Nathan coming up on my back while fending off the father, I saw Malachi.

"Behind you," he yelled.

I shifted to the right with more speed than I knew I possessed, taking me out of Nathan's range and giving me a sudden opening to strike at the father, disabling him with a deep cut across the back of his left leg.

With the father no longer a threat, I turned my attention to Nathan. Malachi had not only shouted to warn me, but he had also engaged Nathan in a heated battle. Nathan wielded his sword and came at Malachi. Being the stronger of them, Nathan was about to deliver a crushing blow from above, so Malachi raised his sword to parry. But Nathan closed the distance between them and, feigning an overhead strike, pulled his dagger and drove it into Malachi's heart instead.

Just like that, Malachi's life was over. My dear friend and Judith's brother was dead.

"No!" I ran to Malachi's side, but it was too late. I cradled his head in my lap, still not quite sure what had happened while the world carried on around me. Numb to the goings-on of the battle, I heard commotion through the fog but did not understand, nor did I care, what was happening.

I later recalled Nathan shouting "On me!" to his men as they moved toward the central square where men from other squads had gathered. I came out of my fog long enough to stop Aaron, who was running by. Together, we carried Malachi to the muster point in the square.

There, Eleazar was standing on a raised platform so he could direct the battle. As he spoke with a bloody sword raised above his head, the unmistakable anguished sound of women mourning their dead husbands reached our ears in ever-increasing crescendos of loss.

Eleazar must have realized the ululating was changing from a general hue and cry to a more full-bodied sound coming at us from each of the thoroughfares of the settlement. The women were assembling, and the sound changed again as they came closer, intent on attacking their attackers.

Rocks rained down on us. Looking up, we saw women and children on the rooftops. They were throwing anything and everything on our heads. But they meant the chaos merely to distract us. From where we stood in the center square, we could see the end of each road and alleyway where our men were preparing to breach the mounds of sticks, branches, and furniture the women were piling up to prevent us from leaving. And then, to our horror, we saw the barriers catching fire.

"Commanders, to the barricades," yelled Eleazar, as screams of "Fire" were breaking out all over.

The lieutenants shouted for their men, who mustered to their sides with amazing speed. Then they moved to the barricades with their shields up to protect themselves from the rocks and burning brambles being thrown down on them from above and burst their way through the fires before they could become engulfed in the growing inferno.

I did not take part. Instead, I watched on while I stayed with Malachi's body.

As our men breached the obstructions, the women and children of Ein Gedi attacked, but they were no match for our forces, who slashed and stabbed each of them for the temerity of trying to burn us alive.

When the bloodlust had run its course—the massacre complete—and the fires quenched, the others put aside their weapons and stripped Ein Gedi to its barest bones while I found a cart to take Malachi home to his sister. And when we had finished, unable to look each other in the face, we burned Ein Gedi to the ground, trying, without success, to purify ourselves by fire and to purge the slaughter from our minds.

At midmorning, we retreated to Masada in absolute silence, unwilling to wait for the darkness of the coming night to cover our transgressions and unsure if we civilians would ever be able to look our families in the eyes again.

CHAPTER

24

The midmorning sun burned us as we trekked back to Masada as if God had already committed us to *Gehinnom* for our sins. The civilians among us were not the same men as before we left for Ein Gedi. Those men had, by and large, become family men and farmers, with all thoughts of their days as killers far behind them. But today, after the extermination of every man, woman, and child of Ein Gedi, we were murderers once again. All so we could steal their food since we were incapable of creating a self-sustaining and nurturing community of our own.

We made the trek back to Masada, taking twice as long to arrive in the daylight as we did at night, undoubtedly dreading having to face our wives and children and the wives and children of our dead and wounded comrades. The regular soldiers among us were elated, seeing the mission as a grand success and proof of their worthiness in battle. The rest of us dragged our feet, trying to delay the inevitable homecoming.

I was too shocked, or possibly too cowardly, to confront Nathan. And besides, what good would it have done? Physically, I was no match for him, and he would beat me once again, maybe even killing me this time. But one of the other civilians in Nathan's unit, David, sought me out and told me he witnessed Nathan's actions, from when he first attacked me to when he killed Malachi. He told me he would bear witness to both the attack and Malachi's murder.

All day, I led the cart carrying Malachi's body. I had covered him with a blanket I'd found, hoping to delay his bodily corruption in the heat. We arrived back at Masada shortly before sunset, and I saw by the cloud of flies gathered around Malachi's shroud I had failed at this too.

The women, alerted by the cheers of the children, swarmed the Snake Path gate to greet the men. There was a palpable sense of anticipation as the wives sought their husbands in the crowd. As the two groups merged, they looked like troops colliding on the battlefield, as each one quickly immersed itself in the other. The wives felt something was wrong; they could see it in their husbands' posture. Their heads were bent, and they shuffled as the women crowded around them, desperately searching for their loved ones. As the shouts of grief began, the faces of the children went from confusion to sudden understanding. Then, not knowing how to make their mothers stop screaming, they too succumbed to despair.

Leaving Malachi on his cart, I was the last to pass through the gate. Seeing Judith from a distance, I trudged toward her, fearing the moment, and when she finally saw me through the crowd, she ran and threw her arms around me and smothered me in kisses. I tried to disengage to tell her about Malachi, but I hesitated, desperately needing to feel her closeness.

Finally, she could tell something was wrong, and stepped back and said, "What is it, Daniel?" as she looked around from face to face and saw the men glancing away, not making eye contact with their wives or each other. "Daniel, what happened? What's wrong with you?"

I opened my mouth to tell her, but the words did not come. She could see I was struggling, and then I saw the horror in her eyes as she understood.

"Where is Malachi? Where is my brother? Is he all right?" she asked, sounding increasingly panicked. She shook me when I didn't answer.

In my anguish, I blurted out, "He is dead. Nathan killed him."

"Nathan killed him? Not someone from Ein Gedi?" she asked.

"Nathan murdered him while he tried to protect me," I said, and then I told her of Nathan's attack on me.

At first, she was silent as she tried to take in what I said, and then she let loose an anguished scream and fell to her knees while tearing her tunic. While on her knees, she picked up a handful of dirt and threw it on her head, thus beginning her period of mourning for her beloved brother. I bent down and held Judith close, and after a few moments, I took her to our room, where she stayed in an unresponsive state until the following day.

I later learned over twenty of our men had died during the raid, with another fifteen severely wounded. Twelve wives lost their husbands, and thirty children would never feel their fathers' hugs again.

Judith awoke and spoke to me for the first time since I'd given her the news at dawn. "We must bury him today," she said. "Where is his body?"

I was standing in the doorway to our room with my back turned to Judith. I did not answer as I struggled with my own demons. Not only had I killed a little boy, but I was the reason Malachi was dead. If he had not been defending me, he would still be with us. But I could not admit this to Judith, and I could not tell her about the boy or the massacre.

"Daniel—answer me," she said to my back.

"He is by the gate," I said as I slid out the door.

I wandered aimlessly for what seemed like forever in the dawn light, staring without seeing, with no destination in mind. My goal was to get away from everyone and everything and stop my endless, churning thoughts. I knew I had to bury Malachi, but I could not face the task, and I could not tell this to Judith because she would not understand. Truth be told, I'd have preferred to lie in bed forever. But Judith and the others would inevitably have wanted me to tell them what had happened, and facing the reality of the past few days was too much to bear. So instead, I had to settle for hiding behind a crest, hoping Judith would not find me.

As I hid, I turned over the events at Ein Gedi. All I'm sure of is, one moment the little boy was alive, and then he was impaled; and one moment, Malachi was fine, and the next, he had a dagger in his heart—a blade meant for me and put there by a murderous thug.

"Daniel!"

'Oh, dear God, is there no escape?' I said, loud enough for my wife to hear, foolishly. But there was no response. I raised my head and scanned the plateau to see how close Judith was but did not see her anywhere. Concerned, I headed back to our room and found her seated behind a rise in the ground nearby, tears flowing, and her face a shade of red not seen in nature. My wife is the strongest person I know, and her tears broke me.

"Judith, please, please," I said as I bent down toward her, trying to embrace her and reverse time.

"Go away, Daniel. You do not get to make yourself feel better by hugging me."

Collapsing close by her side and waiting until she gathered herself up, I said, "My love, I'm so sorry. I meant you no pain, but I cannot explain to you what I do not understand myself."

She turned to me and, not saying a word, gave me the opening to say what I needed to say in my own time and my own way.

"My mind is filled with images and explanations, or should I say justifications? I don't understand what happened, so how can I recount it? One minute, Malachi was alive, and the next, I was holding his head in my lap. All I'm sure of is we are no longer who we were before Ein Gedi. Today, we are monsters. Poke us, and we will spew the horror at the core of men. Prod us, and the primal hideousness, always just below the surface, will be released by the depravities of war. So please, Judith, give me a little time to understand and to mourn. I love you more than my own life and never want to hurt you."

After a few moments of silence, my wise wife said, "Tell me about these images and what happened with Malachi," and it poured out of me like vomit.

"Blood and fire, and so much confusion. Men are trying to save themselves and their families, and women are screaming as their husbands die. There is a boy impaled on my sword.

Another image of Nathan approaching me from behind, his sword and dagger both drawn. Malachi is coming to my defense, and Nathan is sticking a dagger in his heart. Women are being butchered, and a thriving community is burning to the ground—all of its people dead because Eleazar and his men decided it was necessary."

In absolute silence, we sat side by side until the sun crested, and then we returned to our room to rest.

Before retrieving the children from Dorit, Judith and I walked the short distance to the communal kitchen by the central storerooms to find something to eat. Not feeling jovial ourselves, the celebratory atmosphere we noticed as we approached surprised us. Eleazar's troops were hailing the sacking of Ein Gedi as a great triumph as they unloaded the booty from the settlement into the ancient storerooms.

The atmosphere was buoyant, with most people unaware of the cost of the raid on Ein Gedi and on us. Soldiers carried the bounty to the kitchen and storehouses, and the unmarried women had prepared a luxurious breakfast of dates, figs, pomegranates, and goat cheese. The children joined in the festivities and sated their hunger for the first time in months. Everyone was so excited to no longer live off the strict rations we had been enduring. Many of the soldiers seemed inured to the killing and indifferent to the deaths of seven hundred innocent people, merry as they were. From where I stood, few seemed to care what it had cost in terms of our lost innocence.

"Daniel. Judith. I'm so happy to see you both. How are you?" asked Dorit as we approached. I spotted her noticing Judith's rent tunic. "I'm sorry we didn't find you last night, but we didn't want to wake Hannah and Ari. Is everything all right?"

"What is all this, Dorit?" I said. "Why are people celebrating? Is this how callous and insular we have become?"

"What are you talking about?" Dorit said.

"We should be mourning, not celebrating. Don't they care that our men killed every living soul in Ein Gedi? Don't they know we have twenty dead and more than a dozen severely wounded?"

"Nobody said anything about so many dead. Where did you hear this?"

"Where are all the men?" Judith said. "Why are there only soldiers here?"

"They are hiding," said Daniel. "It embarrasses them to be seen. They don't want anyone asking them questions since they're all killers now, and all they can think about is the blood and the fire."

"What fire?" said Dorit.

"You haven't heard yet? After we killed every person in Ein Gedi, we ransacked every home and burned the settlement to the ground."

"No, that is not possible! Why are we only hearing of this from you, Daniel? Why aren't the soldiers talking about this?"

By now, we had attracted considerable attention, and others gathered around us. The women closest to us posed questioning looks on their faces, and the soldiers further away held expressions of consternation. Finally, I saw one soldier give us a bewildered look as he headed to the Western Palace.

"Is it true? Was everyone in Ein Gedi killed? The women and children too?"

"Who gave the order to kill everyone?"

"Was the settlement burned?"

The questions from those around us were endless, and I did my best to answer them.

"Yes, it is true. We killed everyone."

"Yes, the women and children too, but only after they trapped us in their alleyways and tried to burn us to death."

"When we arrived at Ein Gedi, Eleazar gave us orders to enter every house and kill the men to shock the inhabitants into submission. But it didn't work."

"What is this nonsense?" we heard someone bellow from a distance.

The crowd parted, and we could see Eleazar approaching, looking like a landslide descending a mountain, coming fast, out of control, and without hope of escape.

"What lies are you telling now, Daniel?" Eleazar continued as he broke through the inner circle to where Judith and I were standing. Then, getting right into my face, he sputtered, "How are you trying to undermine my authority now, boy? We've won a brilliant victory and restocked our storerooms to ward off starvation for years to come, and you are telling tales?"

"It is you who lie," I said, knowing over two-hundred men had witnessed his orders and the crimes that resulted from them. Did he think he could hide what they did?

"As usual, Daniel, you exaggerate and ascribe to me what you and your allies have done. Yes, you and your friends killed more people in Ein Gedi than I wished for, but it was your fault. It was you and your accomplices, with your stumbling and murmurings in the dark, loud enough to wake the dead, that warned them we were there and led the men of Ein Gedi to gather their forces and counterattack. If all had gone as planned, fewer would have died. But you wanted to see the plan fail. You made that clear before we embarked on the raid."

"What nonsense," I said. "You gave orders to execute all the men in their beds."

"I did not, Daniel, and I cannot believe you are stooping to such outright lies," said Eleazar.

"Lies?" I said, shocked by his audaciousness. "If I am lying, Eleazar, prove it. Let's convene a special community meeting tonight, and you can put forth your story, and I will put forth mine. And we'll see who the men of Masada say is telling the truth."

"I have nothing to prove, Daniel, but we will meet this evening only so you can stand trial for sabotaging the raid and getting so many of our men killed."

CHAPTER

25

With only a waning crescent moon hanging in the crystal-clear desert air, the expanse of Masada was not as well lit as for a regular monthly assembly. Eleazar and I had made serious allegations against each other, and tonight, the community would address these accusations. For me, people needed to understand the need to split the settlement and get Eleazar's support. For him, I suspect, it was to remove me as a constant thorn in his side and to eliminate the threat I and other like-minded members of the community posed to his military force's source of free labor.

As we gathered at the assembly point, Yitzhak approached me and said in a low voice, "Did you hear Eleazar was out all afternoon stirring things up?"

"What do you mean by 'stirring things up'?" asked Judith?

"I mean, Eleazar and his lieutenants were disparaging you, Daniel, saying you and your coconspirators intentionally planned to sabotage the raid. He said you almost succeeded, but Nathan intervened and killed the man you let escape who sounded the alarm. The man only half succeeded. If Nathan hadn't stopped him, he might have warned the whole settlement. As it is, your target warned his immediate neighbors, and they came out in force and killed many of our men. They spoke to hundreds of people. I think he convinced many of the men on the raid who did not witness things firsthand."

Astonished by these revelations, they struck me speechless. How could Eleazar have inverted the story and placed the blame on me?

"That's impossible," said Judith with absolute confidence. "How can our friends and neighbors believe such fantasies? Some of them have known Daniel for six years."

As she said this, I saw others nearby averting their eyes and shaking their heads. And at this moment, Eleazar called the meeting to order.

Standing on the raised podium and glaring down on the assembled from his commanding height, Eleazar, outfitted in his finest military regalia, positioned himself for dramatic effect between two shoulder-high torches.

"I called this special session of the community assembly so you can hear of the treasonous activities of Daniel Ben Yochanan, whose actions caused the deaths of twenty of our men at Ein Gedi."

A murmur went through the crowd, and I could not tell whether it was for me or against me. Fortunately, Yitzhak had prepared me for Eleazar's lies because the audacity of his attack might otherwise have overwhelmed me. I prayed truth would prevail over his demagoguery.

"Liar," Judith shouted at Eleazar as she rose to her feet. "How dare you accuse Daniel of the crimes you committed? Tell them, Daniel. Tell them the truth of what happened at Ein Gedi."

I stood, but Eleazar shouted, "Silence, woman. Be quiet and learn your place."

This was the wrong thing to say to my wife. Eleazar was about to learn what I had known since meeting this daunting woman; her place is where she decides it to be. And so, Judith unburdened herself of the extraordinary contempt she holds for men who tell her how to behave.

Then I added, "Don't you dare talk to my wife that way. The likes of you will not dismiss her."

"The likes of me? Of course, Daniel, I am only the man who led the Sicarii out of Jerusalem. All I have done is make us secure. I always put the safety of my people above all else."

"But I accuse you of much worse than lying," I said. "I accuse you of murder and of corrupting our community by turning every man who went on the Ein Gedi raid into a murderer, myself included." Then, turning to my right and left, I looked at my neighbors and friends and said, "Tell them what happened at Ein Gedi. How he ordered us, right before the raid started, to kill every man in his bed to break Ein Gedi's resistance. Tell how the strategy failed and how we had to kill women and children, guilty only of trying to help their husbands and fathers. Tell them how the women gathered and resisted and how Eleazar ordered us to kill them all—every resident of Ein Gedi. And David, tell them what you saw Nathan do. Tell them that while I was fighting off an attacker, you saw Nathan approach from behind with his sword drawn, stealthily advancing to kill me, and how Malachi died at Nathan's hand after he warned me Nathan was sneaking up on me."

A quick murmur went through the crowd. The women were shaking their heads, and the men were snapping awake, remembering the blood and embarrassed by the savagery.

"And the biggest crime is having made these good husbands and fathers complicit in your transgressions. You created an impossible situation and left us no choice but to kill. You corrupted us in a way God will never forgive."

David stood, and all attention shifted to him. "What Daniel says is the truth. Eleazar commanded us to kill the men in their beds, and when the women and children blockaded us in the alleyways with fire, we attacked and slew them all. And yes, I saw Nathan sneaking up on Daniel from behind with his sword drawn, and only when Malachi shouted to Daniel, warning him of the danger, did Nathan shift his attack to Malachi. I saw Nathan pull his dagger from his tunic and stab Malachi in the heart."

I scanned the crowd to see their reactions and noticed Nathan being restrained by the other lieutenants. Nathan, his face raging, was trying to get at David to do him harm. It relieved me to see he was being thwarted by his companions, but Nathan's aggression was frightening.

I hadn't noticed, meanwhile, but Judith had moved away when David was speaking, and I glimpsed her as she moved to the front of the crowd.

"Murderer," she screamed as she ran to where Nathan was being restrained and launched herself at him from behind. She landed on his back and held on while she alternately scratched his face and tried to choke him.

The crowd gasped as I yelled, "Judith, no!" and moved to the front rows in anticipation of Nathan's reaction.

Nathan broke free of his comrades and tried to shake Judith loose, but she did not let go, and she beat him with all the strength she had.

"You killed my brother!" she shouted. "Die, you bastard. Why won't you die already, you son of a whore?" With these last words, she slipped off his back into a heap on the ground.

I gathered her in my arms as Nathan stood still, unable to respond, while the soldiers did their best to calm the crowd.

After settling the audience, Eleazar returned to the matter at hand and asked, "What is the point of these lies? Do you seek to divide us and destroy our community? Where will we go if we cannot live here in peace?"

Tiring of Eleazar's never-ending falsehoods and distortions, I said, "I have said this so many times, but you insist on believing your own rhetoric. I do not want to destroy us. The opposite is true. I want this community to thrive, but I don't believe it can, not with the number of people living here and the limits on food production. Instead, we should split the community and let those civilians who want to create another settlement close by leave. I am sure our current path is not the correct one. Violence and thievery can never be the path of the righteous, and we must stop, or God will forsake us."

"Eleazar," said Yitzhak, "tell us why this raid was necessary when splitting the community will work better?"

Unused to being challenged, Eleazar was at first taken aback by the question. But his answer silenced everyone as he looked into my eyes and proclaimed, "Daniel Ben Yochanan, if you no longer want to be a part of this community, you don't have to be. I banish you. You will take your belongings and leave this place by the next full moon. If anyone else wants to join him, speak now. That is final. I won't say another word on this matter."

Nine hundred people stared at Eleazar and, glued to their places, were uncertain what to do.

Eleazar's lieutenants broke the silence and began urging the people to return to their dwellings. "Go on. Go home, everyone. No more to see here tonight."

"What just happened?" said Yitzhak. "Can he do that?"

"Tyrants can do anything they please," I said. "Ask our Roman enemies."

"What will they do?" people asked, eyeing my wife and me. And as I turned to Judith, I realized her eyes were asking me the same question.

"Don't worry, my love. We'll figure it out," I whispered.

As we dispersed and walked back to our room in silence, we could hear the buzz of agitated voices all around us. Here and there, we caught the gist of the conversations, which focused on whether Eleazar could banish someone for disagreeing with him. The consensus seemed to be that while Eleazar had fewer men, he had all the soldiers and weapons. That meant he could do whatever he wanted. Not because it was right, but because he could. To most, it seemed wrong that the soldiers, representing only a quarter of the community, could lead us into violent situations and affect the fates of everyone. I was glad to hear it because an idea was forming in my mind.

CHAPTER

26

Judith and I woke early and were lying in bed discussing my banishment when Hannah, who we thought was sleeping, said, "*Abba*, what is banissed?"

I didn't understand at first, but Judith explained to me in a whisper, "I think she means banished, but she still doesn't pronounce sh quite right."

"Hannah, did you hear *Eemah* and *Abba* say the word banished?" Judith asked.

Hannah, who was about to turn four, said, "Yes. What is it?"

"It means to send away," I said.

"Is the mean man sending us away?" she asked.

"Not yet, sweetie. There is nothing to worry about," said Judith.

"But I don't want to be sent away," Hannah said as she sniffled. "Can my friends come with us?"

Judith got out of bed and went to Hannah to make sure she understood. "There is nothing to worry about, Hannah. We are staying right here."

"All right, *Eemah*. I like it here."

"I like it here too," Judith said, as she smiled at Hannah and then looked at me across the room with a look to crush the soul of the most heartless husband.

With a nod, I signaled to Judith we should continue the discussion later. Meanwhile, I left for the fields to work. As I made my way there, I noticed people glancing at me as they walked by, and most gave me a slight nod as they caught my eye. Usually, others greeted me with a hearty "Good morning" or "Have a great day," but this was different. It was almost as if people were wary of being too friendly but still wanted to show solidarity with me. I took this as a good sign as I continued developing my plan.

I spent the morning working with Yoav to plow the fields to prepare for planting, and we spoke in between grunts of exertion. Truth be told, Eleazar's decree devastated me, and I wasn't sure what to do. There was no question of me leaving Masada without my family, but taking them with me exposed us to uncertainty and danger. If he forced us to leave, where would we go? Neither Judith nor I had any living relatives. How would we eat and find water on the way? How would we defend ourselves from wild beasts and brigands? And how would I earn a living once we reached our ultimate destination…wherever that might be?

But working the fields gave me time to think, and after discussing the options with Yoav, I thought up a new approach; one that would solve my predicament and help the community at the same time.

After I finished for the day, I invited Yoav, Benjamin, Yitzhak, and others to join Judith and me that evening to discuss my plan.

"I know this seems self-serving," I said, as we gathered indoors, so the guards above us didn't overhear, "but my banishment could help us split the settlement and be the impetus to start a new village of our own."

"It's not self-serving at all," said Yitzhak. "Eleazar's capricious action of exiling you last night has frightened many people. And the raid, while it solved the immediate starvation problem, has also scared many people. The civilians don't want to live this way."

"And no one sees this as a viable long-term strategy," said Yoav. "We've already stolen everything there is to steal in the vicinity, so what's next?"

The room was packed, with some of our guests sitting on our pallet and others leaning against the walls, so I could not pace back and forth as I like to when I am nervous. A lot was riding on the next few minutes for my family and me, and I wasn't at all sure how this would go.

"It seems to me there are only two viable long-term options," I said. "Yoav and I have calculated Masada's fields can only support a community of four hundred people. Of course, the number could be higher if we had goods to trade, but we produce little of value and minimal surplus. Besides, Eleazar's strategy of stealing from and killing our neighbors has ruled out the possibility of any trade.

"The first option is to split the community and establish another settlement nearby, or further away if we want to put distance between ourselves and Eleazar. The alternative is for the civilians to leave Masada and scatter themselves among the diaspora." This was a new idea and was immediately met with resistance.

"I know dispersing the community is a frightening idea. People would either have to go to Galilee, Alexandria, Rome, or other places with Jewish communities throughout the empire. And Eleazar was right about one thing: we are stronger when we are together. But we have been discussing the idea of splitting off for a long time but were never sure how to overcome some of the logistical problems. Last night, Eleazar made it clear he will never support our efforts, and without his material support of seed and tools, we will fail, which is why I believe dispersing the community might be our only choice."

"Either solution will require an enormous effort, and I think the people will have to decide for themselves," said Yitzhak.

The others agreed, and to conduct a referendum, we would have to find a way for the people to vote. But how could we organize a secret ballot without Eleazar becoming aware and ending our efforts? Leave it to my brilliant wife to provide the solution.

"I suggest we use broken pieces of pottery with names on them like we do to allocate food," Judith said. "Let's have everyone who wants to build a new settlement write their names on the curved inside of pottery shards, one piece for each member of their family. And people who want to disperse should write their names on the curved outside of the shards. Then Daniel and I will place an empty bowl here, inside the door of our room, and everyone should walk by before Shabbat begins this week and place their shards in the bowl. This group will then gather after Shabbat and count the shards."

"Brilliant," Yoav and I said at the same time.

"Is everyone agreed?" I asked.

After a chorus of yesses, I asked everyone to spread the word carefully so the count could take place the same week. We then scattered for the evening.

Judith and I fell into bed, exhausted from the past several stressful days.

"Regardless of the outcome of the vote, we should see if Eleazar will delay the banishment," Judith said quietly, so we didn't have a repeat of the morning conversation with Hannah. "Twenty days is not enough time to prepare, no matter what the decision."

"I agree, but I don't know how to get more time."

"Maybe you should just beg. It won't cost you anything except a little pride, and we all know you have a bit of that to spare," she said, and I could hear the smile in her voice.

"Yes, love. That might work. We can go to him tomorrow, and I will grovel. Perhaps God will soften his heart, and he will let me stay longer."

The following day, we gathered up our little family and went to the Western Palace to see Eleazar. Luckily for us, Ruben was overseeing the changing of the guard and came over when he saw it was me.

"What are you doing here, Daniel? Are you back for more? It didn't go well for you last time."

"I know, but I've come to beg Eleazar to change his mind. As my time to leave draws near, I find I will miss this place immensely, and I would like to stay."

"He might allow it," Ruben said under his breath. "All right, follow me, and when I signal you, stop and wait." So, we followed him down the hallway, and midway down, he turned to the open door on his right and said, "It is Daniel and his family, sir. He would like to speak with you if that is all right."

After making us wait a while, we were ushered before Eleazar. Speaking to an advisor in low tones, he did not so much as look up at me.

"What is it, Daniel?" he finally said. "Why are you still here? You exasperate me and have overstayed your welcome. I don't know why I let you come with us in the first place. I should have expected the son of a priest to be trouble."

"I don't know why you let me come, either, but I am glad you did. Otherwise, I wouldn't have this wonderful family," I said, hoping to tug at his heartstrings. "And I regret any problems I've caused you."

"Really? You do?"

"Yes, truly. There were a few times you were nicer to me than my father had ever been, and I liked that. But you resort to killing too easily, and I can never accept that about you."

"You think you can soften me up by telling me you like me but that I'm a killer?"

"My father taught me to follow the commandments blindly, but I realize now, even if I accept that we sometimes have to defend ourselves, I can never bring myself to believe in the way of the Sicarii."

"I'm surprised by this confession, Daniel, but it is too late."

"It might be too late for what could have been, but will you please let us stay? I know I have offended you, but—"

Cutting me off, he said, "Don't you dare ask for special dispensation after all the times you've challenged me."

"But please," I said, trying again, "I need more time to make proper arrangements."

"That is not my problem."

"*Abba*," said my daughter, "what did you do? Why is he shouting at you? He sounds so mad."

"You are right, child," Eleazar said. "I am angry at your father. He did something wrong, and that has upset me."

"*Abba*, say you're sorry. That's what you tell me to do when I hurt someone."

"Hush, Hannah," said Judith. "Let the grown-ups talk."

"But she's right," Eleazar said. "When you hurt someone, you should apologize. So, apologize, Daniel, and then we shall see."

"That's all it will take? An apology?"

"Yes, if you apologize to me before the entire community, I will reconsider your banishment."

"Fine, call another gathering of the community tonight, and I will apologize."

"Excellent. All you have to do is apologize and admit you were wrong. Then tell everyone violence is sometimes necessary to protect the well-being of the community. What say you?"

"That is not what I agreed to. I agreed to apologize for my behavior, not to endorse your approach."

"But that is what I offer. Either apologize and admit you were wrong or pack your things and leave tonight."

Several hours later, we gathered as a community to put me in my place. They set up the torchères on Eleazar's left and right, as always, to focus all eyes on him. His troops gathered early and were standing in formation below him and on either side while the civilians arrived.

"Gather round, gather round," Eleazar said, gesturing to the civilians to come closer. "The traitor, Daniel, has a few words to share with us, and I have given him this opportunity to say his piece."

A ripple went through the crowd as I approached the raised platform. I couldn't hear the words, but I sensed the anger. I wasn't sure if it was directed at Eleazar or me. Just before I ascended the stage, Eleazar hissed at me and made it clear I should not continue. Then, with his chin, he pointed to where I was standing and said, "From there."

I didn't understand what he wanted. If it was humiliation, wouldn't it be better if they could see me clearly? Or was it to deny me any standing? Who knows? But it was apparent he didn't want to share the stage with me. A hush descended as I spoke.

"Friends, you have known me for many years, and I hope you have found me a committed member of our community. I have worked hard and always contributed the most I could to the community's well-being." Nods of support coincided with my comments. I saw I had the support of almost everyone.

"Get on with it," yelled Eleazar from above me.

"I will, but let me do it my way," I said.

"Get on with it already."

I gathered myself up and said, "Eleazar and I don't agree on much, but the way I expressed myself at the last assembly was inexcusable. I should have made my concerns known to Eleazar in private and not in public. For that, I apologize."

"And?" Eleazar said.

"And sometimes we might need to resort to violence in self-defense. I'm sure the community can decide when that is necessary."

"This is not what you committed to, Daniel, but I'm feeling generous tonight, and I will allow you to stay until the full moon after next. But after that, I expect you to be gone. Understood?"

While I sensed a groundswell of support from the community, it relieved me that no one objected to Eleazar's actions.

After sacrificing my personal pride, the last thing I wanted was to give him an excuse to backtrack on his promise.

Now, I had the time I needed to complete the planning, and all that remained was to count the shards.

For the next two days, people stopped by to greet us and drop their shards in the bowl. Curiosity was getting the better of me, but somehow, I restrained myself and did not count the pieces as they turned into an enormous mound, so large that we had to add three more bowls to collect them all.

As Shabbat ended, my friends once again gathered in our room. I divided us into four groups, each responsible for counting one bowl. The final tally was one hundred and six in favor of establishing a new settlement and a massive five hundred and seventeen in favor of dispersal.

In some ways, it surprised me, but in other ways not. Life on Masada was difficult, mainly because its physical size constrained our growth, and its location was isolated, making us even more dependent on each other. I concluded people were tired and ready to try life on their own. Now, we could begin planning in earnest.

CHAPTER

27

We met in our room many times to plan our departure. There were so many questions to answer, and on one such occasion, Yoav, the most organized of us all, summarized them for us.

"Where will people go, and how will we get them there? What supplies and belongings will they be able to take with them? How will we transport the elderly and convalescing if we can't take any of the carts belonging to Masada? When is the best time of year to depart, and what will be our departure date?"

It took us weeks to answer these questions to our satisfaction and slowly and surreptitiously communicate the decisions to the six hundred people leaving.

But the most troubling question of all was whether Eleazar would let us go, and if he wouldn't, what would we do then? The answer always came down to whether the troops would try to stop us, and we simply did not know the answer to that question.

A few days before Yom Kippur, an alert guard observed a Roman scouting team from the eastern ramparts. Small dust clouds from the cavalry unit lingered in the air all morning as the squad traversed the foothills and explored the gorges around Masada. We also saw a group of Masada residents intercepted by the scouts on the plain below. Some soldiers detained them and took them to the Roman commander for questioning. If the Romans were not sure Masada was occupied before taking our comrades into custody, they certainly were after questioning them. The appearance of the advanced scouting unit did not bode well for us since their presence meant a Roman force was in the vicinity, and our friends not being released from detention hinted at the ill-intent of the Roman troops.

Our anxiety increased the following morning when children playing on the ramparts began shouting about a sandstorm approaching from the direction of Ein Gedi.

"See the cloud?" I could hear them yelling. The screaming attracted nearby adults and a few of Eleazar's troops, who, in turn, called their commanders to the wall. We experienced occasional sandstorms in the area, which were not uncommon at this time of year, but they never came from the direction of Ein Gedi. Instead, they came up the valley rift from the Sinai desert. Since we were in the cloud's path, we had to wait and see what it visited upon us when it arrived. The nervousness was profound and only increased as the cloud grew in size. Everyone pretended to carry on as if there was no expanding dust cloud on the horizon. Still, the furtive glances were proof of everyone's increasing worry. It was closing on us by late morning, and I estimated it would arrive by late afternoon.

Considering the presence of a scouting party the day before and the cloud's apparent speed of advance, I decided it was likely a large Roman force, not a sandstorm, that would arrive by the end of the day. Thus, I gathered the other leaders together.

"I know this is not what we had planned for, but events have overtaken us," I said, "and I believe we must leave immediately. Otherwise, a Roman legion will surround us, and we will have lost our opportunity to escape. Of course, we have planned for this, even though it is happening faster than we want, but we should warn our people to gather at once and be ready to depart when we give the signal. I expect Eleazar to resist our departure, but we will have to force our way past his troops."

Having survived the siege of Jerusalem, Yitzhak warned us what the Romans would do upon their arrival. " You have never seen the likes of the Roman war machine. First, they will surround Masada with their troops so no one can escape. Then, within days, they will build a circumvallation wall to further ensure no one leaves. At the same time, they will build camps for their troops. They will surround us in days and finish us at their leisure."

"If that is the case," said Yoav, "I agree with Daniel. We must leave immediately. My only question is how? We have not prepared to leave with such short notice. We have to warn everyone to gather their belongings and to pack food and water."

"And we must do all of this without alerting Eleazar. I'm not sure how we can accomplish that," said Yitzhak.

"It will come to a confrontation. I don't doubt that. But all we can do is pray God is on our side," I said.

We discussed our plans a little longer and then dispersed to set them in motion.

While packing, Judith and I heard some shouting from the direction of the Snake Path gate. We went to investigate and saw the backs of dozens of our friends and Eleazar's soldiers standing in stunned silence as they craned their necks to peer over the ramparts. No one said a word, which was very distressing. We wended our way through the crowd to a chorus of annoyed grumblings. Judith climbed the stairs to the battlement to see, and when she came back down, it was with a look of fear in her eyes. This look from my mighty wife cut through me like a sword.

"What is it?" I asked.

Her curt response sent chills down my spine: "A force of Roman troops," she said.

I pushed past her and climbed the stairs to the top of the wall. On the coastal plain below, I saw a Roman force arrayed against us. Having lived in Jerusalem most of my life, I recognized the standard of the Roman Tenth Legion: a gold boar sitting on a perch over a banner of brilliant red. Around the standard-bearer, mounted on horses, were the general and his guards. The troops were outfitted in crimson tunics, and the sun reflected off their armor. I tried to estimate the number of soldiers before us and realized we were only seeing the vanguard of an entire Roman legion. Only a small portion of the whole force was visible since the nearby hills still obscured the remaining cohorts, auxiliaries, Jewish slaves, baggage, and rear guard. Once the full force arrived, the Tenth Legion would be a terrifying sight as it advanced across the plain, resembling the vicious snake that it was.

As we gazed out at the Roman troops, we could hear the lamentations of our neighbors praying to God for protection.

"O Lord, grant that this night we may sleep in peace. And that in the morning, our awakening may also be in peace. May our daytime be cloaked in your peace.

"Protect us and inspire us to think and act only out of love.

"Keep far from us all evil; may our paths be free from all obstacles from when we go out until we return home."

By the time Eleazar arrived at the ramparts, the leading formations of Roman soldiers had broken ranks. We assumed they were forming temporary camps before nightfall since they were being built in the floodplain. If we did not act soon, it would be too late.

Eleazar climbed the tower closest to the palace and looked over the rampart. Upon seeing the Roman vanguard, he turned to us with a look of rage. But the themes for his improvised address to those of us gathered below led me to suspect he was as honored as he was affronted.

"Friends. By now, you all know what confronts us—a sea of Roman soldiers sent here by Emperor Vespasian to end my rule. Well, we must be an important enemy for them to warrant sending an entire legion into the field to confront us. They will outnumber us fifteen to one, but still, they will all die by our hands. Masada is impregnable, and if they had sent ten legions, my troops would still prevail. They are the best trained and most loyal soldiers, and each is worth ten, no, one hundred of our enemy. They cannot reach us in our fortress in heaven, and we can bombard them day and night with missiles.

"Who do they think they are? Which divinity has granted them the right to attack us? Not our God, king of the universe. The mere thought their gods could stand against ours is blasphemy. For our God has granted us dominion over this place forever, so who are they to challenge us?"

I thought Eleazar's comments were ridiculous and wrong-headed. The Roman army was powerful, and its leaders determined. In all its history, it had never abandoned a siege, and its mastery of logistics and engineering made it a formidable enemy. It was relentless in pursuit of its goals, and I did not believe they would leave without retaking Masada, killing all the men, and selling our women and children into slavery.

But this did not matter to us, for in a few minutes, we would be leaving. The signal had been given, and as I crossed the plateau, I could already see our people gathering by the Western Gate with their meager belongings and food packed in blankets. With the Romans having set up temporary camps on the northeast side of Masada, our descent through the Western Gate and into the gorge to the west would not be visible to them for several more hours. After that, we would descend into the Judean desert and make our way to Arad. From there, we would head south to the Sinai desert or north to the Galilee or the coast.

But our people gathering in the wide-open area next to the Western Palace exposed our intentions to the rest of Masada. It was time to find out if Eleazar would let us leave, and if not, would we be able to get past his troops?

CHAPTER

28

Seeing the sizable crowd milling about with large bundles and all facing the Western Gate agitated the guards, and they sent for their lieutenants and Eleazar. Except for the monthly assemblies, large gatherings were highly unusual on Masada. Meanwhile, I had dispatched two men to see if they could free Jacob and Sarah from their imprisonment so they could leave with us.

Eleazar soon appeared, climbed to the Western Palace roof, and raised his hand over his eyes to judge the size of the crowd in the bright sunlight. "What is happening here? Why are you gathering? Are you worried about the Romans?" he asked.

The people tried to answer, but shouting on top of one another, they soon realized they needed a single voice to speak for them.

The crowd shouted, "Daniel," and those closest to me urged me to the front. Over six hundred people had gathered, and it took me a few moments to move through them all. I stood there, looking back and forth between those who had chosen to leave and Eleazar. I realized it must have been a very frightening sight from his vantage point. More than half of his community stood before him, and he must have understood by then what they intended. His worst nightmare was about to come true.

"I should have known Daniel was at the root of this trouble," said Eleazar. "I don't know what you people think you are doing, but if you want my soldiers to protect you from the Romans, I insist you return to your rooms immediately." However, Eleazar's demand was rejected, so he ordered his troops to block the Western Gate nearby.

Looking up to where Eleazar was standing and to the casemate walls, I noticed dozens of troops watching events closely. Of course, we outnumbered them four-to-one, and they knew it. But it would be easy for them to prevent us from leaving through the gate since they were armed and it was a narrow chokepoint.

Shouting so all could hear, I said, "We are gathered here because this is our last chance to leave before the Romans encircle Masada."

"Who are you to speak for these people, Daniel, and how long have you been planning this insurrection?"

The crowd answered him with shouts of "He is our leader."

"Are you a leader of men now, Daniel?"

"I am what I am," I said. "But let us focus on what matters now. These families want to leave for the good of the community. It has been obvious for a long time that Masada cannot support this many people. They have had it with watching their children starve, and those who remain will be better off too."

"So, you will run away like cowards just when we need you to defend Masada against the Romans?"

Having lost my fear of Eleazar in the moment, I said, "It was never our dream to confront the Romans. That was your vision. All we wanted to do was live our lives in peace, raise families in safety and security, and be good people. You have made that impossible. Your attack and massacre of the people of Ein Gedi attracted the Romans here like flies to a cadaver. You made us killers, and we don't want to live this way anymore, so we will depart and scatter ourselves throughout the diaspora."

Gesticulating like a madman on his rooftop perch, Eleazar said, "You will not abandon us. Our fortunes are one, and if you try to leave, I will have my soldiers prevent you by force if necessary." He then instructed his lieutenants to send archers to the battlements and prepare to fire into the crowd.

"You are here to protect us, not for us to service you," I said. "And now you threaten with violence the very people you are sworn to protect. Don't you see how you are the same as the Romans? We don't want their yoke around our necks, and we don't want yours either."

By now, dozens of archers faced us on the parapet, and on the ground were dozens of foot soldiers armed with spears, drawn swords, and shields between the Western Gate and us.

Despite the odds, the people refused to back down and surged forward.

"Archers, nock," ordered Nathan. "Archers, draw."

And as the archers drew their bows, Eleazar ordered his foot soldiers to raise their shields and weapons.

Still, the crowd moved forward.

When the lines were a mere arm's span apart, and the danger of an exhausted archer's arm letting loose an arrow was real, my Judith stepped forward from the front line with Ari in her arms and Hannah by her side and closed the gap with the soldiers. As she did so, another mother with two children joined her, and soon, a new front line, composed of mothers and their children, had formed to meet the soldiers, nose-to-nose. We had been living together for years, and we all knew each other, so

I did not believe the soldiers had it in them to attack, but you never know; they had already shown themselves willing to kill women and children when ordered to.

The mothers asked the soldiers to put down their weapons and let us pass while the archers started to tremble from holding their drawn bows. The standoff went on and on, but it must have been too much because, finally, a single soldier's conscience overwhelmed him, and he lowered his shield and weapon. And then another joined him. And another. And soon, archers dropped their arms too. The entire force lowered their weapons, as did the archers above, while the lieutenants and Eleazar shouted orders to no avail.

The muted response to Eleazar's directions had become palpable by the time he'd descended to the front line between the mothers and the soldiers, yelling at his men to push back the civilian line. Then, when he realized his men would not follow his orders, he attacked one of his own soldiers in a frenzy and ran him through with a sword.

A gasp went through both lines as people understood what had happened, and one last time, I heard a mother ask to pass. This time, the soldiers opened their ranks and cleared a passageway for us to leave through the Western Gate, flanked by dozens of armed men on either side. As they did so, one of the men I'd sent to release Jacob and Sarah approached and whispered they had opened the cell, but Jacob had been killed by the guard. Nevertheless, they had managed to free Sarah, and she was hiding among the women.

As this happened, ten men moved into position around my family and me to protect us from attack as we shepherded our people through the gate and to the beginning of our long trek to freedom.

The Western Gate opened onto a narrow dusty path that switched back and forth a few times and then joined with a natural spur leading down to the flat plain on the western side of Masada. The path is narrow at the top, allowing only two people to walk side by side, and later widens to allow three or four to walk comfortably. Unfortunately, the narrowness of the gate and paths impeded us, and it took more than an hour for us to leave Masada entirely behind.

The responsibility of leading six hundred people weighed on me as I realized the magnitude of what we were trying to do. Not only did we have to evade the Romans as we made our escape, but we also had to navigate across the desert with insufficient food and water. Moreover, because of the sudden arrival of the Roman legion and the speed at which we had to depart to avoid them, we could not gather carts to transport our elderly. The brutal reality was they would have to walk, or their families would have to carry them. This would not be an easy trek, and even if we'd had more time, Eleazar would never have allowed us the resources we'd need to facilitate our journey.

The Judean desert is a harsh environment, and keeping everyone fed and watered and our elderly moving was among my greatest concerns. We would have to hunt ibex and gazelles for food, as we did on our way to Masada all those years before, only this time without trained soldiers to help us.

Water would be more challenging to come by, although we knew of hidden cisterns along our proposed path, dug by Nabatean merchants. But this relied on us being able to find them. We had learned about the concealed cisterns from passing traders but did not know their exact locations. The Nabateans hid them well so they could travel across the desert without having to travel to Ein Gedi and Jerusalem to reach the Great Sea coast. Our intention was to send out scouts on either side of the trade route and check all oases along the way under the assumption vegetation grows near the cisterns. It was a gamble, but we had no other choice. The Romans had Masada under siege and had positioned themselves between us and Ein Gedi, the only close source of water we knew of in the region.

We made our way down the path with great effort, and within the hour, it was clear the elderly could not make the journey on foot. Many had tripped or fallen during the descent, and their pace would cause us to spend many extra days in the desert, exacerbating our food and water situation. As we reached the bottom of the spur, we came upon a high cone-shaped hill we would have to circumnavigate before continuing our journey. I climbed a few paces up the side so all could see me, and I spoke with the people.

"Because of the rushed departure, our food and water supplies are more constrained than we'd anticipated. Circumstances have also denied us the wagons we'd hoped to use to transport the elderly. So, I put it to all of you, what should we do?"

There were several shouts for us to continue, and just as I was about to turn back to the path to resume our journey, Yoav stepped forward and said, "My friends, as much as it pains me to say this, I think those who believe they cannot make the journey should volunteer to stay behind for the good of the rest of us."

Judging by the reaction to Yoav's comments, the crowd vehemently opposed the suggestion, and I feared there would be blows, but just then, one of the elderly spoke up and asked, "How long will this trek take?"

"We are not sure, but we expect the journey to Arad to take three to five days without delays," I said. "From there, those seeking ships to elsewhere in the Roman Empire will begin dispersing north to Galilee and Caesarea Maritima. Others of us will head south to Alexandria. Traveling north to Galilee and the port will take at least another seven to ten days, and to Alexandria, possibly as long as a month."

"What about the terrain? What is it like?" asked another of the elderly.

"At first, we will be in the desert where the terrain is rolling hills and ravines. But, then, much of the journey will be uphill, and the ground itself is much like here—dusty with a combination of loose and jutting rocks."

The man who asked the first question turned to his son and said, "I have aged a lot these past few years since we arrived at Masada. Judging from this walk down the ramp, I don't think I will survive such a long trek, and even if I do, I will slow the rest of you down too much. So please, I beseech you, leave me here, and I will make my way back up to the gate and beg Eleazar to take us back in."

"Me too," another said, and then others joined in.

We had over twenty elderly with us, and all of them volunteered to stay behind. If I was looking for an example of familial love, I needed to look no further. These parents and grandparents were all willing to return to a life with Eleazar, and who knows what future, so their loved ones would survive.

The elderly gathered in a small group at the rear of the larger body, and all around me, I saw husbands and wives in urgent conversation. As these discussions wound down, more and more families moved to the rear to be with their relatives, and when the movement of people ended, not a single elderly person stood alone.

Yoav stepped forward then, and I knew what he was about to say before he said it.

"Daniel, Dorit and I have also decided to remain, but we insist you and your family go on. You and Judith are the community's leaders, and you have brought all these people this far.

They look to you, so you must see this through and lead them away from here."

I embraced my friend and cried, and Judith did the same with Dorit. This was ripping my heart out, but Yoav was right. I had an obligation to lead the remaining five hundred souls away from the clutches of Eleazar and the Romans, and to do so, they needed to depart immediately. But I could not leave without knowing if Eleazar would take the elderly and their families back in, and so, charging Yitzhak with leading the others further into the desert, Judith and I led the returnees back to the Western Gate. We would catch up to the main body of marchers once we'd succeeded in returning the elderly and their families to the fortress.

Judith and I gathered our children and headed to the back of the line to better lead those staying behind while those departing began their march into the Judean desert. Everyone had bunched up in confusion, so as I passed Aaron, the stonemason, I asked him to help me straighten out the line and get everyone back inside the fortress.

The climb back up to the Western Gate took longer than the descent, given we were now in the full sun, the incline was steep, and our charges were tired. But we arrived at the gate eventually, just as the sun was close to setting, and I consider it to be a miracle no one slipped off the path during the ascent.

The gate into the fortress is not like the door of a house with a knocker, and we stared at its smooth surface for a moment as we wondered how to signal those inside we wanted to reenter. I tried knocking and then more vociferous banging, but nothing worked. Finally, I picked up an ostrich-egg-sized rock and banged on the gate with both hands.

As we waited, someone further down the path shouted, "What's that rumbling?" and others took up the call.

I felt the ground shaking under us and then detected a muffled sound coming from beyond the Northern Palace. The northern tip of Masada obscured the view, but the sound soon distilled itself into the thundering of numerous galloping horses. Next, I heard the clinking of saddle straps and weapons and the occasional neighing and snorting of Roman cavalry making its way toward us. Apparently, the rest of the Roman force had arrived, and this approaching vanguard was meant to scout and, eventually, surround Masada. Unfortunately, we were trapped on the incline outside the gate. I prayed the Romans would discover neither our defenseless friends nor us in the desert, still visible to us from our higher elevation but perhaps not to them at ground level.

Finally, a guard looked over the parapet and said, "What do you want? We let you go, and now you're back again. You should make up your minds."

"The Romans are coming. Let us in," I hissed, not wanting to yell in case the Romans would hear.

Then, from the back of our line, I heard a whispered, "Hush. They're coming."

"Down everyone," I said quietly so the Romans wouldn't hear. "Behind the rocks."

Everyone moved as fast as they could, and I prayed the Roman patrol had not detected us.

Then, waiting a few more minutes and not hearing any sounds except for the laughing of hyenas in the distance, I resumed my entreaties. "Let us in now, before the Romans see us."

"Now you want my protection?" boomed Eleazar, who had apparently been alerted to our reappearance.

"Quiet," I said, "or you'll get us killed."

"What concern is that of mine?" he asked. "You left the protection of my troops; now you can live with the consequences."

"Always the child, aren't you, Eleazar?"

"Do you think insulting me will convince me to let you in? You all made your choice to throw in with Daniel, so live with it. Be gone."

We hid the best we could, but within moments of Eleazar turning us away, I noticed the cavalry force slowing down directly below us but behind the rounded hill at the bottom of the ramp. Judith nudged me and whispered, "I can still see the other group. Do you think the Romans have seen their dust cloud?"

We soon had our answer as the cavalry unit formed up and headed west into the desert, apparently in pursuit of the other group. From our vantage point, we saw the cavalry catch up and attack our friends, dispersing them and running them down mercilessly. They were never heard from again, and all five hundred must have died at the hands of the Romans.

After an hour of stunned silence on our part, not knowing where to go and what to do, it surprised us when Eleazar's men again thwarted his will. Much to our relief, Ruben and two soldiers opened the gate and signaled we should follow them quietly. Would Eleazar tolerate our return? There was only one way to find out.

I was standing at the gate urging people through quickly when I heard the sound I dreaded more than any other: Nathan's voice.

"What is happening here? Who let these people in?" Nathan asked in a furious state as he approached from the direction of the Western Palace. "Close that gate. Eleazar didn't authorize them to come in," he seethed. "Get these people out of here."

More than half our number had managed to get through the gate by the time Nathan appeared, and I was going to make sure no one was forced out and that the rest got in, so I headed in his direction to protest. Fortunately, I didn't have to.

"Nathan," I heard someone else shouting. "Come back here, and let's discuss this." It was Ruben, and he didn't appear willing to push one hundred people into the arms of the Romans.

"Eleazar already said they can't come in, but your men disobeyed his orders—again," Nathan said.

"We're going to need these people," Ruben said as he finally caught up with Nathan. Then Ruben called out to the guards at the gate, "Get them in before the Romans figure out what's happening. Hurry!"

"I said no," Nathan said as he grabbed Ruben's arm.

Ruben turned on Nathan and said, "I will not let these people die. Maybe you enjoy murdering your own people, but no more. This insanity must stop."

Nathan tussled with Ruben, and when Ruben responded, Nathan pulled his dagger and attacked. My remaining people passed through the gate as Ruben drew his own blade, but there was a sudden shout from the ramparts.

"Close the gates!" one of the guards yelled. "The Roman cavalry is coming." And just as he shouted, an arrow hit him, and he fell to the ground between Nathan and Ruben.

"Hurry, close the gate now," shouted Nathan as Ruben climbed to the battlement with a squad of archers.

"Archers, nock," Ruben ordered. "Aim. Release," he shouted, and the archers on the battlements let loose on the Romans below, blunting their attack and sending them scurrying back to their own lines.

"Get these people out of the way!" Nathan shouted. "Go back to your rooms and stay away from the walls. We have to prepare our defenses."

I was surprised Eleazar had not come out when he heard his troops let us back in, but I later learned he had been asleep. Now that he was awake, he called an assembly for midmorning to address our return and the arrival of the Romans.

"I will allow your return," he began, "But only because I am generous and will not see my people harmed, even though, by your behavior, you demonstrated you are no longer part of us." Warming up now that he had an audience, he held forth on why the Romans would bother pursuing us in the middle of the wilderness. "Just now, I sat in my office and gazed out the window onto the desert. Unfortunately, the view outside is no longer the calming tan color with a slash of blue I am so used to. Now, it is entirely the red of Rome."

I could tell this was going to be another long speech.

Eleazar continued. "I can get no rest, and when I close my eyes, I still see them. Why won't they leave us in peace? I cannot believe these Romans. What are they thinking? This is our land, and they have stolen so much of it already. Who do they think they are? The rulers of the world? Why won't they leave us this little corner? But we can't let them have it. It is ours, and if we don't save it, where will the Jewish people go?"

Still not finished, he added, "Watching their efforts, it is now clear they intend to wipe us from this earth. If their overlords in Rome have the patience, they can starve us out. Otherwise, their only alternative is to breach the walls, and that means fighting us. Either way, our path is clear. Death, or a lifetime of slavery for those of us who survive—men, women, and children. I would prefer to die, and I'm sure everyone else will agree with me."

Addressing my people again, he finished his public statement. "Now that the Romans are here, you must follow my orders without hesitation. Anything I tell you to do, you must do. We must have complete discipline, and you must follow my orders without challenge."

CHAPTER
30

We found ourselves waking in our old room the following morning, almost as if nothing had changed. But, of course, so much had. So many of our friends and neighbors were now likely dead or enslaved.

We were still in bed when Judith nudged me and said, "Daniel, what will we do now?"

"What is there to do? I failed to get our people to safety, and the Romans have exterminated them. What else is there but to remain here and fight for our survival?"

"Daniel, stop these self-recriminations. Our odds of success were never high, but you couldn't know the Romans were coming or that they would send a scouting party so quickly. We all did everything we could. Now, we must focus on how our family is to survive."

"*Eemah*, why are you angry with *Abba*?" asked Hannah from her bed.

"I'm not angry, my love. Sometimes adults get excited, and they speak loudly."

"What are you excited about?"

"Hush, Hannah." Then, hearing shouting from outside, Judith said, "What is that, Daniel?"

We rushed out, and I climbed the casemate wall near the synagogue and looked down to see a sizable Roman force arrayed two deep all the way around Masada. It was a massive demonstration of strength and a very effective way to intimidate us. But this was only the beginning. Soon, we would understand the scale of the resources and time Rome was willing to invest in eliminating the last bastion of rebellion in Judea.

Later that day, I heard dozens of people shouting at their neighbors on the wall.

"What are they doing now?"

"Have they moved?"

The fear was palpable, but Eleazar's soldiers were hardened and looked over the walls impassively.

I felt Judith nudging me with a sense of urgency as she said, "Daniel, look! They are breaking ranks and dispersing." Then, shortly afterward, "No, only half of them are leaving. Where are they going?"

She was right. Only the second line of soldiers was leaving, and it wasn't apparent where they were going. We watched them as they moved, much like watching the actions of ants from above. We heard their commanders shouting orders we couldn't make out and watched them motion with enthusiasm. Soon, we understood. They were moving to new muster points far away from the base of Masada, and at every muster point, there were many pre-positioned wagons pulled by mules waiting for them.

When they arrived at these distant gathering points, their commanders lined them up an arm's length apart and parallel to the fortress. I expected what was coming because we had done the same several years before, and they began walking toward us, heads down, as if looking for something on the ground. The wagons were ahead of them as they bent over to pick up rocks of all sizes and place them on the wagon beds. They kept going until they filled the beds, and then the drivers brought the overflowing wagons close to the fortress base. Soldiers and slaves were waiting, and they dumped their loads according to the instructions issued by whom I presume must have been engineers. Then, after an hour, we saw them drop the rocks around the perimeter of Masada in contiguous piles, which they would soon build into a barrier around us.

Eleazar was watching, too, and having heard of the siege wall at the Machaerus fortress from a caravan that had passed by, he knew the Romans intended to surround us and prevent all escape attempts.

"Have your troops supply each tower with arrows," I heard him call to his lieutenants, "and order the archers to target the Roman engineers and slaves from the towers. And have the fletchers make more arrows. We're going to need a lot more than we have."

I descended from the casemate wall to join a large group standing near our room, where we gathered for evening campfires. Peppered with questions, I did my best to answer and then described what we had seen below.

"They are dumping large piles of stones around the perimeter and appear to be making a siege wall. We also saw them laying out two rectangles—one large, one smaller—that might be for camps for the troops. There were also large groups of soldiers with wagons and mules gathering below the Northern Palace. I don't know what for, but since they are facing Jerusalem, I think they are being sent to gather supplies."

Someone on the wall said, "They are forming up into a long caravan facing north, probably toward Ein Gedi to bring water back."

"Doesn't this mean they intend to stay a long time?" someone else asked, and I shrugged.

But then the harder questions came.

"What do they want?"

"Can we make them leave?"

By then, Judith had come down from the battlement and rejoined me, but she had no more answers for them.

I kept my honest thoughts to myself, for they did not bode well for the people of Masada. After all, Rome did not send an entire legion to the middle of the desert only for them to turn away, and Roman commanders knew their fates if they failed their mission.

Soon after, the first of a continuous volley of arrows was released onto the Romans below, so I climbed back onto the battlement to continue my observations. On occasion, our arrows hit their targets, but, in truth, the barrages were a waste of valuable projectiles and inflicted no more damage than mosquitos might. Even so, the Roman general would not tolerate Jewish rebels firing on Roman legions, and shortly after, we observed centurions ordering their catapult teams into place outside the reach of our archers.

Moments later, the Romans began a massive catapult bombardment, and hundreds of skull-sized rocks rained down upon the plateau. Where they landed seemed absolutely arbitrary and caused panic in their wake.

"To your rooms," I shouted as soon as the first rocks began to land, and havoc broke out on the plateau as people sought shelter. My shouts were picked up by Eleazar's troops, but Eleazar himself ordered his archers to continue launching flight after flight of arrows. As people ran to their rooms, some received direct hits or near misses, and screams of the injured contributed to the chaos. Clearly, the bombardment was meant to instill terror and send a clear message from Rome: We will do whatever it takes to prevail.

All I could think to myself was, *Will this never end?*

Later that night, being a very light sleeper, I was startled awake when I heard banging against the gate, much like we had done the night before to get back inside the fortress. The pounding continued in fits and starts for the next while, so I went to the gate to see why it did not stop, and as I expected, the guards were asleep.

"Guards," I snarled to wake them up. "There is banging at the gate."

They leaped up quickly and dispatched someone to the battlement to see who it was.

After a few minutes of mumbling from above us, we heard "Open the gate" from the rampart. "It's one of our patrols. Open. Hurry."

Three guards by the gate lifted the drawbar, and a group of five Sicarii soldiers came through, with two of them carrying a Roman centurion dangling between them, his head lolling and toes dragging along the ground.

"Lock the gate," one of them shouted, and the guards put the drawbar back in place, just in time to hear the thwack of arrows hitting the other side of the gate.

"What's happening?" someone asked.

"We were on patrol when the Roman vanguard arrived, so we stayed below to estimate the size of the force. They launched their surrounding forces so quickly we couldn't get past them to return to base before they completely encircled Masada. We got stuck on the other side and waited to find a gap to go through to come home."

One of the soldiers holding the centurion continued. "When we were sneaking through their lines below the southern fort, we came across this one doing his business behind a bush. We thought he would have some useful information, so we brought him back with us."

"Bring him to the dungeon," said a voice behind us. "We'll find out what he knows." The speaker was Nathan, and I did not envy this poor Roman soldier. The dungeon was in the southern fort, where Sarah and Jacob had been held, and was on the far side of the crops, so the screams of prisoners could not be heard. I went back to my room and did not learn of this fellow's fate until the following day.

Now that Yoav and I were back at Masada, we resumed our daily routine of working in the fields. That morning, we picked up where we left off a few days before and took a group of workers to the onion fields to clear the irrigation paths from the cisterns to the plants. First, I went to our tool sheds near the southern fort with some helpers to gather hoes. As I rooted through the tools, I heard a blood-curdling scream from the fort. My team collected the hoes and returned to the fields. But I decided to stay and went to the cell window where the Roman was being interrogated. Sitting below the window, I could hear the questions being asked, but the Roman's voice was flagging.

"Why are you here?" was the first question I heard Nathan ask, coupled with what sounded like a dry thump and an *oomph* sound.

"Why do you think we're here? This is the last settlement left in Judea. We're going to wipe you Jews out once and for all."

Another voice, I think it was Eleazar's, said, "You don't look like you'll be wiping anyone out. You can barely lift your head."

"Don't worry about me," the Roman said. "Rome will take care of you."

"Why won't you just leave us alone?" That sounded like Eleazar.

"That's not Rome's way. Besides, you attacked Ein Gedi and massacred every person there. So now, you must bow your knee to Rome. Only then will you be left in peace." The Roman let out a small laugh. "You Jews, you think you're so special, with your *all-powerful* god and his promise that this is your land and only you can rule it in his name. The Romans will never accept your god, and we'll destroy you to prove our gods are stronger."

"So," said Nathan. *Thump-oomph*. He accentuated his words with his fists. "You intend." *Thump-oomph*. "To destroy us?" *Thump-oomph*.

There was only silence from the Roman.

Then I heard water splashing, and Nathan continued the interrogation. "How will your commander proceed now?"

Slowly the Roman responded. "I suppose there's no reason not to tell you. We have encircled Masada already. No one will get in or out. The outcome is inevitable." I shifted my position to hear better. "We'll do the same thing we did in Jerusalem. The engineers have already scouted the surroundings and decided where they will build the circumvallation wall and the base camps."

"They can't build a circumvallation wall around Masada," Nathan said. "There are steep gorges."

"You think that will stop Roman engineers? We have built siege works from Britannia to Syria and have seen everything. A few ravines won't stop us."

"And then what will they do?" asked Eleazar. "Masada is impregnable. Doesn't your general know that?"

"You think Masada can't be breached? Nothing can stop the Roman army."

I saw Yoav approaching and signaled him to not speak. Then, when he was close enough, I whispered, "Listen. They're interrogating the Roman soldier."

"Then what?" asked Eleazar. "How will your vaunted engineers scale our cliffs?"

"They have their ways, like at Machaerus."

Eleazar and Nathan could both be heard laughing.

"Assuming you reach the wall. Then what? How will you breach the walls?" asked Nathan.

"The same way we breached them in Jerusalem."

"My men will kill you before they let you get that close."

"How many times have we heard that?" asked the Roman. "We have ways to protect our builders and soldiers."

"I think we've heard enough, Nathan. Send this man to his Roman gods."

Yoav and I were appalled to hear a sword being drawn and then absolute silence.

CHAPTER
31

The following day at dawn, we heard unfamiliar sounds and sights below our room. Roman engineers, recognizable due to the lack of cheekpieces on their helmets, were gathered at the bottom of the spur below us. It was hard to determine what they were doing, but things soon became apparent as we saw soldiers marching toward them with digging implements and baskets.

The troops climbed to a high point about halfway up the spur, and when they arrived, the engineers issued instructions. Within minutes, the legionnaires arrayed themselves around the hilltop and dug holes here and there. Other soldiers stood next to them and placed baskets on the ground, which the diggers filled once they had enough loose soil. Then the basket carriers would heft the basket on their shoulders and walk about one hundred and fifty paces down the hilltop into a dip in the spur. Once there, they dumped their loads and climbed back up the hill, and started the process anew.

We watched in bewildered silence as this went on for hours. By then, Eleazar had arrived to observe as well. He ordered his archers into place and said, "Shower them with a barrage of arrows. Stop them."

Once the archers were in place, a lieutenant set a steady cadence of aerial volleys loose on the soldiers below. Then, without saying a word, Eleazar looked around at the crowd and walked away toward the palace as his archers fired wave upon wave of arrows.

"How many arrows do we have that they are using them with such abandon?" I asked no one in particular.

The Romans soon figured out how to reduce their casualties after the first day. They built sheltered paths over the entire length between the hilltop and the dip to protect their troops, used a big mounted bow-like weapon to launch metal bolts at our archers, and erected catapults to bombard us for hours at a time. They could hit us anywhere on the mountaintop, and the bombardments took a severe toll on everyone's nerves as the rocks exploded randomly across the summit.

It took the Roman legionaries fifteen days to move the hilltop into the valley and another ten days to put down a finer layer over the rough to create a uniform road from ground level up the side of the mountain. Long before they finished their work, we determined it was a ramp up to the wall, created by filling in the dip between the hills. You have to admire the Romans for their commitment to eradicating us and their willingness to do the hard work of moving mountains—especially under a constant shower of arrows.

Still, the ramp didn't reach the fortress walls, and we decided they didn't want to expend the effort. Working right up under the walls would be hazardous since we could slow them down by throwing rocks and boiling oil down on them. So instead, I thought they would build a siege engine to reach the ramparts, as they had done in Jerusalem.

The next day proved me right as the Romans moved the siege tower pieces to the bottom of the ramp. Many Jewish veterans of the Jerusalem siege recognized what the Romans were doing. When they told us, it sent chills through us all. Those pieces, once assembled, would comprise a siege tower and battering ram that would knock down part of the fortress wall and let Roman troops stream into the fortress to finish us.

Most of the remaining civilians gathered around the campfire that night, with a few of Eleazar's soldiers above us on the casemate wall, as always. The discussion was lively but soon quieted when people realized what moving the siege engine pieces into place signified. When people stopped talking, I could hear sobs and outright crying by many. A few railed against the unfairness of it. Others cursed the Romans, Eleazar, and even God.

"What has Eleazar brought us to?" someone outside the light of the fire asked. I had no answer, for I agreed.

From the ramparts, a soldier in the shadows said, "What's wrong with you people? I'll tell you what Eleazar has brought us. He brought us the ability and willingness to fight against Rome. He taught us to fight for our land and way of life, and he taught us how to be excellent soldiers so we can defend all of you thankless people." The soldier yelled loud enough that his comrades heard him.

We could hear shouts of "He's right" and "Eleazar! Eleazar! Eleazar!" as more soldiers converged on us from the palace. At first, they came in ones and twos, but soon, larger groups of soldiers arrived and surrounded us with their shouting. There were at least one hundred of them. I looked for familiar faces in the campfire's light and saw more fear of this immediate threat in the faces of my friends and family than of the Roman danger below.

Unable to stop myself, I shouted back at the shadow soldier, "You're wrong. Do you think it's a coincidence the legion arrived so soon after the attack on Ein Gedi, an imperial city under Rome's protection? Of course not. Your violence brought them here."

Moments later, Eleazar himself appeared, perhaps sensing the discord and internal danger to his community.

"I understand your concerns. But we cannot let our fears overcome us. Each of you is important to this war effort, and I will call upon you to help. Tonight, we intend to send a patrol out to investigate and destroy those pieces at the bottom of the ramp. We don't know what they are, but they're important to the Romans, and so we will destroy them."

"We know what they are," someone said. "They're parts of a siege engine. You can see the battering ram. They called it Big Julius in Jerusalem."

"Yes," Eleazar said. "You are most likely right. I didn't mean to be coy, but I didn't want to alarm you."

"Stop patronizing us by trying to keep us in the dark. We are not children and deserve to be told the truth," someone else said.

"If you want the truth, I will give it to you. Eight thousand Roman legionaries, together with their auxiliaries and their slaves, have surrounded us. They intend to eliminate us, and they will try to break through our walls soon to get to us. We will do everything we can to stop them, but likely, they will break down the walls enough to stream through and attack us. Once they do, we will fight to the death. Death is almost certain for the men, as is slavery for the women and children. That is the truth.

"Stay away from the wall tonight. We don't want to give the Romans any hint of our mission. Tomorrow morning, we will let you know how it went. Good night."

Eleazar's men had a few hours until dawn to complete the mission. They'd leave by the Water Gate, descend the slope, kill the guards posted near the siege engine pieces, and destroy as many as possible. Straightforward, but not easy. Nathan led the operation, and I noticed he took some of the best soldiers with him.

I stood close to the Water Gate to watch the squad leaving. The hinges of the gate had been oiled at dusk to minimize any noise from opening and closing it, but a squeak escaped just before the men could finish closing it, making Nathan and his men hold their breaths.

There was no moon that night as they made their way down. I climbed the battlement to watch what I could as they huddled behind a few boulders before the descent, making sure not to alert the Romans to their presence. Satisfied they had not triggered an alarm, they began their covert journey down, moving from rock to rock, careful not to cause small avalanches that would be a telltale sign they were coming. It was a balancing act, choosing between using the path and forging an alternative way down. The Romans were guarding the preexisting path, but taking a new pathway could lead to someone loosening rock and causing a gravel landslide, prematurely alerting anyone below.

Before long, they disappeared into the darkness, but I later learned the Romans were waiting for them when they arrived. As they approached the siege engine site, dozens of legionaries ambushed them and killed five of them immediately. Nathan and one of his men evaded capture and hid, but the Romans caught the remaining men. Later, still watching and hoping to see survivors, I noticed a Roman soldier starting a campfire. This made no sense to me, but looking closer, I saw the soldier run behind a boulder. Next, I heard muffled shouting, and then I understood one of the surviving men had set a part of the siege engine on fire, destroying it. The Romans quenched the fire, but it was too late. They found the soldier in his hiding place and killed him.

When the inhabitants of Masada woke in the morning, they witnessed Rome's revenge as they crucified three captured men for all to see. I can still hear the screams reverberating in my head. Only Nathan returned from the mission, embarrassed, I suspect, having lost all his men and not dying himself. His only gratification was a prize he took from a Roman officer he encountered on his way home—a Roman sword in its sheath he took while defending himself.

• • • • • • • • • • ● ● ● • • • • • • • •

We woke to animal-like sounds of several voices screaming in pain. The source was not immediately apparent—it could have been on our mountaintop or somewhere nearby. But then I noticed the screaming only bothered the civilians, not Eleazar's men, who were going about their business.

Soon after, the screams ended abruptly, and the men and women came to me to explain the silence.

The civilian mind, so different from the military, led them to ask, "Who would order the killing of our own men?" And it came to me again; Eleazar's behavior was not much different from Rome's, and he had built a militarized community at Masada, with him as emperor. His men followed his orders without question.

As I approached the communal kitchen for breakfast, I saw Aaron hunched over, seated at a table, and talking intensely with Yoav. When I joined them, they barraged me with questions about the situation and asked what we could do.

"What would you have us do?" I asked. "The Romans will rebuild the damaged siege engine piece by this afternoon, and they will probably bring the pieces up today and assemble them tomorrow. Then they will knock down the wall and attack. After that, it will be too late for any other course of action but to fight."

"We should send an envoy to the Romans, asking to surrender," said Aaron.

"Eleazar will never allow it," I said.

"We don't have to ask his permission."

"Assuming the Romans accept our proposal, how would you surrender if Eleazar doesn't agree?"

Aaron suggested we shoot an arrow with our proposal wrapped around its shaft down to the Roman camp below, having them wave a red flag if they accept.

"That part works," I said. "But then what? How do you get Eleazar to agree to a surrender?"

"Eleazar believes our fate is what he calls an honorable death," Aaron said, "He won't let his soldiers go, and most likely, won't let the civilians go either."

"So, what is the point of trying?" I asked.

"Surrender was originally your idea, Daniel. I'm surprised by your resistance," said Aaron.

"I'm not resistant, but we need the details laid out, so we have a chance of success. Eleazar is becoming more erratic by the day. Who knows what path he would lead us down?"

We stayed together and hashed out the plan, and we designated Yoav and Aaron to take it to Eleazar.

Alas, Eleazar's response was a predictable and straightforward no. He said nothing to justify his position; just a simple and emphatic no. His self-restraint impressed me.

After Eleazar rejected the idea, we went to retrieve Aaron's bow to let loose a simple message:

We want to discuss surrender. If you agree, wave a red flag at the bottom of the ramp during daylight.

We prayed the Romans would wave a flag in response. If they did, we would deal with Eleazar then.

Aaron fired the arrow with the message from the fields, so I went with him, intending to check the roots of several bulbs of the onion crop to see if the rot we'd discovered was spreading. We didn't know what was causing it, but if the onion crop failed, we would again face starvation since onions were a mainstay of our diets. But my mind was elsewhere, and as I kneeled by the carpet of onions, I worried how Eleazar would react when he found out about the message arrow, and the Romans' steady progress toward our eradication was scaring me senseless. They are like a swarm of locusts, with nothing to stop them in their never-ending and mindless destruction. What would it hurt the Romans to leave us alone? What harm could an isolated little group of Jews do to the Roman Empire? But I knew the answer to that. We, too, were like a plague of locusts and had recently killed seven hundred of our closest neighbors.

Violence begets violence. But not being naïve, I knew the Romans would have come for us anyway, regardless of whether we attacked Ein Gedi. They cannot tolerate dissent, and in that way, Eleazar was no different. Which was the real reason for my concern. I was equally afraid of the enemy without as I was of the enemy within. So, now, I was worried for Aaron and the rest of the civilians. If the Romans didn't get us, I worried Eleazar might.

The fear of Roman progress was palpable. Children clung to their parents' legs, and husbands and wives held each other, people would sneak up the walls to peek over and see the progress, and everyone spoke in hushed tones. If I wasn't so afraid for Judith, myself, and our children, the Roman force would have impressed me with their single-mindedness. They had military might and expertise and were so well trained. They had crossed the desert and built eight camps and a siege wall out of nothing but the rocks on the ground. And then they constructed a ramp hundreds of paces long and a siege engine to invade our home.

Shouting from atop the battlement closest to the ramp interrupted my thoughts. I couldn't see what the commotion was about nor hear clearly because the orchards stood between me and the source, so I went to the wall to see.

"The Romans are moving the siege engine up the ramp," someone said.

I climbed the stairs to the ramparts and looked down. Our archers were already releasing continuous volleys onto the Romans below, but it was useless. Legionaries held interlocked shields over their heads and the heads of the troops carrying the siege engine pieces. They resembled a turtle moving up the ramp, with the haulers and components well protected under their shields. To emphasize we could not interfere with them, the Romans fired bolts as long as a man's arm span from mounted bows to clear the walls of archers. It was just as well since I heard a nearby soldier say we were almost out of arrows.

By midmorning, the Romans had all the pieces at the top of the ramp and began constructing the siege engine. So ingenious and practiced were they at building weapons of war, they managed to assemble the siege tower from the inside, never once exposing themselves to our attacks from the walls. Moreover, they had flattened a large area atop the ramp, which we thought was to stage their troops before the big raid. Now, we understood it was to provide a platform for the siege engine to sit on.

Dozens of men worked on its assembly, and they finished building the tower by dusk. Its total height was higher than the casemate wall by a few paces. It was an impressive weapon of war, clad in iron plates so we could not burn it, and at the top was a ramp they would lower onto the wall to act as a rampart from which they would fire salvo after salvo of arrows at our defenders. Halfway up the tower was a door. The men inside could raise or lower it, as needed, to expose Big Julius, a monstrosity with an iron boar's head mounted on a massive hanging beam. Slaves heaved the shaft back and forth between the front and back of the tower like a pendulum. It would pound the walls until they yielded, which they inevitably would.

Accompanied as we were by the constant sound of construction throughout the day, I came to notice an absence of noise as we prepared our evening meal, but did not realize it meant the Romans had completed their assembly of the tower. The yelling and hammering were replaced by an ominous silence, which had to mean the Romans were ready to begin their assault. But they didn't. We waited for hours, but the silence continued, with us ready to explode with unmet anticipation. Finally, after a long and exhausting day, we went to bed but did not sleep.

In our bed that night, Judith and I snuggled close, taking comfort in each other's warmth as we drifted off to sleep.

Later, emerging from a deep sleep, I knew something was wrong. A drinking cup had fallen from a shelf and exploded on the ground. Then I felt an *oomph* sound in my chest more than I could hear it with my ears. It was the thud and all-permeating pounding vibration of the battering ram as it hit the casemate wall near our room.

Thud-throb, thud-throb, thud-throb.

It hit the wall every ten seconds throughout the night and the next day, and we could not sleep as the menacing sound drove us out of our minds.

One day later, at midday, Aaron told me the Romans would breach the wall that day, or at the latest, the next. But as a stonemason, he said he knew of a way to reinforce the wall to give us more time and asked me to go with him to tell Eleazar.

Aaron must have had more credibility with Eleazar and his troops; he was able to get us in to see Eleazar more quickly than I'd ever managed.

"Aaron, welcome," Eleazar said, greeting him warmly.

"Eleazar, the Romans will breach the wall today or tomorrow, but I have an idea on how to slow them down and gain us more time."

"More time for what? To listen to the endless thumping?"

"No, more time to surrender, to escape."

"We will not be doing either of those things," Eleazar said. "We will wait for the Romans here and prevent them from having this victory."

"What do you mean, 'prevent them from having this victory'?" I asked.

Eleazar looked at me and said, "I mean, we will die before letting them enslave our women and children and kill our men."

"We will die?" I said. "By whose hand?"

"By our own hands. Would you give the Romans the satisfaction of conquering the last Jewish enclave in Judea?"

"But what about the civilians?" Aaron asked.

"What civilians? In the war with the Romans, we are all soldiers; men, women, and children. But proceed. Reinforce the wall. We can use the extra time for our planning. You can recruit whomever you want to help—except my soldiers. Dismissed."

I went back to work in the fields, but later in the day, as I returned to my room to find Judith, I saw a work crew dismantling a fifty-foot stretch of the inner casemate wall in the exact spot where the Romans were pounding the outer wall. I approached Aaron and asked how it was progressing.

"We are dismantling the inner casemate wall because it is rigid and will crumble under the assault of the battering ram. We'll replace it with a flexible wooden wall right behind the outer casemate wall. Then we'll build another parallel wall about twenty paces back and fill the space between the two wooden walls with packed earth. It will absorb the blows of the battering ram."

"Ingenious," I said. "What can I do to help?"

"I've calculated we need about four thousand wooden beams to build the two walls. There's a work crew dismantling roofs to get to their beams. Take your sword back to your room, then find Levi and help him. I have to get back to work now."

Hundreds joined the work crews. At one point, I saw Eleazar come to watch our work and then walk away without comment. Everyone worked without stopping to dismantle the inner wall, uncover beams, and haul and compact the soil between the walls. So many worked on the wall, Eleazar had to move the assembly to the next night. It had been a long time since I'd seen members of our community working together so well, proving nothing focuses attention like trying to save your own life.

We worked through the day and night, with the never-ending *thud-throb* accompanying our labors. Finally, we finished by midday on the second day, and I couldn't help but notice the sound and vibrations of the battering ram had softened. Between that and the exhaustion, we could finally get a brief rest, knowing we had all worked together to save ourselves.

Before sunset, the Romans broke through the outer wall and discovered the inner wall. After several unsuccessful attempts to batter the inner wall into submission, the Roman general ordered his men to launch torches and fire arrows at it, which, being made of dry desert wood, immediately caught fire. It soon burned enough away, and once the fires had extinguished themselves, the battering ram made quick work of what remained of the wall. Once the wooden wall gave in, enough of the soil and desert sand we'd compacted behind it spilled down the hill, creating a loose path into the fortress for the Romans to finish us off.

And yet, after breaching the walls and laying us wide open to attack, the Roman general had his forces retreat to the bottom of the ramp, leaving only a defensive force to guard the tower and the breach.

In the dark, and after we saw the Romans move to the bottom of the ramp, Eleazar assembled us one more time. It was a somber group that faced him as he began his prepared remarks.

"Long ago, we decided we would never let the Romans be our masters and that we would only serve our God."

I didn't realize we had decided that.

"Until now, it has been easy to honor this commitment because we never had to live up to our oath."

What commitment? Who swore an oath?

"But the time has arrived to honor the oath we swore as a community."

What does he mean by "the time"?

"Now that the moment is upon us, we cannot turn back. We cannot accept slavery as an alternative to death because we are committed to the oath we swore to each other and to God."

Oh, dear God, he wants us to kill ourselves! What about surrender? Maybe they'll let the women and children go if the soldiers and civilian men surrender.

"We were the first among our Jewish brethren to revolt and the last to hold out against Rome. It is our destiny, and God has granted us this opportunity, to die a glorious death in a state of freedom and not be dragged away in chains."

What is a "glorious death"?

"I have concluded we cannot win against the might of Rome. Once I thought this fortress gave us the advantages we needed to be safe, but I was wrong. The Romans are masters of war—it is the basis of their entire society."

If we cannot win, we can still try to surrender. Maybe a few will survive. All these people cannot die because of one man's stubbornness and megalomania.

"The Romans will be here within the day, but it is not too late. We can take our fates into our own hands. The Romans cannot stop us."

What would he have us do—commit mass suicide and deny the Romans the pleasure of sacking the place and killing us?

"We still have food and weapons, but God has decided we will not be delivered, and so we will end our lives and deny Rome its victory."

How does he know God's decision in this matter? Our God is a loving God who would not see his people slaughtered or die by their own hands. So, where does it come from, his need to see us all dead?

"That God would allow the Romans to destroy the outer wall and burn the inner wall despite the heroic efforts of so many of you is proof God will deprive us of deliverance. It is God's way of saying our time is over. Therefore, we must fulfill God's will in this matter and end our lives."

This is not a message from God. If anything, it proves Eleazar would choose to see every one of us dead by our own hands so history will say he was a brilliant commander, never defeated by the Romans.

"God is angry with us for our multitude of sins, and we cannot avoid his punishment. He will have his way, and we will be his hand in this."

What sins have the women and children committed? Did they murder every person at Ein Gedi? Did they drive daggers into the hearts of priests in Jerusalem? We would not face this dilemma if you did not insist on violence at every turn. Yoav! Aaron! Say something!

Yoav stood, and glaring at Eleazar, he said, "There is another way."

"Silence! There is no other way, for God has decreed it!" Eleazar bellowed. "Sit yourself down."

But Yoav, a much-loved leader in our community and so well respected for raising the food that has fed us for the past seven years, stood his ground.

"We will not sit, and we will not be silent. People need to hear the options," I said as Yoav looked around at the assembled crowd and nodded his agreement.

"How many of you want to die?" I asked. No one knew how to respond, but obviously, no one wanted to die. It was almost a rhetorical question, but it wasn't. I continued. "How many of you are willing to die as a punishment for sins you did not commit?" Still no answer. "You are not assassins. The assassins are up there," I said and pointed to Eleazar and his men. All this while Yoav was moving closer to the front of the crowd, and with my last statement, he mounted the platform where Eleazar stood and planted himself an arm's length away.

"Yesterday, we sent a message to the Romans, asking if they would consider our surrender, and they replied yes by waving a red flag at the bottom of the ramp—" said Yoav.

"Grab them," Eleazar shouted to his men. And as they moved to restrain Yoav, Aaron, and me, Eleazar shouted, "Traitors! What do you mean you sent them a message? Who helped you send this message? Who else is a traitor? Tell me now or die!"

"We will never tell you," said Yoav.

As he said this, Eleazar told his men to grab the still standing Aaron. Then, while his men moved through the crowd, Eleazar drew his sword and ran Yoav through, yelling again, "Traitor!"

Everyone froze in place, except for the men moving toward Aaron. Dorit screamed at the horror of seeing her husband of forty years murdered. The scream released everyone, putting them in motion. The crowd split like oil and water, with the men surging forward to protect Aaron and the women and children running like a scattered flock to the rear to escape the melee. I remember realizing the answer to my question: no one wanted to die.

As the crowd broke apart, I grabbed Judith and Hannah's hands and pulled them to the side. "Follow me and don't look back," I said to them. We had arrived late to the assembly and, positioned on the edge of the crowd, were able to make a run for the orchards.

"But Daniel," Judith said to me, "What about the others?"

"It's too late for them," I said. "Eleazar will never let them live."

We hid among the date palms, Judith covering Hannah's eyes as I watched the events unfold. It was an unwinnable battle for the civilians. Even those who had started carrying swords after the Romans had arrived at our door were no match for Eleazar's well-trained troops.

His soldiers moved into a defensive phalanx around him, and the men approaching Aaron formed up like the Romans do, using interlocked shields to protect themselves.

We could hear Eleazar shouting commands above the fray, "Fulfill God's commandment. He wants us to be his hand in their punishment. God wants them dead!"

The civilians threw rocks and tried surging toward Eleazar, but this only incensed his troops, and they started, hesitantly at first, to carry out his orders. In the end, though, they slaughtered every civilian man, woman, and child of Masada without hesitation.

From between the palms, Judith and I watched the carnage. My closest friends were now dead: Yoav and Dorit, Aaron, Benjamin, and Yitzhak.

After his men killed all the civilians, Eleazar called his bloodied and frenzied troops together and spoke again.

"We have fulfilled God's will, but we are not finished. We, too, must perish, as God has decreed. Now, it is time to finish what we started. We, too, are guilty of great sins, but we'll not let the Romans punish us. We will be as God's hands and we will punish ourselves. We will bestow a magnificent death on each other and show the Romans we prefer our death to theirs.

"Life is a calamity, but death is not. On the contrary, death is liberty, and it releases our souls to a pure place beside God. And there, we will feel no more the pains of earthly life.

"This is God's design, and we will execute his will, for he has determined the Jewish people will live no more.

"Those of us remaining will each now write our names on a piece of pottery, and I will select ten shards. Those chosen will execute God's will on those of us whose lots were not drawn, so we do not violate the prohibition of suicide. Then I will finish the final ten lot holders before dispatching myself, for I will be the last standing and will show the Romans my army was a worthy opponent.

"But first, we'll collect the bodies and put them on a funeral pyre. The remaining ten will do the same for all of you, and I will do the same for the remaining ten. We will die next to the funeral pyre, so I can add each of you to the cleansing fire, and so the Romans will not have the satisfaction of seeing our tormented bodies."

We had been hiding among the palm trees all night with the horrible smell of burning bodies filling our nostrils.

Finally, when the slaughter was over, and when I saw only Eleazar remained, I turned to a horrified Judith and said, "We must escape this place before Eleazar realizes we are not among the dead, and before the Romans arrive. Come with me. I know a place we can hide." Judith, my fearless wife, and touchstone looked at me with dead eyes, then followed in silence, holding our children tight.

Slowly and quietly, to avoid detection, we moved through the orchards to the area of the ritual baths on the eastern side of Masada. I knew there were caves on the slope below the *mikvah*. The path to the caves was treacherous, but I thought we could make it. After climbing carefully for a while, we found a cave and slept for a few hours.

CHAPTER

34

The following day, I made my way back up to the orchards to see what I could learn while avoiding Eleazar and any Roman soldiers. I was immediately struck by the stench of death and the absolute silence of this once vital community. The enormous loss of life owing to the folly of men impressed itself upon me, and I was at a loss for words. I was transported back to my argument with Father, and I decided he had been right all along. Killing should never be condoned, for killing only begets more killing, and I was seeing before my eyes the logical conclusion of when men disobey God's commandment.

Eleazar's troops had not collected all the dead, and as I meandered, I saw so many friends, their wives, and children, their bodies contorted in death and the vultures already gathering to feast on their remains. The loss was enormous and on a scale my mind could not fathom.

I returned to our room to gather a few belongings and heard voices down below the ramp. Climbing to the battlement near the destroyed Western Gate and peeking over the edge, I saw a Roman commander muster his troops to attack.

"We will strike with overwhelming force, but since it will be impossible to move an entire legion through the breach quickly enough to affect the battle, I will have cohorts one and two breach first. Without good intelligence on the rebel numbers, we will hold cohorts three and four in reserve at the bottom of the ramp, but two cohorts should be able to manage whatever we face. The remaining troops will continue to man the siege walls in the event the Jews break for a different exit."

The troops were in formation and ready to begin the ascent. Their general gave the order, and the centurions commanded their men to "Turtle Up," and a thousand shields snapped into place.

"Forward, march," the general commanded, and the soldiers began the slow march up the ramp, awaiting the bombardment of arrows and stones. The turtle formation did not protect the vanguard or the commanders on horseback, leaving them completely exposed. But it didn't matter, for no one stirred on the battlements, and the counterattack did not come. There was no one left alive to launch the salvos. As they made their way up the ramp, I imagine the tension for those Roman soldiers must have increased by the minute, every step bringing them closer to the expected rebel ambush. But it was not to be.

I hid in the *genizah*, a storage room for scrolls in the synagogue, and was able to peek out and watch as they quickly breached the opening. As the Romans streamed onto the plateau, they were undoubtedly struck by the eerie silence and appeared perplexed. Having broken through the wall fully expecting to confront their enemies, the silence confused them, but they stood their ground while looking for opponents.

"Look! There, on the far wall," a soldier shouted, and the entire Roman force turned as one to see a lone rebel soldier standing on the parapet looking down on them. As they watched, he did a little jig and then bent down quickly, picked up a fist-sized stone, and threw it in the general direction of the general. I guess it was too heavy to throw far because it fell short, but I heard a snicker from above when it hit the ground.

I looked up and saw him raise his tunic, and he said, in a clear voice, "I piss on you, Rome," which he then did. Someone shot an arrow at him but missed as he ducked behind a crenelation in the wall.

Eleazar was the last Jewish rebel alive, either too cowardly or too brave to have taken his own life.

I continued watching from my hiding spot as the general sent a few men to bring their enemy down. When they returned, they brought Eleazar who appeared soaked in blood, with bloodshot and crazed eyes.

"Who are you?" the general asked.

"I am your very worthy opponent, Eleazar Ben Yair, commander of the Sicarii," he replied.

"Well met, sir," the general responded. "But where are your troops?"

"God told me we were to deny Rome the honor of ending our lives and ordered me to do it, so you will return to Rome and tell them Eleazar Ben Yair bested you in combat."

I watched Eleazar in disbelief, seeing the insanity that was gripping his mind. Who knows? Maybe it was the stress of the last few weeks or the guilt of ending so many lives, but the man was obviously mad.

The general turned to his men and said, "Arrest this man, and have cohorts three and four join us. Then have the commanders organize search parties to see if he has left anyone alive," he ordered.

"Yes, sir."

Thus ended the Roman invasion of Masada. They had finally eliminated all Jewish resistance to Roman rule everywhere in Judea, and I snuck back to my family without incident.

Everybody Judith and I knew had been massacred. Our families, our friends, our acquaintances, and our enemies. Crazy and brutal men had ended their lives. The enormity of the carnage and the sheer number of people dead was of such a magnitude that Judith and I were in a stupor for days while we tried to make sense of it. Finally, on the third day, we decided to make our way to Alexandria. We hid in the cave until sunset, mourning the deaths of our friends and waiting until we were confident the Roman legion had departed, so it would be safe for us to come out of hiding. Then, heading around to the western side of Masada, we followed the same path to Arad we had been on before. We did not make much progress that first night, so we decided to rest in the shallow cave we found before when collecting firewood years before.

"Judith, I'll put the blanket out for the children—"

"Who goes there?" a woman's voice further back in the cave asked, sounding very frightened.

"Who are you?" I asked, drawing my sword and pointing it toward the rear of the cave.

"Daniel, is that you? This is Sarah, from Jerusalem," she said while sobbing. "Thank God, it is you. They killed my Jacob."

"We heard," Judith said as Sarah emerged from the shadows. "*Baruch dayan emet.* I'm so sorry for your loss."

"*Baruch dayan emet.* I, too, am so sorry for your loss," I said. "Why are you still here? How have you survived all this time?"

"When the groups split, I went with those leaving for the diaspora, but Roman cavalry soon caught up with us. It was horrible. They crashed through us and murdered so many from atop their horses. I hid and was not spotted, so after they left, I gathered abandoned supplies and headed to this cave, which I had noticed on the way out. I've been here ever since, mourning the loss of my Jacob. I didn't know where to go or what to do. I thought of going to Alexandria, but I have no idea how to get there."

"You're in luck then," Judith said before I had the chance. "We are on our way to Alexandria too. You can travel with us."

The five of us left for Alexandria at sunset, and the last sight we had of Masada was the vultures as they circled above the remains of our friends.

We departed undetected, crossing the desert between Arad and Alexandria on foot. We were lucky the cooler season had arrived, for I'm sure we wouldn't have made it in summer.

It took us thirty days to cross the desert, sleeping on the ground with the crystal-clear sky above us and God's glory revealed in the breathtaking sight of millions of flickering lights in heaven. There were many adventures along the way, including the ever-present scorpions, nomadic desert people on camels, and wild animals that wanted to taste human flesh to see if they liked it. Yet, with God watching over us, we evaded and eluded all dangers, surviving on the prickly pears of the cactus plant. But after a month, we were on the edge of death from insufficient food and water; we were blessed to complete our journey at all, so well-worn were we.

We arrived in Alexandria barely alive, with cracked lips and gaunt faces, as well as bloody blisters on our bare feet because we had worn through our sandals, and we threw ourselves at the mercy of the thriving Jewish community.

Before long, we encountered Shula, who could have been our dear friend Dorit's sister. She was of the same stocky build and temperament, and this generous and motherly soul took us in, telling us exactly what she thought while overwhelming us with concern. As a recent widow, she had plenty of room to host us at her farmhouse on the outskirts of the city, and after she nursed us back to health, it was apparent to me she needed help to manage her farm. So, when I had recovered enough to work, I proposed that we stay with her and help her. In exchange, she let us build a house next to hers, and we would live there like a family. This overwhelmed Shula with happiness, and not having children of her own and having warm feelings in abundance to share was a perfect solution for us all.

There were many Sicarii in Alexandria when we arrived, so we never told our new community where we had come from. Within a few weeks, word of a mass suicide at Masada had made its way to Alexandria, for that was the emerging narrative, as told by a few Jewish slaves who claimed to have escaped from the Roman forces at the fortress. Our new friends and neighbors responded with gasps of shock; many of them had been made refugees by the destruction of Jerusalem and had had friends and relatives at Masada. A number had even visited when deciding where to live after the exodus from Jerusalem.

I prayed none would recognize Judith or me.

I love the predawn hours, when I can lie on the pallet I share with my best friend and wife, Judith, and let my mind wander before the day's work begins. Today, I thought about our luck in surviving those years at Masada, escaping the massacre, and crossing the desert. We live in a new home Judith and I built and have beautiful children and a new and loving mother and grandmother in Shula. We survived the nightmare that was Eleazar with minimal damage, although we often have bad dreams about those times.

As Judith woke, I whispered to her, "I love you, and I love our little family. Thank you, Judith, for being the wonderful woman you are. Who would have thought a child raised in the tunnels of Jerusalem could grow into such a marvelous wife and mother?"

"And who would have thought the spoiled son of a Temple priest could grow into such a wonderful husband, father, and leader?"

"It is all your fault," I said with a humph. "You were with me every step of the way, guiding me and being my conscience when the one provided by my parents was insufficient. Thank you, my love."

"*Eemah* and *Abba*, what are you talking about?" asked our ever-curious Hannah in her not-quite-awake voice.

"We were talking about how much we love you and Ari, little one. Now go back to sleep for a while. It is early."

"We should go to the market today," I whispered. "We need to refill the oil amphora and buy a few things."

Barely awake, Judith grunted her assent.

At midday, I took a break to join Judith and Hannah at the market. We weaved through the crowded marketplace, going from vendor to vendor, choosing a few wares along the way. I love the market in Alexandria. It reminded me of the one in Jerusalem I left behind so long ago, with its familiar spice smells, hanging goat carcasses, and jostling crowds.

Daydreaming as we meandered, I got caught up in the market's rhythm; the vendors hawking their goods and the constant bumping against too many people in such a confined space. Judith and Hannah were a few steps behind me as we approached the stairs to the lower market. I heard a tussle behind me and turned to see someone rushing toward me.

The crowd parted, and suddenly I heard, "*Abba, Abba*," as my little Hannah came at me with outstretched arms, her mother behind her, with Ari held tight to her chest. "Catch me," she said as she flew into my arms.

The End

Glossary

- *Abba:* Father.
- *Afarsemon balsam*: The persimmon fruit produced a balsam unique to Ein Gedi and the Dead Sea region during the Roman period and was used to produce perfume.
- *Baruch dayan emet:* "Blessed be the one true Judge"; a Jew recites these words upon hearing about a death.
- *Eemah*: Mother.
- *Gehinnom:* Hell.
- *Genizah*: Storage room for damaged scrolls in a synagogue.
- *Pikuach nefesh*: The principle in Jewish law that the preservation of human life overrides virtually any other religious rule, meaning when the life of a specific person is in danger, almost any negative commandment of the Torah becomes inapplicable.
- *Shabbat:* The Jewish sabbath, celebrated from sunset Friday evening to sundown Saturday evening.
- *Sicarii*: The Sicarii were a group of Jewish rebels who specialized in political assassinations to eliminate Jewish collaborators with Rome and force the expulsion of Rome from Judea.

- *Tanakh*: The Hebrew Bible, including the Torah, Nevi'im, and Ketuvim (Pentateuch, Prophets, and Writings).
- *Tisha B'Av:* The ninth day of the month of Av marks a day of grieving for the destruction of both the First and Second Jerusalem Temples and is observed by fasting and prayer.
- *Tzedakah:* Charity.
- *Yimakh shemo:* A strong curse meaning "may his name be erased."

Historical Afterword

The basic outline of the Masada story, as told by Josephus, is well known. Around the time of the destruction of the Second Temple, nine-hundred-and-sixty-seven Jewish rebels retreated to Masada. As one of the few remaining pockets of Jewish resistance to Roman occupation, Emperor Vespasian sent the Tenth Legion to eliminate them. After a rousing speech from their leader, Eleazar Ben Yair, the rebels chose to have husbands and fathers kill their own wives and children rather than be enslaved or slaughtered by the Romans. The remaining men elected ten to kill the surviving men, and finally, the last of the men were killed by one man, who then killed himself.

This recounting of the story comes to us through Josephus in his book *The Jewish War*, which he finished writing in 80 CE, only a few years after the events of Masada. While Josephus was a witness to other Roman military actions in Judea, he was already in Rome when the siege of Masada was purported to have occurred. Thus, he had to rely on second-hand accounts, such as Roman field reports and possibly the recounting by Jewish slaves taken to Rome, to gather the *facts* of this story.

Despite a remarkable archaeological record, historians and archaeologists do not agree about the events described in this novel. One area in dispute includes the basic story of Masada itself, especially as it relates to mass suicide. Unfortunately, there is no evidence of this event in the archaeological record as the skeletal remains of hundreds of people have not been found.

For me, having served in the Israeli army as a combat medic in the infantry, the primary problem with the Masada story was born of the disbelief that soldiers would follow orders to murder their own wives and children. I've always had a sense of incredulity when hearing the Masada story since I could not imagine following such an order myself, especially when the weapons available to the Jews on Masada would have required a very personal and face-to-face killing by sword or dagger. And if Josephus had this part of the story wrong, it always made me wonder if other elements were incorrect too.

During my time in the army, I spent one-and-a-half years stationed near Masada, often climbed the Snake Path, and spent hours wandering around the site. It was this exposure in my early twenties that generated my curiosity about what really happened there. You cannot help but be taken in by the story when you touch a stone and realize a rebel handled that same stone almost two thousand years ago.

Having lived on a small kibbutz in the Arava desert a little south of Masada, I also tried to imagine how these people survived the desert isolation. According to Josephus, King Herod the Great had vast stores of foodstuffs laid in over a hundred years before, and this is what the rebels at Masada ate during their time there. I always thought of this explanation in the vein of the oil that lasted eight days at Hanukkah. A delightful story but highly unlikely. I, for one, would not want to eat one-hundred-year-old dates, day-after-day, for seven years. Instead, I would crave fresh food.

From my kibbutz experience, I also knew what was required to grow food in the desert. So, I always wondered how these people survived and what they did to ease the boredom of living in an isolated place. This led me to the firm belief that the rebels must have raised their own food, which would help address both their nutritional and psychological needs. But then I did some math and realized Masada simply could not support over nine hundred people above starvation levels and that there must have been enormous pressure for people to leave Masada and seek refuge elsewhere.

The population density at Masada exceeded that of current-day New York City, which also led me to believe that tensions must have been high between the residents who likely split into various factions over time. For example, a rift might have emerged between the Sicarii and those I refer to as civilians. The Sicarii believed in targeted assassinations as a strategy, which would have conflicted with the beliefs of most other Jews of that period. During the Second Temple period, Jewish norms focused on obedience to the Ten Commandments. The Sicarii's willingness to violate the sixth commandment would have clashed with the societal values of most other Jews. The likelihood of starvation and societal rifts between the Sicarii and other refugees contributed to my imaginings of how society functioned on this small and isolated rhombus-shaped plateau in the middle of the desert. There must have been enormous pressures that are hereto undocumented in the historical record.

There was definitely a siege of Masada, as evidenced by the remains of the Roman camps, circumvallation wall, and ramp. In addition, a section of the Herodian casemate wall is missing above the ramp, where Josephus says the Romans used a siege engine to breach the wall. Archaeologists have also found numerous ballista shot and arrowheads atop Masada. But what is not agreed upon is the siege's date and length, so I allowed myself some artistic license.

In place of historical certainty, I offer this novel as one of many plausible explanations for what transpired at Masada during that very turbulent time in Jewish history. For history purists, please forgive me for taking dramatic license with the exact timeline. I hesitated to change details such as the year in which the Ein Gedi massacre took place, but I realized that I would have to write a different book if I was to hew to the exact dates as put forward by Josephus. So instead, please consider my interpretation as one of several plausible scenarios that could explain what actually happened almost two thousand years ago. And as Jodi Magness says in her excellent book, *Masada: From Jewish Revolt to Modern Myth*, (p. 196):

> "I am often asked if I believe there was a mass suicide at Masada, to which I respond that this is not a question archaeology is equipped to answer. The archaeological remains can be interpreted differently as supporting or disproving Josephus's account. Whether the mass suicide story is true depends on how one evaluates Josephus's reliability as an historian—a matter that I prefer to leave to Josephus specialists to resolve."

Based on my military experience and time spent living in an isolated desert agricultural community, I have added my thoughts to the postulations of the scholars who have come before me. I hope you have enjoyed my imaginations.

Shimon Avish
Massachusetts, 2022

Dramatis Personae—In Order of Appearance

Daniel: Protagonist
Jonathan: Daniel's twin brother
Mother and Father: Daniel's mother and father
Eleazar Ben Yair: Sicarii leader on Masada and antagonist
Nathan: Eleazar's cruel lieutenant
Menachem: Eleazar's cousin and Sicarii leader in Jerusalem
Malachi: Judith's brother and one of Eleazar's soldiers
Judith: Malachi's sister and Daniel's wife
Aaron: Stonecutter and Malachi's friend
Ruben: Eleazar's kind lieutenant
Yoav: Head farmer, Dorit's husband & Daniel's father figure
Benjamin: Head of the orchards
Dorit: Midwife, Yoav's wife, and Daniel and Judith's mother
  figure
Hannah: Judith and Daniel's daughter
Sarah: The wife of Jacob and niece of Zealot leader, Yochanan
  of Gush

Jacob: The husband of Sarah and former lieutenant of Zealot
     leader, Yochanan of Gush
Yitzhak: Leader of the Jerusalem refugees
Arieh (Ari): Judith and Daniel's son
Shula: Daniel and Judith's mother figure in Alexandria

Book Club
Discussion Questions

1. Daniel struggles with the idea of using violence as a means to an end. Did he resolve this conflict to your satisfaction?
2. Which character did you like the most? Which character would you most like to sit with around the campfire?
3. Why did Eleazar resort to violence and thievery? Do you think this was a viable long-term strategy? Do you agree with Eleazar's statement that violence solves all problems?
4. Was Judith able to break with the expectations for women in her time successfully? If yes, how?
5. What did you think of the relationship between Judith and Daniel?
6. Why was Nathan so against Daniel? Did his life experiences at all justify the level of violence he directed toward Daniel?
7. Did any of the plot points take you by surprise?
8. The book was written from the first-person point of view. Do you wish you could have heard from other characters in their own voices?
9. Have you been to any of the places mentioned in the story, and if yes, did you find them recognizable?

Bibliography

Ben-Yehuda, Nachman. *Masada Myth: Collective Memory and Mythmaking in Israel.* Madison, WI: University of Wisconsin Press, 1995.

Ben-Yehuda, Nachman. "Questioning Masada: Where Masada's Defenders Fell." *Biblical Archaeology Review* 24, no. 6 (November/December 1998).

Borowski, Oded. *Daily Life in Biblical Times.* Atlanta, GA: Society of Biblical Literature, 2003.

Davies, Gwyn. "The Masada Siege—From the Roman Viewpoint." *Biblical Archaeology Review* 40, no. 4 (July/August 2014).

Davies, Gwyn, and Jodi Magness. "Recovering Josephus: Mason's History of the Jewish War and the Siege of Masada." https://lessons.myjli.com/debates/index.php/lesson-2/recovering-josephus-masons-history-of-the-jewish-war-and-the-siege-of-masada.

Domsky, Ronald Z. "Taxation in the Bible During the Period of the First and Second Temples." *Journal of International Law and Practice* 7, no. 225 (1998).

Gill, Dan. "It's a Natural: Masada Ramp Was Not a Roman Engineering Miracle." *Biblical Archaeology Review* 27, no. 5 (September/October 2001).

Goldfus, Haim, Yoav Avni, Roy Albag, and Benny Arubas. "The Significance of Geomorphological and Soil Formation Research for Understanding the Unfinished Roman Ramp at Masada." *CATENA* 146 (April 18, 2016): 73–87. https://doi.org/10.1016/j.catena.2016.04.014.

Goodman, Martin. *Rome and Jerusalem: The Clash of Ancient Civilizations.* New York, NY: Vintage Books, 2008.

Horsley, Richard A. "High Priests and the Politics of Roman Palestine: A Contextual Analysis of the Evidence in Josephus." *Journal for the Study of Judaism in the Persian, Hellenistic, and Roman Period* 17, no. 1 (1986): 23-55. http://www.jstor.org/stable/24657973.

Horsley, Richard A., and John S. Hanson. *Bandits, Prophets, and Messiahs: Popular Movements in the Time of Jesus.* Harrisburg, PA: Trinity Press International, 1999.

Issar, Arie S., and Dan Yakir. "Isotopes from Wood Buried in the Roman Siege Ramp of Masada: The Roman Period's Colder Climate." *The Biblical Archaeologist* 60, no. 2 (1997): 101–6. https://doi.org/10.2307/3210599.

Josephus, Flavius, and E. Mary Smallwood. *The Jewish War.* New York, NY: Dorset Press, 1985.

Lev-Yadun, S., D.S. Lucas, and M. Weinstein-Evron. "Modeling the Demands for Wood by the Inhabitants of Masada and for the Roman Siege." *Journal of Arid Environments* 74, no. 7 (2010): 777–85. https://doi.org/10.1016/j.jaridenv.2010.01.010.

Levine, Lee I. *Jerusalem Portrait of the City in the Second Temple Period (538 B.C.E. – 70 C.E.).* Philadelphia, PA: Jewish Publication Society, published in cooperation with the Jewish Theological Seminary of America, 2002.

Magness, Jodi. "Masada: Arms and the Man." *Biblical Archaeology Review* 18, no. 4 (July/August 1992).

Magness, Jodi. *Masada: From Jewish Revolt to Modern Myth.* Princeton, NJ: Princeton University Press, 2019.

Magness, Jodi. "The Siege of Masada." Accessed November 10, 2021. https://popular-archaeology.com/article/the-siege-of-masada.

Magness, Jodi. "Masada: A Heroic Last Stand Against Rome." Accessed November 10, 2021. https://press.princeton.edu/ideas/masada-a-heroic-last-stand-against-rome.

Mason, Steven. *History of the Jewish War: AD 66-74.* Cambridge, UK: Cambridge University Press, 2019.

Netzer, Ehud. *Masada III: the Yigael Yadin Excavations 1963-1965.* Jerusalem, Israel: Israel Exploration Society, 1991.

Netzer, Ehud. "The Last Days and Hours at Masada." *Biblical Archaeology Review* 17, no. 6 (November/December 1991). https://www.baslibrary.org/biblical-archaeology-review/17/6/13.

Ngo, Robin, ed. *Masada: The Dead Sea's Desert Fortress.* Washington, DC: Biblical Archaeology Society, 2014.

Ngo, Robin. "The Masada Siege: The Roman Assault on Herod's Desert Fortress." Accessed November 10, 2021. https://www.biblicalarchaeology.org/daily/biblical-sites-places/biblical-archaeology-sites/the-masada-siege/

Richmond, I. A. "The Roman Siege-Works of Masada, Israel." *The Journal of Roman Studies* 52, Parts 1 and 2 (1962): 142-155.

Wiener, Noah, ed. *Life in the Ancient World: Crafts, Society and Daily Practice.* Washington, DC: Biblical Archaeology Society, 2013.

Yadin, Yigael. *Masada: Herod's Fortress and the Zealots' Last Stand.* Great Britain: George Weidenfeld & Nicolson Limited, 1966.

About the Author

Shimon Avish (She-mone Ah-veesh) is an author who came to writing novels later in life. His stories draw on his adventures in soldiering, farming, industrial design, cabinetmaking, political science, international business consulting, and living in the U.S., Canada, and Israel.

This novel is part of a planned series on significant events in Jewish history, including:

- Rome and the Jews: Prelude to War (First Jewish–Roman War – 6 BCE–70 CE)
- Jerusalem: Siege and Destruction (First Jewish–Roman War – 70 CE)
- Masada: Thou Shalt Not Kill (Siege of Masada – 66–73 CE)
- The Second Jewish Rebellion Against Rome (Kitos War – 115–117 CE)
- The Third Jewish Rebellion Against Rome (Bar Kokhba Revolt – 132–135 CE)

Shimon currently resides in the Boston metro area with his wife and rescue pup, Luna. His website is shimonavish.com, where, after signing up, you can find supplemental stories about Daniel, Judith, Eleazar, and Nathan.

Acknowledgments

This book would not exist in its current form without my editors, Dan Cross at The Open Book Editor, and Julie Gray at Julie Gray Editing. It would also not have been possible without the unwavering support of my family. I would especially like to acknowledge my wife, Chris, who saw I had a book in me that had to come out. This was during COVID, when the industry I worked in for twenty-five years collapsed, and I found myself out of work. Chris agreed it would finally be a good time for me to complete the novel I had kept locked away in my drawer for the past ten years, and the push to finish Masada was born. I could not have done it without her patient support as I learned what I needed to create my first work of fiction. And to my children, Emma and Nate, my best beta readers, thanks for the gentle but honest critiques. All my love to the three of you.